# THE BOOK OF NAMES

## FORBIDDEN BOOKS, VOLUME VI

DAVID MICHAEL SLATER

LIBRARY TALES PUBLISHING

PRINTED IN THE UNITED STATES OF AMERICA

Published by:
Library Tales Publishing
511 6th Avenue #56
New York, NY 10011
www.LibraryTalesPublishing.com

Copyright © 2017 by David Michael Slater
Published by Library Tales Publishing.
New York, New York, 10011

For general information on our other products and services, please contact our Customer Care Department at 1-800-754-5016. For technical support, please visit www.LibraryTalesPublishing.com

Library Tales Publishing also publishes its books in a variety of electronic formats. Every content that appears in print is available in electronic books.

ISBN-13: 978-0998333496
ISBN-10: 0998333492

*For Heidi, the reason for my good name*

*"A book is not an isolated being; it is a relationship, an axis of innumerable relationships."*
— Jorge Luis Borges

# PROLOGUE
## ONE CLEAN STROKE

iny beads of sweat trickled down the young man's forehead as he hurried through the dark with a book clenched under his arm. There were no streetlights on the little horseshoe-shaped street.

It was one a.m.

He stopped several times to check behind him, but continued on each time. Fortunately, the houses' address plaques all had lights trained on them.

The moment he spotted the one he was looking for, he froze.

Directly in front of the house—it was the largest one by far—a vehicle quietly idled, a black Cadillac SUV, almost invisible in the night. With his heart pounding, the young man bolted behind a car parked across the street. Quickly, but carefully, he laid his book open on the hood, then crouched down to conceal himself.

The SUV's engine cut out, then the driver's door opened. A figure got out, a silhouette scarcely differentiated from the darkness.

The young man peered over the hood, placing a trembling hand on one of the pages of his book.

The figure approached the house, but hesitated at the front door. It appeared to look up at the windows of the second floor. It put a hand in its pocket. Then it turned away, moving stealthily toward the garage.

"No!" the young man cried, leaping to his feet.

With one clean stroke, he swept his free hand across the page he'd been marking.

The figure vanished.

# CHAPTER ONE
## A Better Place (Part I)

"'Penelope Posey,'" Daphna read, leaning over the newspaper with an unpeeled hardboiled egg in her hand, "'seven pounds, five ounces.' I like that name. Has a nice ring to it."

Dex ignored this. He was chewing on a yolk, looking around at the fancy kitchen they were sitting in: the giant stainless steel oven and sub-zero fridge, the hanging racks of expensive-looking pots and pans, the gleaming hardwood floors. It was all stuff right out of a glossy magazine. There was a pool in the basement that made waves you could swim against and a rec room with Ping-Pong and pool tables. Dr. Fludd even had a giant flat-screen with a game system installed for them in the den. It was like they'd won the lottery or something, getting taken in by the most famous scientist in the world.

On the grand tour last night, Dex had done his best to act like it was all so wonderful.

"'Zachary Kaplan: seven pounds, seven ounces,'" Daphna read, setting her egg back in the shiny yellow goblet-type thing with the others. Despite the alarming way her T-shirt and jeans hung on her this morning, she just couldn't muster any kind of appetite. "'Gino Palantonio: nine pounds, nine ounces.'"

Dex continued to ignore his sister. He was now focusing on all the high-tech gizmos and gadgets on the granite countertops—some sort of wine-serving mini-fridge, a giant espresso machine that looked both brand new and a hundred years old, and a silver contraption he was pretty sure was a homemade ice cream maker. There was even a door in the wall with one of those elevators that lifts food to the upper floors.

As he made these inspections, Dex absently massaged his arm, which was still sore from the endless cycle of giving blood and getting it back. Dr. Fludd had put him and his sister through the process every day for the last four weeks up at Oregon Health Sciences University.

The upshot of it all was that the cure and the vaccine, both based on a unique protein extracted from the twins' blood, were everywhere now. It had been barely a month, and the plague was completely wiped out. It was as if the panic on the streets of the Northwest had never happened.

Dex probably ought to care.

"'Justin Blake: eleven pounds, four ounces.' *Ooof*, poor woman."

*"Fine,"* Dex sighed. He popped what was left of an egg white into his mouth. "What's with the birth announcements?"

Daphna had spent most of her time in the hospital with her head in a newspaper. Dex would sometimes wake up at night to find her poring over one or another from the stack that kept growing on the floor next to her bed. Of course there was nothing much else to do up there; he'd been bored out of his mind the whole time. Even so, he'd not once asked what she was up to.

Daphna looked at him, flashing those flecks in her green eyes that always seemed like charged particles when she got emotional. Dex wondered if his matching eyes did the same when he got worked up. Daphna's eyes still had dark circles underneath them, too. Not sleeping well in those lumpy hospital beds was understandable, but how she couldn't get rest on their new supersoft mattresses last night was beyond him. He'd slept like the dead. And she was losing weight.

Daphna took a deep breath. Now was the time to end this charade, to make her brother admit that, plague or no plague, a disaster of epic proportions was going to strike at any moment.

It made her furious that Dex wouldn't talk about it in the hospital. He wouldn't talk about anything, really—nothing important, anyway. He'd acted how he used to act: brooding and withdrawn. But things were supposed to be different now! After all they'd gone through together, it was painful to endure. But she'd respected his need to process things alone, if that's what he was doing. What galled her the most was his acting like they weren't in the slightest bit of danger. But now that they were out of the hospital, Dexter needed to start facing reality again. He needed to start facing it *now*. Daphna set the paper down.

"Dex," she said very carefully, as if simply saying his name wrong would set him off, "you know all the other Lamed Vavniks were killed. So any of these newborns could be one of the new ones." As she said this, Daphna unconsciously touched the raised skin above her ear in the shape of those two Hebrew letters, Lamed and Vav.

Then, in the face of the incredulous look her brother was giving her, she said, "I've been thinking about it—how it must work. See, so, there's thirty-six of us at any given time, right?

"I know, Daphna."

"I know. But let me talk it through. You know I need to do that."

Dex sighed, but didn't object.

"So, the thirty-six of us have the extra rib that can produce life all by itself, at least in girls, but they all can after we die—if the rib is buried. I know, I *know*—you know this," she said, seeing Dex's impatient slumping, "but I think the ribs can only do that—create new life from the earth after we die—until we're replaced by a new Lamed Vavnik, a new baby. Think about it. Otherwise there'd be a growing pile of these buried ribs waiting to start life again if humanity got wiped out. There'd be millions of them—billions, eventually. See what I mean? No one would have to worry about humans going extinct. For this secret really to be something to worry about protecting, I've concluded that there's only ever thirty-six ribs with the stem cells capable of producing life at one time. They are either in a living person or in the ground, *but there are only thirty-six*—I'm sure of it."

Dex opened his mouth to speak, but Daphna kept rambling.

"But hold on. That's not all. Remember how the Secret Keeper made that call about burying us in the Church's secret cemetery—"

"Yes, Daphna. I remember the time we were shot."

"He said something about increasing the guard, but also about—"

"He said triple the guard in the cemetery for the six-week term."

"How do you do that?"

"I really haven't thought about that," Dex admitted, shrugging off the compliment. "What does it mean?"

"Well," Daphna said, "we know the whole secret cemetery was about burying our ribs so humans could come back if the plague wiped us all out. But if it *didn't,* I think he wanted them guarded."

"Which would make sense with a monster killing us all and destroying the ribs."

"Yes, but why six weeks?"

"I have a feeling you're going to tell me."

"It fits what I'm trying to tell you," Daphna said. "I think a new baby—a new Lamed Vavnik—is born six weeks after an old one dies. After six weeks, it's just a rib in the ground. So, like I said, there's only ever thirty-six of us."

"Wow," Dex said. "So you weren't just reading newspapers up there."

"Now," Daphna forged ahead, ignoring this, "I know the odds of any of the thirty-four new ones being born around here and listed in *The Oregonian* is, well—it's obviously pretty unlikely. And even if some *are* being born in Portland, how would we know? It's not like they'd have an asterisk next to their name. Unless we could check every newborn in town for the birthmark, which might not even be visible right away—in fact, I'm sure they're not. Though most babies are born bald, obviously, so it might not be too hard to—"

"Daphna," Dex said, shaking his head.

"I know. I *know.*" Daphna knew she'd been obsessing. "It's just," she tried to explain, "those names—" She picked up the paper and showed it to Dex as if it explained everything. "Imagining those little babies, wherever they are, with their tiny little extra ribs—they're the only other people on the planet like us, Dex. They're family in a way, *real family.* People we could count on some day."

"Daphna!"

*"What?"*

"What's wrong with you?"

"What do you mean?"

"You know very well there are no new Lamed Vavniks being born."

"But—"

"You just said yourself the other thirty-four were killed. And you know that monster murdered them all for their ribs so he could throw them into that volcano. And you conveniently left one thing out of your little theory: that if the ribs are destroyed that one way during those six weeks, that's it. They. Are. Gone. *That's* why they were being guarded for six weeks. Face it, Daphna, there are no new babies with those ribs. We're the last two."

"But—"

*"It's us! Just us!"*

Daphna felt tears rising up. The real reason she hadn't pressed her brother to have this conversation until now was obvious: She didn't want to face the truth.

"I don't want us to be the last ones," she whined, her voice cracking. The thought made her want to heave up her insides. "If we are," she choked, "then all human life depends on us staying alive! Don't you see, Dex? Risking our lives means risking *the end of the world!*"

"It's not like everyone would just die if we get—"

"Yes, but if our ribs get destroyed too, life wouldn't come back after a catastrophe, like a *plague*—"

"Well, our ribs won't get destroyed," Dex said, flatly. "I'm pretty sure no one's going to throw them into that volcano. That *thing* is dead. They'll re-enter the earth one way or another, and eventually life would be re—"

"What if there are other ways to destroy them, or they just get kept from re-entering the earth? What if our bodies get blown up? What if they get sealed in plastic?"

"Neither of those are actually perm—"

"What if they get shot into space?"

Dex simply shrugged in response. Daphna could go on like this forever.

*"What if, when we find a way back into Heaven, we get stuck there!"*

Dex sighed. He knew this was where they were heading all along. It was what he'd been trying to avoid by pretty much refusing to talk to Daphna for the last month. But he'd been resigned to things getting ugly when they got "home." "What do you want to do?" he asked. "Go climb one of those goofy towers to pass through a gate that isn't even there? There's no point, Daphna. There's no way back."

"But we have to find a way. Otherwise—"

"Wait," Dex interrupted, again noting the dark circles under Daphna's eyes. They were the worst he'd seen now that he thought about it. "Let me guess," he said. "You've been up all night scouring the Internet for ways into Heaven."

Daphna looked down at the marbled top of the circular island they were seated at. She didn't need to say it had been a waste of time, but last night was the first chance she'd had to do anything productive in so long.

"But," she said, "that book up there in the Light— with the keyhole—the fire that came out—the panic—"

While she spoke these words, Daphna's mind drifted to another book, the book she'd opened in Heaven herself, the book with blank pages that felt so profoundly hers somehow. The experience of looking into it felt so personal that she'd not mentioned it to her brother. She'd thought about it a lot, though. She'd dreamed about it the few moments she'd actually slept. In her dreams, the pages weren't blank. They were flowing with letters like in the other book she'd opened, the one with T's and G's and A's. At least those were the letters she remembered.

And then yet another book came to mind.

"And the missing book," she added, "on that shelf that angel was singing so sadly at. I don't think I should have seen that. But I'm positive that whatever book belongs there is what all the angels are searching the shelves for. *Don't you care what's happening up there?*"

There, she'd said it.

"Of course I care!" Dex snapped. He'd been expecting to hear this for a few weeks now. It was almost a relief to have it finally said. "But, Daphna," he added, "Mom and Evelyn destroyed the Aleph. They don't want us coming back, probably because they know we're the last Lamed Vavniks and don't want us risking the entire world, just like you said!"

"But—!"

"Or maybe they destroyed it because *people who aren't dead don't belong in Heaven!*"

"But—!"

"I don't want to think about problems we can't fix, Daphna! *Why is everything always up to us?* It's been a month and nothing bad has happened. I'm sure they handled the fire and solved whatever crisis there was."

Daphna believed the crisis had been solved as much as she believed the Church had forgotten they'd discovered that their ribs were the real explanation for Jesus' Virgin Birth—that is, not at all. And something told her Dexter didn't either. But she didn't have the strength to fight anymore right now.

"Hey," she said, looking at the oven clock. "We need to get going." It was 6:20, which meant they had an hour before First Bell. "We can't be late for our first day of high school."

"You're right!" Dex said, thrilled the conversation was over, but unable to stop himself from rolling his eyes. "Because *that* would be the end of the world."

# CHAPTER TWO
## *No More Than Two Steps*

"Should we say goodbye to Dr. Fludd?" Dex asked. He was actually feeling grateful to see this recognizably annoying part of his sister. It meant she hadn't completely lost her mind.

"Oh," Daphna said. "She's not here. I heard her leave. It was, I don't know, way past midnight, I think."

"I thought she said she was going to stop working twenty hours a day."

"And I'm sure she will, when the plague scare is officially over." Daphna re-folded the newspaper and returned the eggs to the fridge. She'd have to figure out the high-speed dishwasher later. With all her attention on birth announcements at the hospital, she hadn't had time to wonder about the house they were moving into. She hadn't even been thinking about it on the ride over last night, mostly because the radio was talking about how the towers in the Middle East—"Stairways to Heaven," people were calling them—were increasing the usual tensions there. It wasn't until they came to a stop and Dex elbowed her that she finally saw the gorgeous house. Her first thought was that it was as nice as any *Pops'*.

It looked like it wouldn't matter if all the confusion about their inheritance never got worked out. Daphna now had everything she could ever want, except for her family photographs of course, which were lost in the destruction of their house. She'd trade it all for them in a second.

The only thing Dr. Fludd had forgotten to do for them was make extra keys, but it didn't matter since they could open and close the garage from outside with a code. After Dex cleared his plate, the twins grabbed their new backpacks from the floor and stepped into the garage. A massive yellow Hummer greeted them there. The gargantuan beast of a thing looked like it could smash Dr. Fludd's Caddy flat without even noticing.

"Now that's what I'm talkin' about!"

"Don't even think about it," Daphna warned, though she couldn't help allowing a smile at the memory of their driving adventures, harrowing though they'd been.

"Only in an emergency," Dex agreed, grinning. But then he added, "Which means we should go ahead and buckle up, right?"

"Ha ha," Daphna said. She put her hand on the button to raise the garage door, but took it off and placed it on her brother's arm instead.

"Dex," she said, "I know the teachers at Wilson were told all about your Scotopic Sensitivity, but I'm sure you can't rely on them, not with so many students. I've decided that *I'm* going to help you. I'll read you everything this year if those colored overlays or whatever other tricks they try don't keep the words still for you. You don't even have to go for extra help. I'm sure you hate that. I just want you to—I don't know—I just really want both of us to start *living*. I feel like we've been given a fresh start. After losing Mom and then Evelyn, to have found Dr. Fludd—"

"Do you think she'll adopt us?"

Daphna shrugged. "Maybe," she said. "But what do you think about me helping—?"

"You don't really like her, do you?"

"No, I do," Daphna protested. "I do. It's just...we need to get to know her first, to make sure her intentions are good."

"You don't trust her?"

"I—I don't know. I guess not totally. Not yet."

"Anyway," Dex said, "I guess we better go."

"Dex," Daphna said, looking at him closely, "are you sure you're okay with school starting and all?"

"*Daphna*," Dex sighed, "a monster older than time almost ripped my guts out. I've been nearly asphyxiated, almost burned alive, and I've been *shot*. I've been to *Heaven* and back, for crying out loud. And I'm supposed to be afraid of *high school?*" It was true he wasn't afraid of high school, but for Daphna's sake, he didn't mention that he saw no reason to go, other than maybe to escape her wrath. Now *that* he was afraid of.

16

Despite these rather compelling points, Daphna wasn't so sure Dex was telling the truth. "Speaking of all those pleasantries," she said, "I did find something interesting last night. I can't believe Dr. Fludd got us computers. And cell phones!" Daphna patted her pocket to make sure hers was there. She was happy to see that Dex did the same. Fortunately, with voice command, he hardly ever had to try to read the screen.

"What did you find?" Dex asked, though only to be polite.

"I read that in Judaism, in one of its sacred books, they sometimes refer to Heaven, or the afterlife, as 'Gan Eden.'"

"Is that 'Garden' of Eden?"

"Yeah, they use the terms interchangeably sometimes—'Heaven' and 'The Garden.' Sounds like somebody knew they were similar. I guess the Garden here was just an earthly version of the infinite one there. Which kinda makes sense, really."

"Anyone know they were both *libraries?*" Dex didn't mind that Heaven was full of books. He knew that, perfected in the Light, he'd be able to read them. One of the times he was there, he'd felt a nearly irresistible urge to go find something, something he later realized had to be a book, a book that was his alone. It felt so intensely personal that he hadn't mentioned it to Daphna.

He'd been dreaming about it almost every night.

"Negative on the library," Daphna said. "There's definitely nothing about God having a bajillion books. I found a lot about angels, though. No one said they were librarians, of course, but they've been described as winged figures robed in white with golden belts. That means they've been seen before. And maybe that means people have been to Heaven and came back, maybe without using the Aleph."

"Or because an angel came here."

"What?"

"People could know what angels look like if angels came *here.*"

"Oh, right," Daphna admitted, disappointed. "There are stories about that in the Bible, I think."

Neither twin said anything for a moment.

Finally, Daphna said, "Dex, I'm sorry I acted so

crazy in there. I know it's just us. And I'm glad you're with me."

"Me too," Dex said. And he meant it.

"Anyway," Daphna said, "time to face the music."

Daphna pushed the lift button, and the door began to grind its way up. She took Dex's hand while they waited because she knew she could face anything with him by her side, and it seemed he was finally going to take his place there again.

Dex let Daphna take his hand. He supposed it was better to face the world with someone who had your back, even if she was often on it.

When the door was high enough, brother and sister simultaneously drew in deep breaths and slowly let them out. Then they walked hand-in-hand out onto the driveway.

They'd taken no more than two steps before the loudest explosion they'd ever heard sent them diving face-first onto the pavement.

# CHAPTER THREE
## The Church of Us

The twins cowered on the ground covering their heads, both certain that a bomb—*the* bomb—had been dropped on their house. They stayed lying there, eyes clenched, bodies stiffened, waiting for—what happened when a bomb blew you up?

"Dex?" Daphna finally said. She didn't feel blown up. Peeking out above the crook of her elbow, she saw that the house was fine. All the houses were fine.

Dex looked up too, but just as another deafening boom exploded. The twins could tell this time that it had come from above. Cringing, they looked up. A third explosion came. The sky seemed to shake with it.

These weren't bombs. They were thunderclaps—ungodly loud thunderclaps.

The twins tensed in expectation of the next ear-splitting crash. They stayed silent and waited for a long minute, barely breathing. When Daphna finally felt none was coming, she took in a breath and asked, "Can it thunder with no clouds?"

Slowly, Dex got to his feet. Daphna did the same. They scanned the sky.

Another boom came, and this time lightning immediately followed it, jagged white lines crisscrossing crazily for a moment over the horizon.

"This has nothing to do with us," Dex said, but he couldn't take his eyes off the sky. A spectacular daybreak lit up the world in a thousand shades of rosy red. There were no clouds in sight.

Daphna offered no reply. She was awestruck. It looked like special effects.

But the spectacle dissipated quickly as the light increased. When the display was gone, Daphna lowered her gaze. "Oh no," she said, pointing at the street. "Look!"

Dex looked. Dr. Fludd's black Cadillac SUV was

still parked right there in front of the house.

"Oh no," Daphna repeated, already hurrying over to peer through the tinted windows. "The Church got her," she moaned. "We're just two stupid kids! They know no one would believe us if we claimed Jesus was born from special stem cells—but Dr. Fludd! Oh, God!"

Dexter shook his head at his sister's melodrama. *"Or,"* he said, "a colleague picked her up."

"In the middle of the night?"

"Why not? They're all workaholics. Or more likely, Daphna: She has two cars."

"You mean *three?"*

"Why not?" Dex said, looking back at the garage. There was enough room in there for four cars. "I heard the nurses saying she gets paid to be an expert in trials and on news shows and stuff like that. *Hey—"* He'd noticed something on the ground under the code panel mounted on the house, a yellow square of paper. He walked over and grabbed it—a sticky— then handed it to Daphna.

"'Sorry to leave so early,'" Daphna read. "'Have a great day at school—Roberta.'"

"So there," Dex said. "One way or another, she went to work."

"What's it doing out here?"

"Easy," Dex said. "She's not used to having kids and didn't think of leaving us a note until she was in the car, but she didn't want to risk waking us up coming back in, so she stuck it on the panel knowing we'd see it when we closed the garage. But it fell off."

It was reasonable, Daphna had to admit, but she was unconvinced and feeling profoundly uneasy— *more* profoundly uneasy.

After punching in the code to lower the door, she took her phone out and tapped Dr. Fludd's number. She listened, then put the phone away.

"No answer," Daphna said. "I don't like this, Dex. I don't like this one bit. I'll keep calling, but come on— let's get going." After a quick glance at the sky, she added, "Before the sky falls on our heads."

Feeling intensely vulnerable, Daphna shot a look up and down the street. The houses all seemed sinister now, and she wondered why she hadn't checked them out last night. Instead of reading useless birth announcements all that time in the hospital, she should have found a way to research Dr. Fludd's neighbors! Tension yanked her shoulder muscles taut as she walked tentatively to the sidewalk, motioning her brother to follow.

Annoyed with the dramatics, Dexter only very slowly obeyed. Daphna looked like she thought she was leading some kind of lame military exercise. Thunder was just thunder, no matter how loud. A fancy sunrise was just a fancy sunrise. Parked cars were just parked cars. None of it added up to anything— anything he cared to think about, anyway.

Dex caught up with Daphna at the end of the street, where she'd stopped to wait for him, somewhat testily, he observed. Together, they turned right and passed a synagogue with massive Ten Commandments tablets for one of its front walls. They had to be well over a hundred feet tall—God-sized. Neither had noticed it last night, but neither commented on it now. Up on a hilltop next to the synagogue sat a large orange brick church. Three tall white crosses of different heights stood in front of its impressive glass entryway, pointing proudly at the now frightening sky.

Daphna saw Dex looking curiously at the long line of vehicles turning into the synagogue's parking lot, so she said, "The Jewish new year, Rosh Hashanah—it started last night."

Dex shrugged.

It was obvious her brother didn't want to talk any more, but Daphna had to get her mind off that horrid thunder and this new anxiety about Dr. Fludd. "On the radio this morning," she said, "I heard that more people are joining religious institutions right now, especially churches. That apparently happens after near-disasters because people think there was a reason they were spared."

*"We're* the reason they were spared,' Dex scoffed. "They should all join the Church of *Us."*

Daphna didn't even hear this. She could somehow feel her heartbeat in her throat.

"And I also heard," she added, rambling again, "that there's some huge Jesus exhibit opening at the Portland Art Museum today. They're unveiling a bunch of modern works from around the world. Crazy interpretations of famous works of religious art, I guess. One painting has everyone eating fast food at the Last Supper."

When Dex half-heartedly raised a brow at this, she added, "The last meal Jesus had with his—his followers or whatever they were called."

"Disciples," Dex said. "Didn't we see that on a tapestry at the Vatican—next to that one of Jesus on the cross with some guy catching his blood?"

"Right!" Daphna said. "Anyway, it's sold out and people are scalping tickets for hundreds of dollars! To an art museum! The news guy said we need a new vaccine for Jesus Fever. What?"

Now it was Dex who wasn't hearing his sister. His annoyance about so many people suddenly finding religion had turned to outrage.

The powers-that-be had decided it would be safer to keep the twins' special blood a secret. Daphna had readily agreed that it was safer that way. She didn't mind a bit that they'd not been part of the "official" story, which was that Dr. Fludd had come up with the cure on her own at pretty much the last second. The one and only mention they'd gotten was a brief write-up in the papers saying that though the twins had been present at the first site of infection, and though their adoptive mother was the first to die of the disease, they did not have the virus nor any special immunities to it (although they were under observation at OHSU as an extra precaution).

It also said that the nationwide manhunt for them had been an "unfortunate distraction" and that they were no longer wanted for questioning in connection with the deaths of two local clergymen. Daphna thought this was a more than adequate consolation prize, but Dexter thought it stunk. He didn't care what was wise or prudent. He wanted to be recognized for what they'd accomplished, for *all* they'd accomplished against such incredible odds. But of course he couldn't say that. Of course he had to bite his tongue and agree.

But now, hearing that so many people wanted to thank *God* for saving them when He would never, ever help, lest He encroach on the free will that was His ultimate gift to mankind—the gift that required Him to hide himself from the world He made and supposedly loved so much—it was an insult Dex suddenly couldn't bear.

Daphna had forgotten what they were talking about, even that they'd been talking. She was oblivious now to her brother's degenerating mood because her own already sour mood was doing the same. Wilson High School sat just beyond the top of the long hill. How could it not have occurred to her until now how exposed they'd be on the way there? As they walked up the main road into Hillsdale, Daphna turned around every few steps, scanning for trouble. Whether or not anything had happened to Dr. Fludd, she was absolutely certain their lives were only seconds away from ending once and for all.

# CHAPTER FOUR
## Something Bad

Daphna had been battling this paranoia for a month, though she didn't think it could be called paranoia since the danger was real. But the dread hadn't been this powerful since they'd first gotten set up at OHSU, when she'd been fully expecting every moment that a Church assassin would come to murder them. *Another* Church assassin.

It would have helped if she could talk to someone, but Dex was being...Dex, and Dr. Fludd, despite what she'd seen with her own two eyes, was sure that there was a rational explanation for everything. And their stem cell producing ribs only made her surer. The thought of telling her their father was *Adam* and that she and Dex were adopted by Eve after he died in Turkey was absurd.

Each day did get a little bit easier, and after two weeks, Daphna let Dex convince her that the Secret Keeper of the Church was satisfied that none of them was going to call a press conference. Dr. Fludd kept a guard at their door, but the twins were eventually allowed to leave their floor for a part of each day to alleviate their boredom.

Dex had taken to going out on the deck to watch the tram run up and down the mountainside between the hospital and the waterfront below. Daphna tried to stay holed up with her newspapers, but one of the nurses badgered her into going to use the fitness center. She agreed when she realized she could walk on a treadmill and continue reading the papers, along with a Bible she'd found in the hall.

However, this required Daphna to leave the hospital proper, which she almost couldn't get herself to do. As she hurried across the driveway for the first time, she could have sworn someone stepped out of the shadows behind her and was walking quickly to catch up. She'd spun round, but no one was there, no one but some cops and a boy in a baseball cap sitting on a bench taking notes in a book. She only went a few more times before she couldn't take the stress anymore.

Now Daphna wondered how she'd forgotten all that visceral fear. Maybe it was having given up the usefully distracting fantasy about the birth announcements. The killers were surely just waiting until they all left the hospital—and for all she knew they'd already gotten Dr. Fludd! Daphna reached for her phone again, but she saw something, a movement behind her as they crossed the street in front of an ice cream store. She wheeled around.

It was a mother pushing a triple stroller with three crying babies fighting over a stuffed snake.

*"Dexter,"* Daphna hissed, barely suppressing panic as the woman went by, "this is stupid. We're sitting ducks out here! After school we need to visit the synagogue and church back there to see if we can learn anything we don't know about Heaven."

"I don't think so." Dex had been watching Daphna spin around in the street like a demented ballerina, as if snipers were aiming at her from imaginary balconies. Maybe she thought one of those babies was a ninja assassin in disguise.

"What do you mean, you 'don't think so?'" Daphna demanded, stopping mid-whirl as they reached the opposite sidewalk. They were standing at the merge point between the main road and another that joined it, curving down from their old neighborhood, Multnomah Village.

"By, 'I don't think so,'" Dex said, "I meant, 'I don't think so.' Or to put it another way: *I don't think so.*"

"Dexter, something bad is going to happen. I just know it. I can literally feel it in the air."

"Why now?" Dex asked, not particularly interested in his sister's newfound psychic abilities. "It's been a month. No one murdered us. The sky *didn't*—"

At that moment, another devastating clap of thunder cracked overhead, obliterating Dexter's last word. The twins covered their ears because it actually hurt. Everyone else on the street did the same. The lightning flashed just after, a spider's web that for a moment seemed to drape itself over the globe. Cars screeched. There was a collision up the hill a bit, a multi-car collision, followed by more screeching as traffic came to a halt behind it.

Horns blared, but Daphna just stared at Dex, waiting for him to accept the obvious. *"Well?"* she demanded.

"Look, Daphna," Dex said. "Let me put it like this: I'm retired from the Saving-the-World business."

Daphna continued to glare at her brother with the embers flaring up in her eyes.

"What's the worst that can happen?" Dex asked, thinking about the blissful feeling he'd experienced in Heaven, the feeling he'd thought about pretty much all day every day at the hospital. "We get killed, right? So we die. You seem to have forgotten that our friend in the Church is very concerned about our ribs. He'll bury us in his little secret cemetery, back in the earth, safe and sound. And six weeks later two more lucky winners will get born to deal with two new fancy stem cell ribs. Meanwhile, we get white robes and gold belts and wings. And we'll be with Mom and Evelyn forever." And he could find that book—*his* book. And read it.

Hot blood flowed to Daphna's face during this little speech. It was as if her old brother, the stubborn, negative one she'd nearly forgotten about, had come back from Africa, and the new one, the confident, caring one who turned his challenges into his advantages, had been tossed into that volcano there. How could this happen after all they'd been through? It infuriated her. And his words had pricked a tender spot in her festering fears.

"But Dex!" she said, throwing up her hands. "Don't you see? We brought that assassin—a *kill-er*—into Heaven. Dead Face caused the fire, but *we* brought him there. The fire is *our* fault. Whatever is happening there is *our* fault! Mom and Evelyn practically threw us out afterward, and you said it yourself: By destroying the Aleph, they pretty much banned us from coming back!"

"So what? *You* said it yourself: They probably don't want us risking—"

"The Lamed Vavniks, the Thirty-six—" Daphna interrupted, "We're supposed to be the *Righteous Ones!*"

"We don't even know what that actually—"

"HOW CAN YOU BE SURE THAT IF WE DIE, *THAT'S WHERE WE'LL GO?*"

There. She'd said it. They might never get to see their mothers again. Or that book again. *Her* book.

Dex's face twisted up. His spiky hair felt like needles in his scalp. "We—we *had* to," he protested. "Dead Face *shot* us! It was the only way to save ourselves, to save everyone! And he got vaporized, just like he deserved!"

Up the hill, people were out of their vehicles complaining to a pair of police officers who were somehow already on the scene. There was also the distinct sound of kids crying coming through open car doors. Screaming, really.

"Moses," Daphna said, turning back to her brother after taking in the noisy scene.

"Moses?"

"When he was leading the Hebrews through the desert, he made some small mistake. I know it's only a story, but we keep finding out that there are truths behind them. That's why I read that Bible at the hospital while you just—! Anyway," Daphna said, trying to keep to the point, "he disobeyed God in some small way—I forget how, but it was completely minor—and do you know what his punishment was, despite all he did for his people, risking his life to lead them out of slavery?"

"No," said Dex. And he was sure he didn't want to know, either.

"He wasn't allowed into the *Promised Land*. Get it? I'm thinking that letting a murderer open a locked book that set Heaven on fire might qualify as a bit more than completely minor!"

Dexter was speechless. If after all the thanklessness they had to put up with in this life they had to put up with more in the next...the thought of it made him want to implode.

Before Daphna could say anything further, the thunder crashed again. A moment later, someone screamed, "Watch out! Behind you!"

The twins turned and looked up the street coming down from the Village. A dirty white van was swerving around, honking at cars that had no room to get out of its way. It sideswiped a bus, jumped a curb, crashed back off of it, and barreled on.

The driver, a man with long black sideburns, had his beady black eyes trained directly on the twins. His murderous intent was clear as day. Dex and Daphna looked at each other, but neither was able to react.

"WATCH OUT!" the voice called again.

The van was nearly on top of them when Daphna finally registered the situation. She dove away, taking her brother down with her.

But the van did not drive over the spot they'd been standing in. Instead, it swerved back into the street.

Sprawled on the sidewalk, the twins watched it lurch wildly up the hill toward the school. There was screaming from pretty much everyone on the street as they flung themselves out of its way.

Finally, the van bounced like a pinball between three idling cars, then slammed head-on into a telephone pole.

# CHAPTER FIVE
## *Over Fifteen-Hundred*

The twins got back to their feet at the sound of all the shattering glass. Many of the drivers and passengers who'd thrown themselves down were now back up as well and running over to the van. The cops ordered them to return to their vehicles, but they paid no heed. Someone shouted, "Idiot! You could have killed one of us!"

"You could have killed *all* of us!" someone else corrected.

It was clear the little mob wasn't an impromptu rescue team.

"Dex, what's going on?" Daphna asked. Her stomach was turning over.

Just then thunder smashed the sky again. Everyone stopped in their tracks, holding their ears and crying out as they looked up at the crazy lightning spreading its electrical net overhead. But then it was gone, and they resumed their charge to the van.

The first person to reach it, a large man with tattooed arms, ripped open the mangled driver's side door, which came clean off in his hands.

"The driver!" he shouted. "Where's the driver?"

A woman at the passenger's window called out, "Check the back!"

Three people were already there. One opened the doors, a deliveryman. "There's no one here!" he shouted.

A siren sounded, silencing the group. Everyone turned to look back up the hill to see a police car slowly making its way onto the scene. It had one of those double-sided megaphones attached to its roof.

"Get back in your cars!" one of the two cops inside called through it, a woman. "Return to your cars immediately! If your vehicle has been damaged, we will approach you for details. Leave your car and you will be cited for obstruction!"

"Wait a minute," Daphna said, "where did those two other cops go?"

"Richards and Madden?" Dex said. "Maybe they're looking for the—"

"The cops that came to our house?"

Dex nodded, but Daphna had already forgotten about cops.

People were obeying the order, though from the sounds of all the grumbling, they were doing so very unhappily. Gawkers on the sidewalk walked off in all directions, so Dex and Daphna headed up the hill, striding quickly with their heads down. Daphna's legs were rubbery. She couldn't process a coherent thought. Dex was processing them all right, but he didn't want to.

When the school came into view, Daphna needed a moment to collect herself. Several moments, actually. She detoured down a set of concrete steps leading to a little strip of shops they'd been walking past and sat down on a bench at the bottom. She put her head in her hands for a few seconds, then looked up. "Dex, *what's going on?*" she asked again, barely able to keep her voice steady.

Dexter had reluctantly followed her down the steps, but he didn't sit down.

"I thought that was it," Daphna said, trying to settle one shaking hand with another on her knee. "I was sure it was coming after us. But I—I couldn't move."

"Me neither," Dex admitted. What he didn't say, because it shocked him to think it, was, *I didn't want to move.* In the hospital he'd decided to let events take their course, not to lift a finger to help even himself—but now that Daphna had cast doubt on where he'd wind up in the afterlife, he should have tried to save himself. As the van bore down on him he shouldn't have had the crystal-clear thought: *Who cares?* "Will someone shut those kids up!" he shouted at the street.

"He *was* coming after us," Daphna said, her voice a low growl. "I saw the driver. He was looking right at us, Dexter. Did you see what happened to him?"

"He probably took off after he crashed."

"Without any of those people right there on the street noticing?"

"Everyone looked up at the thunder and lightning. Maybe he ran away right then. Who cares, anyway? Those screaming kids are driving me crazy!"

Daphna responded with only a long, hard, and very cold look. So this was how it was going to be. "By the way," she said, "you're welcome for saving your life."

"It wouldn't have hit us," was all Dexter had to say back.

Simmering, Daphna took out her phone and called Dr. Fludd.

Again, nothing.

Daphna shoved the phone back into her pocket. "Let's just get going," she said, swallowing a barb of indignation at having to be the one to face all of this, at having to be so scared when she should be full of excitement, when she should be about to jump joyfully into a world of new experiences, experiences that didn't include being run over like a—"Oh, my gosh—look!" Daphna jumped to her feet, pointing at the strip of shops.

"What?" Dex looked over, but with no sense of urgency. Daphna seemed to be indicating a glass door next to the sub shop.

"A new bookstore! All it says is 'Rare Books.' It must be upstairs. It must be one of those appointment-only deals. I'll have to check it out after school. I'm so excited!"

Dexter smirked. It was as if Daphna had spied a pot of gold at the end of a rainbow. From the shining look on her face, he could see she'd magically forgotten everything else going on.

"Fantastic!" he said. "That's just what we need around here!"

Daphna took in a deep breath and let this go. A new bookshop! She was so pleased in fact, that she took her brother's hand again and pulled him back up the steps, now brimming with anticipation. All it took was the prospect of a new store, even if discovering the last one was the start of all their nightmares. *High school!* She tried to head uphill toward campus again, but Dex resisted her tug. Daphna stopped and turned to him, irritated all over again. *Enough of this already!*

At first she thought he was watching the escalating fracas in the street. Drivers from wrecked cars had apparently had enough of waiting their turn. They were all back on the road, complaining loudly about something, each other it seemed, and the two new cops seemed aggravated with all of them. An ambulance was now wending its way toward the wreck, though no one seemed to have located the driver. Someone was demanding to know what was going on with the weather, and kids were *still* screaming.

But Dex wasn't watching any of this. He was looking beyond it all, down the hill.

"Ah, Daphna?"

"What, Dex? We gotta go. We're gonna be late." Daphna tried to pull her brother again, but he wouldn't budge. She didn't need this from him right now!

"How many kids go to Wilson?"

"I don't know. Over fifteen hundred I think. Why? We have to—"

"What are the chances we're the only two kids who walk to school?"

Now Daphna saw what Dex was seeing—or not seeing. There should have been dozens, if not hundreds of kids coming up the hill.

"Weird," she admitted. "I don't see anyone our age at all."

"There was one kid, on the other side of the street down near where we almost got flattened."

"That's right! I mean, I didn't see anyone, but it sounded like a boy who yelled to watch out. Was that him?"

"I don't know."

Daphna scanned the streets suspiciously for a moment, then said, "Well, c'mon—let's go find out what the heck is going on."

Dex shrugged. Shrugging was becoming his new signature move. Something had snapped in him this morning. Maybe it was that thunder. Regardless, the result was that he felt... *free*, was the word.

The pair crossed the street and finally headed into campus. Daphna hurried down the long drive that ran along the back of the school, past the football field and outdoor community swimming pool. Dex kept up, but only halfheartedly. The parking lots were jammed with cars.

"This is weird," Daphna said, checking her cell

again. They were right on time. "There must be some-thing going on we didn't know about. An orientation or something?"

Daphna ran now, dragging her brother by the sleeve the rest of the way down the drive, and then up the steps and in through the school's main rear entrance.

The long gleaming hall that greeted them was completely empty. It was eerily silent too, but both Dex and Daphna had the distinct feeling there were a great many people around. There had to be with all those cars. They walked down the freshly waxed hall, looking left and right into empty classrooms. Dex pointed to a sign nestled among dozens of welcome and club posters indicating that the Main Office was straight ahead. They kept going.

"Dex," Daphna said, stopping halfway down the hall, "listen."

There was music, some kind of soft background type with no lyrics. It was coming from somewhere ahead, so the twins picked up their pace. Across from the office, which was at the end of the hall, and also disturbingly empty, they found two large doors—the Auditorium. The music was coming from inside, but so was something else, a powerful mood or feeling that gave them pause.

"Whatever's going on in there isn't good," Daph-na warned.

"And your point is what?" Dex asked.

"I guess I have no point."

"There *is* no point."

"Good point," Daphna retorted. "So—you're wrong."

"Point taken."

With that settled, cracking something that could almost be mistaken for smiles, the twins pushed open the doors.

# CHAPTER SIX
*A Better Place (Part II)*

The auditorium was packed. Every seat was filled with students, teachers, and what looked like random adults—parents, presumably. The awful feeling that was seeping into the hall was nothing short of stifling. All eyes were on a slideshow set to depressing classical music. Since no one looked back, Dex and Daphna stood in the doorway and watched.

Two dimply babies were on screen. The boy looked a year or so older than the girl, who had to be his sister. After a while they were both toddlers. There were a bunch of church photos, various ceremonies the kids took part in. Lots more were of birthdays at expensive venues: onboard the Portland Spirit; at a circus; what looked like a private box at a Blazer game. Fun at out-of-town mega-amusement parks followed those.

Lots of sniffling and a few outbursts of both sad laughter and despairing sobs came from the crowd as it watched.

"Oh my gosh," Daphna said when the thought crossed her mind that the kids looked a bit like she and Dex. "It's Teal and Jasper."

Dex nodded. They'd missed the news about this gathering, obviously, but it was no surprise. Teal and Jasper were the only two kids from the school to die from the plague. Jasper had been a freshman, and Teal was supposed to be one now, along with them. Dex couldn't help reflecting on how much the two looked like him and Daphna, even as little kids. If Teal had shorter hair and didn't have a tan all the time. If Jasper cut his hair and spiked it more....

Daphna's eyes burned as the pictures flashed by. A million emotions were kicking up inside. There was one slide from elementary school with Teal and her friends skipping rope on the playground. And there was Daphna, a small figure half cut off at the edge, sitting on a balance beam with a book, pretending to read but actually looking longingly on.

Books, Daphna understood, had been more than bottomless wells to slake her endless thirst for knowledge. They'd also been her escape from a world that wouldn't treat her right. In the end though, she'd gotten the better deal, because books were the only things that never let her down.

Teal had pretended to be her friend just to have Daphna do her work for her and her buddies. It was despicable, true, but she didn't deserve to *die*. Yet, her and her brother's deaths made it possible for everyone in the room to be there right now. If they hadn't looked enough like Daphna and Dex to fool that monster, everyone—*everyone*—might now be dead. *What does that mean?* Daphna thought. *How is that okay?*

After one final montage—brother and sister dressed for a fancy affair; football and cheerleader outfits; a princess and a caveman on Halloween—it ended. The screen went blank as the music faded away. The only sound left in the auditorium was muffled crying.

A paunchy man with prominent ears stood up from a row of chairs on stage and approached the podium. Daphna realized the glazed-eyed couple who'd been seated between him and another man, a big splotchy-faced guy with ginger hair, had to be Teal and Jasper's mom and dad. They looked completely absent, utterly lost in grief.

*"Mr. Haslam,"* Daphna whispered. *"The Principal."* She'd seen him on the school's website last night.

"I'd like to introduce Edward Jons," Haslam said, gesturing to the splotchy-faced guy. "Pastor Emeritus of the Taylor's church. Their current pastor is ill but sends his most heartfelt condolences to the Taylors and our entire community." He paused a moment, then added, "Pastor Jons has been kind enough to share just a *few* words."

Static burst from the walkie-talkie clipped to Haslam's belt, and a voice called his name. Looking concerned, he silenced it, said something to the Taylors—who didn't seem to notice—then hurried off through a door backstage.

Pastor Jons watched Haslam leave, then got up and charged to the podium, loosening his tie like he was ready for a fight. With no preliminaries, he shouted into the microphone, "We're at school, right? Am I *right?*" Without waiting for a response, he barked, "Well, what we have here is a test! *Life* is a test! *Death* is a test!"

This was met with a general murmuring of grief-stricken agreement, if surprise as well.

"But I'm here to tell you what you need to know to pass these tests!" Jons told the crowd. "Here it comes. You *ready?* You prepared to take *notes?* Here come the *answers!*"

Though this man came across as more than a few cards short of a full deck, Daphna actually felt breathless standing there still holding her door open. She wanted to hear what he was going to say.

Dex thought, *This ought to be good.*

"*Obedience!*" Jons yelled. "You got that? Obedience to the Word of *God!* That plague was a test! It was a *plague*—get it? A *plague!* You so-called survivors may have passed the test, but are you gonna pass the next one? These kids, Neal and Jasmine, they took their *final* exams, and they FAILED!"

Gasps sounded from all over the auditorium, either in response to the pastor's having gotten the deceased's names wrong or his having spoken ill of the dead—or both. Everyone looked to the Taylors in their chairs behind the podium, but the couple continued to stare blankly at nothing.

"Each and every one of the faithless sinners blighted by this plague—" Jons ranted, "they *all* failed! What's gonna happen when it's your time? You gonna be in a better place? How you gonna get there? You gonna climb on a tower and sneak through a trapdoor? Well, I'm here to tell you, you can't *cheat* your way through the Pearly Gates! You best choose your paths wisely my friends, because they don't all lead to the same place! You best *pray* for your immortal souls!"

The room had gone silent. Dex scoffed at the suggestion that praying could have any effect on, well, anything. Daphna wished it were so. She'd be happy to pray if God would respond to her.

"Are you going to *earn* your just deserts?" Jons

continued, still building steam. "Will you be among the believers who will rise from their graves? Will you be among the faithful who will meet the Lord Jesus in the air when he raptures his chosen people? Those who have lived by the testament written in his blood will be caught up with them as they rise into the sky to be with the Lord forever!" He paused a moment, then roared, "WILL YOU BE AMONG THEM, *OR WILL YOU BE CONSIGNED TO ETERNAL PUNISHMENT IN A LAKE OF FIRE?*"

"Now wait just a minute!" someone called out. It was Mr. Taylor, who'd evidently tuned into what was going on. He was on his feet now, red-faced and sputtering. Mrs. Taylor, perhaps unaware of what her husband was reacting to, was trying to pull him back into his seat.

"But let me tell you the real reason I came here today," Jons said, ignoring the interruption, or changing the subject because of it. "I came to point a finger at the *true* source of our troubles!"

Dex and Daphna had both been thinking about that odd phrase, 'testament written in his blood,' how they'd seen the same thing on that plaque under the painting of the Last Supper at the Vatican. But now their eyes went wide. They both had the same panicked thought: *This crazy pastor is talking about us.*

"I'm here to tell you who brought this plague down upon the good people of our land!"

Suddenly, Haslam was hurrying in through the door he'd gone out of backstage. "That's enough!" he shouted.

"They are here!" Jons railed, in full lather now. "I tell you they are here among us right now as we—!"

Before Haslam could reach the podium, before Jons could name the culprits, before the twins could back out of the auditorium and run for it, someone screamed, "Shut up!" from the crowd—a girl in the front row who had gotten to her feet. "Shut up! Shut up! Shut up!" All the twins could see was a cascade of spiraling white-blonde hair. "You don't know!" the girl challenged, though in a quavering voice. "You don't know for sure what will happen when we die!"

The pastor looked stunned, as did Haslam, who'd frozen a few feet behind the podium.

"Hey!" someone shouted before either of them

could respond, someone else now. The ringing, nasal voice was a dead giveaway. It was Wren, Teal's best friend. She was on her feet next to a seat at the end of the center aisle, pointing at the twins. Her eyes were pink and swollen. Make-up had run down her face. She looked devastated. But she also looked great in a designer tank top and swirl skirt. Daphna realized all the girls there had dressed up, everyone but her. "Hey!" Wren shouted again. "It's *them!*"

That's when Dex and Daphna realized that they had in fact been naïve to imagine a single measly news article about their having had nothing to do with the plague would undo so much news about their having had everything to do with it.

While Jons, Haslam, and both the Taylors remained on stage looking stupefied, and while the crowd processed what Wren was talking about, the white-blonde girl up front screamed, "I'm sorry! I'm sorry!" Then she tore down the aisle. Dex and Daphna got a good look at her because she sprinted right between them. Her features were delicate and ghostly pale. Tears streamed down her face.

When the girl disappeared into the hall, the twins turned their attention back to the auditorium to find themselves facing two thousand cutting eyes. It was not something either had ever experienced. Now *they* were stupefied.

"*They* did it!" another girl stood up and shouted. It was Branwen, the third and most polished jewel in the middle school crown. Beautiful Branwen. She was sporting her usual flowing raven locks and wearing her famous "Little Black Dress." She wore it every year on Dress Your Best Day, when it never failed to have the effect it had on everyone now. The entire crowd stared at her, evidently forgetting everything else. "It was *them!*" Branwen repeated when she'd absorbed enough staring. "*They* killed Teal!" Her make-up was perfectly in place.

An oppressive silence suffocated the auditorium for a moment. Daphna knew something really bad was brewing. It was an ironclad law of life: If you looked into Branwen's big, beguiling eyes, you did whatever she wanted. Lots of kids believed she was actually the Queen of the Pops, that the others did her bidding without her ever having even to bother moving her pouty lips to give orders. The only reason the crowd wasn't doing anything yet was because they weren't sure exactly what she wanted them to do.

Finally, Branwen started to boo. Then someone else started to boo. Haslam, turning back from watching Jons storm off stage past the Taylors, called for attention, but he was ignored. The booing was coming from everywhere now.

Branwen bent down, picked up a purple piece of paper, some sort of flyer or program, balled it up, then threw it toward the twins. It missed by a mile, but a few seconds later hundreds more went flying. The room now smelled of lavender.

Daphna, who'd somehow left her body for a moment, came back when she realized the flyers were scented with Teal's favorite fragrance, but she was paralyzed by all those eyes. *"Dex,"* she whispered, *"get me out of here."* If this is a test, she thought, I fail. A wad of paper bounced off her face. Then another.

"Attention!" Haslam demanded. "Attention—!"

Teachers all around were up now and calling for order, but they were also ignored.

*"Dex, please!"* Daphna was seeing the room spin.

"No," Dex said without looking at his sister. He was staring down the two thousand eyes, scanning two by two to meet every last one. They weren't going to make him move an inch. Getting *blamed* for the plague? Sure, why not? Why should he have expected anything else?

The booing got louder.

"Attention! Stop this at once!"

The bell for Zero Period rang just then, but no one got up. Dex wouldn't let them. He stood his ground up to his ankles in smelly crumpled paper, trading hate for hate with all those ignorant eyes as the booing flowed over him, justifying his every thought since leaving Dr. Fludd's that morning. *If this is a test,* he thought, *I. Don't. Care.*

But enough was enough.

"You're welcome!" Dex shouted. "It's been an honor and a pleasure to serve you!" He turned to take in Daphna's approval for this marginal witticism, but she was no longer there.

Sighing, he stepped out of the auditorium, letting

the door close on the sound of Haslam still hollering lamely over the boos.

Daphna was just down the hall, bent over a water fountain.

"We should have expected something like that," Dex said when he reached her, still feeling rather pleased with himself. "Can you believe that loony preacher guy? What a loon!"

Daphna straightened up, touching the corner of her eye with a wet finger. She wasn't crying, which was a good sign, Dex thought, but her face seemed disturbingly unstable, like a continent about to collapse in on itself. She was taking deep breaths. "*Come on*," he sighed. "Who cares what those—"

Daphna slapped him. Hard.

"*I* do!" she snapped. "I. Do! *Get it?* Or is that too hard to get through your thick skull! Do you know *anything* about me? I needed you back there—and you just—!"

At that moment kids erupted from the auditorium and streamed into the halls. Daphna went silent and put her head down, while Dex just stood there with his hand on his cheek, thinking about slapping his sister back. She *had* lost her mind.

There was no booing. No one threw anything, but everyone kept as far away from the twins as possible as they passed by. One boy simulated a heart attack stumbling past. He and some others were clearly trying to be cruel, but most seemed genuinely afraid.

Daphna pulled the schedule she'd downloaded last night out of her back pocket, read it over, then walked off without even acknowledging her brother.

After watching his sister head through a crowd that parted for her like the Red Sea, Dex took a few deep breaths of his own. Daphna had read his schedule to him last night, so he knew what Homeroom he was in, but why bother?

*If life is a test,* he thought, *who needs school?*

# CHAPTER SEVEN
### *The Next Thing She Knew*

If hell was a high school, Daphna was now enrolled in it. She didn't hear the jeers, the fake puking noises, or the foul insults. The grotesque faces drifting past her in slow motion were more than enough. *I'll make things right myself,* she thought, fuming. *If he doesn't care about seeing our mothers again, he can go jump in a lake—a lake of fire!*

Was it really all a *test*? Deep in her heart, Daphna thought it might just be. God left humans to their own devices, surely to *prove* themselves worthy of his gift of free will. *That* was a test. Despite everything she and her brother had seen and done, Daphna suspected she was failing it. She had always believed that the ends don't automatically justify the means. Just because they *thought* they had to take Dead Face into Heaven didn't mean they actually *had* to, did it? How could anything good have come of such a thing?

Maybe she should have stopped him before he got his hands on that locked book, thrown herself at him or something before he turned the key in the cover. If they would have just let themselves die properly when he'd shot them, he never would have been in Heaven to begin with. Things couldn't possibly be like that pastor described them. Could they? God didn't get involved. But what if that was only until you died? What if he was up there in some secret part of Heaven somewhere, waiting to pass judgment on you when you got there—when you were *supposed* to get there? Surely they were wrong to step foot in the Light with or without Dead Face. Dex was right— they weren't dead! *What was happening up there?*

*Wait!* Daphna thought. *Taking Dead Face into Heaven was Dexter's idea! Maybe I won't have to answer for that!*

Now Daphna was utterly disgusted with herself,

sickened by having even entertained that thought—she'd reached a new low. And it wasn't even entirely true. She deserved whatever she got for that selfish thought alone. But alone is how she felt. It was Dexter's fault she was even having these thoughts!

Flustered by the effort to keep it together, Daphna went the wrong way, so she had to trek back through more abuse, which she could hear now. Finally, mercifully, there it was—her homeroom, about as far away from the auditorium as she could get. She paused before going in, taking a moment to hope she got a good teacher. Because parents had a history of flooding the school with requests for Homeroom changes based on teachers' reputations, Wilson didn't include their names on the schedules.

Daphna walked in—and froze.

Wren was there. Just her luck. Branwen too. She'd forgotten that they tried to place kids from the same middle schools together in Homerooms if possible, based on recommendations. Her old teachers probably thought they were all friends, just like Daphna used to. There were a few others there, too.

Naturally, the Pop girls were chatting up the Pop and potential Pop boys. Branwen had one trapped by the rear wall, little-black-dressing him to death. He was tall and lanky, with longish black hair that fell into a wide part and flipped a bit over a pair of large, dark movie star sunglasses. Actually, now that she looked closer, Daphna thought the boy seemed rather uncomfortable. *Extremely* uncomfortable, in fact, which was very, very strange, since right about now his tongue should be on the ground. He was fidgety and looking around the room too much, nervously stretching a bright yellow elastic cover on a large book he was holding.

Was she supposed to have her textbooks already? No one else seemed to. It was going to be the last straw if she got an assignment she couldn't do.

Incredibly, the boy seemed to be searching for a way to escape the situation. Maybe he was blind? If he wasn't, resistance was futile. Pop girls went right in for the kill. It was a well-known fact that no boy Branwen had ever targeted as boyfriend material ever got away. Daphna had seen it a thousand times, but she couldn't help watching how Branwen operated with Wren as her wingman and the other girls as her audience/shield/distraction. Did they get together to plan actual strategies, or was it some kind of pack instinct?

For a second, the boy seemed to look at Daphna as she watched the scene. He smiled. A big smile. A gorgeous smile. Daphna didn't smile back. Instead, she choked a bit on her suddenly dry throat.

Just then the hubbub in the room died. The other kids had noticed her, too. Everyone looked repulsed. Everyone but Wren, who looked as if she could barely contain the urge to come over and rip Daphna limb from diseased limb.

Daphna swallowed hard. She saw an empty seat and took it. The kids in the nearby desks stood up in theirs and began to drag them away.

"Don't. You. *Dare.*"

Daphna turned at the sound of the adult's voice—and beamed. It was Mr. Guillermo! *Mr. G!* She didn't even know he'd moved to Wilson. His class had been her favorite in middle school, and not just for the obvious reason that he'd unwittingly set her and Dex on the path to finding the truth about Eden. He was the most open-minded teacher she'd ever had, and the most excited about what he taught. Daphna wondered if he'd be teaching World Religions there as well. Maybe he could help her get some answers about Heaven! She should have thought of that before!

"Sit down," Mr. G snarled at the class, taking his glasses off the way he always did. She'd never heard this tone from him before, though he did, of course, have to deal with high schoolers now.

Everyone sat down as he stormed over to his desk. Wren sat directly next to Daphna, unleashing her infamous glare, a look known to reduce its targets to quivering heaps. Daphna used to be mortally afraid of provoking The Look. Now she rolled her eyes at it.

"I have been teaching for nearly thirty years," said Mr. G, putting his glasses back on. "I've taught in elementary school, middle school, and high school. And I have to tell you something: That debacle in the auditorium was the most shameful display I have ever seen.

"Now, I'm not going to stand here and say I subscribe to that supposedly holy man's belief system, but I'll tell you this: If *that* was a test, you did not pass. Not an impressive debut, my friends. Not impressive at all. Something has brought out the worst in you today. I'm just going to hope it's this crazy weather. Daphna, I sincerely apologize on behalf of everyone at Wilson. This is not what we stand for here. I am beside myself." He took his glasses off again.

No one had spoken through the speech, and no one spoke now. Most kids had their heads down, but they didn't look especially ashamed. Some were manifestly sneering. Wren didn't even lower her eyes, let alone her head. She continued to glare openly at Daphna.

"It's fine," Daphna said, recalling that Dex had at some point mentioned to her that Mr. Guillermo used to be at their elementary school as a counselor. Dex would know of course, because he always had to see counselors. Daphna just wanted to move on. She just wanted to start high school, to start *life*. *Why couldn't she just move on?*

Mr. G scanned the room, looking for challenges. When he was satisfied none was forthcoming, he picked up a clipboard. "Fine," he said, still irate. "Find a locker partner, line up, and I'll hand out combinations."

*Great*, Daphna thought. She didn't bother to get up. Everyone else practically jumped out of their desks. The moment the commotion began, Wren leaned over and whispered, *"It's your fault she died. I know you did something to us in the park and at the party. You're a* freak. *You* should be the one who's dead!"

Daphna wasn't sure how to reply to this outrage, but it didn't matter because Wren and Branwen rushed off to be first in line at the desk, no doubt so they could charm their way into the best locker location. Daphna just sat there while the rest of the room negotiated around her. *It'll blow over*, she told herself, taking deep breaths, trying not to hyperventilate. *Soon. I'll start living soon. I'd probably get a partner who'd steal my stuff anyway.*

Tears were coming again, but so was something else: toxic detestation. If she had a Word of Power, she'd vaporize these girls here and now and damn the consequences. *Bring on the Lake of Fire,* she thought bitterly. *I can swim just fine.* She should have choked them all to death in the park when she had the power to do so. She should have drowned them in cleanser at that stupid "party."

*No, that was totally—*

"I'm really very neat."

"What?"

Someone was talking—to her?

"I said, 'Mind partnering with a boy? I'm very neat.'"

Daphna didn't think the question was directed at her, but it was. The boy from the back of the room. He'd folded up into the desk Wren just left and was sitting there looking at her expectantly through his shades with his yellow-covered book on his lap.

He took the sunglasses off, and Daphna looked into his grey-blue eyes. They had an intelligent cast, even if they were still darting around. But there was something unusual in them, something she recognized but couldn't quite identify. Something sad? No, she saw exactly what it was: pain. This boy's eyes radiated pain, and it was very much like the pain she carried around, maybe even worse.

"I've just barely escaped the Sirens' clutches," he said, smiling in a way that seemed both shy and smart. "Maybe I should've stuffed my ears full of desk gum and tied myself to the flagpole."

Daphna laughed. She loved *The Odyssey.* "Oh, they'll skin you alive," she said. "That's how they have so many leather handbags."

The boy laughed too, a giddy sort of, well, nerdy laugh. Daphna liked it.

"Daphna Wax," the boy said, "I know you." He pushed some hair out of his eye. "I mean, not from the news or anything," he hastened to add. "I mean, I do, but not only…My name is Quinn. Quinn Quartich."

Daphna recognized the name. Sort of.

"My father and your father—" Quinn explained, "they were colleagues in the book biz. He was real sorry to hear about your dad's death." Quinn sounded choked up. "My pop had a rare bookshop out in McMinnville," he continued. "The last time we saw your dad he was desperate about some old Latin thing. There was some book he asked about more recently, but he never came to get it." His eyes started to dart again.

"Barney Quartich!" Daphna couldn't believe it. That Latin book! It seemed like forever ago that it had saved their lives.

"Berny, yeah," said Quinn. Then he started talking fast. "We just moved into Portland— which I love," he said. "I swear it's like Never Never Land compared to McMinnville. We opened up a new shop out of our apartment right down the street here, what with that giant store having burned down and your dad not working the area anymore. We heard about the new store you were going to open up, in Multnomah Village, but I guess that didn't work out, huh? It never opened, did it, even with all the stock inside? It sounds like you guys have really had a hard time. Ours is just a little place. I've seen you a few times over the years, with your dad. I was kind of shy though, and small, so I rarely came out of my Hobbit hole. I doubt you ever saw me."

Daphna blushed. Had she ever really blushed before? Not like this. It felt like her cheeks were going to melt off her face. The thought alone that this boy knew her would have been enough to throw her for a loop. How could he have been too shy to meet her? He was, well, a Pop, at least he looked good enough to be one. But it seemed he'd shunned them to come talk to her. And his father sold rare books out of that new shop! Had he mentioned *The Odyssey*, *Peter Pan*, and *The Hobbit* all in the last sixty seconds?

"So, how 'bout it?"

"What?"

"Partners? Locker partners?"

"Oh, yes. Sure. Okay." Daphna couldn't control the connection between her brain and mouth. "Yeah. Locker partners. Good. I need one. For my stuff." She stood up, managing in the process to crash her knee into the desktop.

"Great," Quinn said, getting up too. "But, ah, would you mind signing up yourself? In case they don't allow boys and girls—"

"Sure."

It was only when Daphna looked over to check the status of the line at Mr. G's desk that she noticed everyone not in it was standing as far away as possible along the walls. They'd all been watching the show. Her ears went as hot as her cheeks.

"I'd keep away from her if I were you," Branwen said to Quinn after making sure Mr. Guillermo was still occupied. "Everyone who knows that girl dies. How many people you know are dead, Daphna? A dozen? *Two?*"

"Shut up," Daphna snapped. That was it. This was going too far. Branwen just couldn't stand it if a boy didn't fall to his knees for her.

"All those old people in the rest home," Wren spat. "Your *parents*. How *many* parents, now?"

"Hey, now," Quinn said, looking slightly pale.

"You don't know what you're getting into," Branwen warned him. "Anything you touch her with will probably fall off."

Daphna was way beyond being afraid of these girls, these girls who she'd idolized for so long. But she despaired. It was true. Just about everyone she came to care about *was* dead.

"Hmmm," Quinn said, though Daphna only heard him as if from a great distance. "Let's see about that."

And the next thing she knew, he was kissing her.

Fireworks went off in Daphna's head—the earth moved. She was somewhere else entirely.

It took a while—forever—but cries of alarm eventually filtered through to her.

Quinn stepped back, looking confused and alarmed.

It took another few moments, but eventually Daphna realized there'd been two explosions—one inside her head and one outside of it.

The thunder had crashed again, so loudly that it sounded as if it had exploded inside the school. And the earth was *still* moving.

The building was shaking right down to its foundations.

# CHAPTER EIGHT
*Not a Drill*

When Daphna was out of sight, Dexter headed for the exit. Kids fell over themselves to communicate their horror at the very sight of him, which provided an amusing opportunity. He took a detour, walking up and down random halls holding his gut and coughing toward anyone he could get near. It produced the desired effect: Everyone ran for their lives. When the late bell rang he was still in the hall, but alone.

*Alrighty then*, Dex thought. *Time to get this retirement thing started.*

The nearest door deposited him in front of the school. He needed to think. Maybe he should head to the park and hang out in the Clearing under the Ash tree awhile. Despite the horrors that happened there, he missed it.

*Lake of fire?*

The image had lodged in his head and was growing in there like a malignant tumor. It couldn't possibly be true.

*And this Jesus stuff*, he thought. *First of all, since Jesus was born from a Lamed Vavnik's rib, he obviously wasn't who everyone thought he was. How could he come back from the dead—be resurrected, if that was the right word—and 'rapture' people, or whatever that word was? But there was all that stuff people said he did—miracles. Didn't he walk on water or something? Heal people? Was there one special Lamed Vavnik?* Dex had no idea what to think. It was impossible to dismiss anything anymore.

A lake of fire?

A waste of time even to think about it. He'd probably find out about *that* soon enough, anyway—his just deserts, like that mental pastor had said.

Dex approached the sidewalk in front of the school, but stopped at the sound of some kind of disturbance. Several women were scampering down from their porches across the street. Another came out of her house wrestling a squalling baby, a heavy-set lady wearing a bandana on her head. "What's happening?" she called to the others.

"An emergency at the elementary school!" shouted a blonde woman already heading down the street. "They won't say what it's about, so we're going to find out!"

Dex watched the mad dash for a moment. The elementary school was just on the other side of the athletic field.

"Hey, you!" the woman on the porch called. Her baby would not shut up. Again with the screaming!

Dex assumed she was talking to him, so he intentionally didn't look her way, but then she added, "Get away from my car!"

A long-faced man in running shorts and a zip-up sweatshirt stood up from behind a car across the street.

"Why do you need to be there so long tying your shoe?" the woman complained. "You going to steal my car? Are you one of those people who hang around schools selling drugs? This isn't a bus stop!"

She caught sight of Dex, who was now watching the confrontation. "I don't pay taxes for you to skip school!" she hollered at him now. "There's all kinds of police down there," she warned both troublemakers, waving toward the other side of campus. "I'll go get 'em too. I'll do it!"

The man had looked at Dex, but now turned back to the woman and said, "Get back in your house, lady."

Dex didn't have time for this, either. The thing was, she was right. What *was* he going to do, skip *high school?* Dr. Fludd wouldn't stand for it. *Daphna* wouldn't stand for it. She'd probably take his drop-ping out as a sign of *her* failure, which meant he'd never hear the end of it. But then again, maybe it would do her good to fail at something for once in her life. *Project Dex.* If only he had that inheritance, school wouldn't even matter. But of course they'd set it up so he wouldn't get the money until he was eigh-teen—and probably not until he had his diploma, if that was legal.

"Go on! Git! Move along!"

"Get back in your house, lady," the sweatshirt guy repeated, this time with a dangerous edge to his voice.

*Anyway,* Dex thought, *is being considered contagious any worse than being thought stupid? Sounds better, actually. No one runs away from stupid.*

Impossibly, the baby bawled louder.

"GET BACK IN YOUR HOUSE!"

*The believers will rise up into the sky,* Dex thought, turning back toward school. He broke into a jog. *Been there, done that.*

"That's right!" the woman called after Dex. "You punks just need to know who's boss! Why the whole lot of—!"

The door swung shut behind him. Dex had to be at least ten minutes late now, but, well, it was too late to do anything about that. Luckily, the numbers on the doors weren't acting up. He quickly found the right room.

Dex peeked through the window in the door. Only a few kids seemed to be inside, perhaps half a dozen. They were sitting quietly, looking nervously around. After a deep breath, he pushed his way inside and hurried to the nearest seat, which was in the front row. He'd figured maybe the teacher was yelling at everyone for what happened in the auditorium, but it was immediately obvious that this was not the case. There was no teacher. Maybe he wasn't that late? Unsure what to do, Dex just sat there staring at the whiteboard, listening for clues behind him. There was a very uncomfortable feeling in the room. Maybe everyone thought he'd been the teacher coming, so they'd shut up?

"So, what's your damage?" someone asked in a slightly garbled voice. Dex turned around. It was a boy with large hearing aids and hair he must have cut himself. Dex didn't reply at first, so the kid said, "Dumb, is it? That's a new one. Of course I mean 'mute,' if you know what I mean, unless you don't 'cause you're dumb, by which I mean stupid."

"What?" Dex managed. He assumed he was being insulted, but the look on the kid's face, while not friendly by any means, wasn't cruel. It was mostly curious.

"Not mute, anyway," the kid concluded. "Hmm.

I'll guess in a sec. And I'm not going with the obvious, 'cause any mouth-breather knows they don't let kids come to school with the freakin' plague. But first," he said, waving at the room in general, "let me introduce you to your fellow inmates: I'm the nearly deaf kid, which I'm sure you noticed, unless you're the nearly blind kid. We don't have one of those right now, but one's on order." He stood up and pointed to a short girl in a black skirt and two brightly striped, clashing knee-high socks. She had a pierced lip. "Here we have Odie," he said, by way of introduction.

"Like the dog?" Dex asked.

"O. D., as in 'Oppositional Defiant'," the girl said, sounding proud of her label. "Plus ADHD," she added.

"Sorry, didn't mean to short-change you," the nearly deaf kid replied. Dex almost cracked a smile, but it didn't actually seem that anyone was particularly amused. He finally realized what permeated the room: the dark humor of futility. He knew it well. He'd apparently been placed in a "special" Homeroom.

Home at last.

The boy with the hearing aids was pointing to someone else, but before he could make the introduction an incredible explosion shook the entire school. Everyone looked to the classroom's one window to see that web-like lighting snap across the sky immediately after.

"That thunder!" the clashing-sock girl shouted. "It's not normal! Lightning comes *before* thunder! Lightning *makes* thunder!"

*That's right,* Dex thought, shaking his head. *That weird lightning came* after *all those thunderclaps.* It was amazing how you could fail to note the obvious. But so what?

Now everyone looked at one another, unsure what to do with no teacher in the room. When the shaking finally stopped, it sounded like people were running through the halls.

The fire alarm blared, a shrill, stabbing siren.

Before anyone could decide how to respond, Mr. Haslam's voice came from the speaker on the wall over the door. "Students and staff," he instructed, "please disregard the alert. False alarm. Please remain in your classrooms."

Mercifully, the painful noise cut off.

Moments later, a short, barrel-chested teacher rushed in with a stack of folders in his arms. He tossed them on his desk, then grabbed the phone sitting next to his computer. After punching a single button, he said, somewhat breathlessly, "I saw who pulled it. A girl, the girl who—yeah, that's her," he said. "I chased her, but—yes, a few ne'er-do-wells taking advantage, shockingly enough. Yes." Then he hung up and said, "So sorry to be late!" to his uneasy students. "Tardy on the first day, no less! And I'm the teacher! It's just that—I was in the office—what a crazy day, even for the first—!"

The alarm went off again, as if to prove his point.

"Don't worry kids. It's a copycat, no doubt. These things tend to be contagious, especially on the—oh, Dexter, I'm so—"

"This is not a drill," Haslam interrupted. He sounded much more severe this time. "This is a Lock Out. Students are to remain in Homeroom until notified. I repeat, this is *not* a drill."

"What's going on!" demanded a buzz-cut girl in all black Dex hadn't been introduced to. Her entire head was shaking.

The teacher sat down. *"I'm probably not supposed to say anything,"* he sighed, "but if it makes you feel better to know, there's some kind of incident taking place outside. There was an accident on the street that involved a lot of cars. Authorities are on the scene—some kind of search is going on—and, you see, if any police activity gets within a certain distance of the school, by law we have to declare a—"

"But the building shook!" the clashing-sock girl protested. "Don't we have to evacuate, like after an earthquake?"

"Well, that actually might not be a bad—"

As if on cue, the thunder boomed outside, rattling the windows and walls.

From the hall came the sound of more running feet, many more, and also what had to be skateboard wheels whizzing along polished floors, then a teacher yelling, "Get back in the room!" Their teacher did not continue to offer reassurance. He looked hopelessly flummoxed.

Haslam came on again, this time sounding

downright furious: "The Lock Out is still in effect!" he shouted. "All students must remain in their classrooms. I repeat, all students must remain in their classrooms. This is not a drill!"

"I don't like this," grumbled a boy with an unusually large forehead and watery eyes. "I don't like this. I don't like this. I don't like this." Then he stood up and shouted, *"I don't like this!"*

Someone in the hall yanked open the door, a gangling boy with broken glasses hanging halfway off his face.

"Get out!" he wailed. "Get out! Some older kids—that used to go here—that got expelled—some local gang—they're on campus to fight! Gang war! GANG WAR!" He ran off to the sound of screaming and banging.

After a moment of stunned silence in the classroom, the boy with hearing aids demanded, "What are we going to do? Shouldn't we lock the—"

The thunder crashed again. The entire building jolted. Two boys fell into the room through the open door, wailing on each other. When they crashed through a row of desks and hit the floor, everyone rushed from the room, the teacher included.

Everyone but Dexter, who'd stayed put. He knew one of these boys. Eyeballs was his name. Dex had gotten him out of jail and temporarily set him on the straight and narrow with the First Tongue. But he wasn't afraid. Let Eyeballs get him next. Let the building fall on his—

*No. Wait a second. What was he thinking?*

Dex ran into the hall. It was madness out there, though it didn't look like a gang war, not that Dex knew what one looked like. Some kids were throwing punches, but randomly, in all directions. Most everybody else was simply smashing things. Dexter couldn't help but reflect momentarily that the scene resembled rather closely dreams he'd had many times; dreams in which he was personally destroying a school.

One boy was crushing in lockers with his huge black combat boots. A girl in pigtails was just sitting on the floor giggling while tearing pages out of a textbook and tossing them around like confetti. Inside classrooms, it looked and sounded like everyone was smashing everything.

*Dreams really do come true,* Dex thought, darkly. His backpack was still in the classroom, so he scooped up a random, rather heavy one from the floor. He scanned for an enticing target. *There:* a display case down the hall full of academic awards.

Dex dove into the throng and began bulling his way through bodies. At some point while he pushed and shoved, he heard a powerful voice cry out over the clamor. It was that barmy pastor.

*"There is nothing that keeps wicked men, at any moment, out of hell,"* he bellowed, *"but the mere pleasure of their God!"*

Dex couldn't see the man, but his voice was incredibly powerful. He sounded like God himself might.

*"Satan stands ready to fall upon you and seize you as his own!"*

More and more students were pouring out of classrooms up and down the hall, making any movement at all nearly impossible. Some were clearly trying to evacuate, but most were just flailing around. Dex threw elbows to keep people off of him as he fought his way forward a few feet at a time. But then he tripped and fell on his face. The backpack got kicked away.

*"THE WICKED WILL BE CAST INTO HELL!"*

Something hit him on top of his head, hard enough to set sparks flashing in his eyes.

Furious, Dex looked up from the floor to find Pastor Jons looming over him with a Bible held up over his head and a transported look on his perspiring face. He'd hit Dex with his Bible, a hardback. Dex tried to get up, but it was difficult with legs and knees crashing into him from every which way.

*"YOUR SOUL WILL KINDLE AND FLAME OUT INTO HELLFIRE!"* The book cracked his skull again.

"Stop that!" Dex demanded, which earned him another whack, this time on the side of his head.

Pastor or not, Dex was going to fight back. He got to his feet and shoved Jons as hard as he could, sending him and his trembling jowls toppling over into the frothing crowd.

"Assault!" Jons wailed from the floor. Then it sounded like he screamed, "Jason!"

"It's Dexter!" Dex shouted. "Dexter Wax! Get it

right! *Dexter Wax!*" He turned back to fight the crowd, but nearly fell again. There was a body on the floor right under him, someone in the fetal position, rocking back and forth. It was a girl, and she was pretty much wrapped around his leg.

Dex was starting to tear his foot free when he noticed all the white-blonde hair.

"*YOU WILL BURN FOR ALL OF ETERNITY FOR YOUR SINS!*" the pastor shrieked from wherever he was on the floor. He was invisible now, swallowed by the riot, but his voice was indomitable. "YOU! WILL! *BURN!*"

Dex made another attempt to free his foot, but an eye opened to him from over an arm in the midst of all that hair, an eye so full of fear that it pierced him. It pierced him so powerfully that he suddenly felt as if he were alone with it. Dex had never encountered fear like this before, not even in his own heart, not even after all he'd been through.

Something compelled him to kneel down next to the girl. Maybe she was hurt. She was muttering something, though he couldn't tell what. Dex put a hand on her back and shook her a bit. "Are you okay?" he asked, helping her sit up. She didn't resist at all. He was quite sure she didn't even know where she was. "Are—are you okay?" he asked again, louder this time. "Do you need help?"

"*THE LAKE OF FIRE!*" thundered Jons' disembodied voice.

The girl's lips stopped moving and she seemed to register Dexter, however weakly.

"I can help you," Dex promised. He had no idea why he had to do this, but he did. He absolutely did. "Come with me." He helped her to her feet.

"THE LAKE OF *FIRE!*"

"What's your name?" Dex shouted, pulling the girl into the moving crowd.

"Nora," she whimpered. "I don't want to go to Hell."

Jons' voice was fading now, but they could still make it out. "BURN! YOU WILL *BUUUURN!*"

Dex straight-armed a boy coming right at them, knocking him aside. "Why would you go to hell?"

"Jesus!" Nora yelped as she stumbled forward, her eyes glazed over. "Please take me! I want to go to Heaven!"

A wicked clap of thunder cracked outside, setting off screams all around, but Dex scarcely noticed them. Finally, everyone was heading for the exits.

"Funny you should say that!" Dex said, leaning into Nora's ear while getting them moving again, aiming for the door.

"What?" She focused on Dexter for the first time. "Why?"

"Because if Jesus won't do the job, I might be able to take you there myself!"

They'd reached the door at last, but now Nora stopped.

"What?" she said. "Are you mocking me?"

For a moment, Dex scanned the mob scene outside for Daphna. How could he have forgotten about her? But he looked at Nora again and said, as seriously as he knew how, "I'm Dexter Wax. My sister and I have been to Heaven—and I promise you that pretty soon we'll be going back."

# CHAPTER NINE
*This Is For Real*

"What's happening?" Daphna asked. She was still not processing thoughts clearly. Had she just been kissed for the first time in her life? It felt like the world had dematerialized around her, leaving her floating in some blissful alternate dimension.

"Quiet!" Mr. Guillermo ordered. "All of you!"

Reality was coming back, but only in fits and starts.

"Duck and cover! This is for REAL!"

*"What?"* Daphna gasped.

The alarm went off again. Everyone was on their feet, crying out, ignoring Mr. G completely. When the building finally stopped shaking, one shout rose up, cutting through the clamor: Branwen's. "It's *her! She's* doing this! She's a *witch!"*

*Super,* Daphna thought.

But before anyone could react to this, the crashing and smashing commenced in the halls. Someone threw open the door to see what was happening, then ran out. Mr. Guillermo tried to block the exit to prevent others from following, but when he reached it, whatever was happening out there evidently demanded his immediate attention, because he rushed out as well, ordering someone, or everyone, to cease and desist immediately. A stampede followed him out.

Daphna, standing at her desk, finally back on Planet Earth, watched these developments with dread twisting in her gut. This was all wrong. *Everything was all wrong.* She had to get out of there. She moved toward the door but stopped when she heard Quinn yell, "Watch out!"

Before Daphna could react to hearing that phrase for the third time that morning, she was hit flush in the face with a stinging spray of billowing white gas. She couldn't breathe, and her face went simultaneously icy cold and burning. All she could do was fall to the floor, choking and gasping.

Quinn called Daphna's name, but then there was the whoosh of spraying again, followed by the sound of Quinn falling to the floor, groaning and gasping himself.

Writhing in pain, Daphna tried to rub the freezing fire out of her eyes, but that only seemed to make it worse.

"This is all your fault!" someone screamed. Daphna forced an eye open. Through pouring tears and a haze of lingering white smoke, she saw who it was: Wren. She had a fire extinguisher and was about to smash Daphna's head open with it.

*She's going to kill me,* was all Daphna could think. *After everything I've been through, a Pop is going to kill me.* And she produced something that resembled a laugh.

"Teal was the only thing that kept me going," Wren sobbed.

Daphna closed her eyes again and curled up in a ball with her arms over her head. *Please,* she prayed, *please let me go to my mothers.*

*No!* She hadn't made things right yet!

"You took her from me!" Wren wailed. "And now I'm going to—!"

Daphna rolled blindly away.

There was a ringing clang when the extinguisher hit the floor and released another blast of chemical fog. The canister rolled against Daphna's leg.

Wren missed!

Daphna opened her eyes, which weren't burning quite so much now. Through the misty tendrils of spray wending up and around desk and chair legs, she saw—no one.

Wren was gone.

A movement across the room attracted Daphna's attention. Quinn was also on the floor, but with his tear-stained face pressed to—a book? His yellow textbook?

Quinn—he'd kissed her! *But*—

"What—what happened?" Daphna asked, slowly getting to all fours, then to her feet. She couldn't see much more than blurs, but Wren was definitely no longer in the room. No one else was. "What are you doing?"

Quinn was back on his feet now, too. His sunglasses lay broken on the floor. It *was* that book with the yellow cover.

"What is that?" Daphna demanded, trying to get her vision to clear, but a sound at the door made her spin round. It was Branwen. Daphna now heard the raging that accompanied the continued sounds of destruction from the hall.

"Wren?" Branwen demanded. "Where's Wren?" Seeing that her friend was not there, she turned and beckoned someone. A moment later a group of boys, half of whom were bleeding from one place or another, came storming into the room. "Wren never came out!" she shrieked. "That witch did something to Wren!"

Daphna backed up and bumped into Quinn, who seemed to be fumbling with his book again. His eyes were red and swollen. It was clear he was having trouble seeing whatever he was looking for.

A boy at the front of the group started kicking aside the desks that blocked the way to the posse's prey.

*"What are you doing?"* Daphna yelled at Quinn.

"Can't see! I just need a second! I just need a second!"

But there was no second. Daphna leapt to snatch up the fire extinguisher. With no hesitation, though with poor aim, she sprayed it at the three boys who were nearly upon them. They all fell to the floor, wailing with their fists in their eyes. Branwen ran.

"Sorry!" Quinn shouted, finally looking away from the book. "I guess it was your turn! Follow me!" He headed for the door directly enough. Daphna ran behind him.

*Why did he kiss her?*

It was bedlam in the halls. Hundreds of students were throwing themselves at one another, swinging backpacks like maces or hurling heavy textbooks like grenades. At least one other person had sprayed another fire extinguisher at the far end. It sounded like that pastor was somewhere, shouting about the devil. Quinn put his shoulder down and simply charged into the mass of bodies like a running back. Following closely behind, Daphna remembered Dex.

*How could she have forgotten about her brother?*

"Dex!" she called. "Dex!"

Quinn managed to find a stream in the melee moving toward the exits.

"Dex!" Daphna called again, craning her neck to scan the crowd as she moved through it. Eventually, they forced their way out through the front doors.

The rioting outside was just as bad. Students were on cars in the smaller front lot, stomping hoods and spider-webbing windshields. The fence surrounding the pool was down, and kids were running up and down the dry slides. Daphna could hardly believe what she was seeing—many of these hooligans were mild-mannered and studious! Some kids were trying to get away on bikes or scooters, but as soon as someone was on one, they were knocked off. One bike was wrapped around a light pole.

Some teachers were trying to get everyone to evacuation spots, but they mostly seemed to be arguing with each other. A few seemed ready to fight. There was a brutal clap of thunder followed by that insane lightning spreading over the sky. The ground shook violently, causing hundreds of bodies to fall. Everyone screamed.

"Dex!" Daphna wailed, back on her feet after a tumble. It was like being in Turkey all over again! When would it end? And it was really hot, much hotter than it had been on their way to school. "Dex! Where are you? *Dex!*"

"There!" Quinn called out from his knees. He was pointing toward the street.

Daphna followed his finger, but there were so many people between her and—but, yes! She saw him! Dexter was in the crowd with a girl—that white-haired girl who'd yelled at the pastor in the auditorium. He was leading her through the shifting maze of bodies. They stopped at the large tree by the sidewalk and looked back toward the school. Surely he was looking for her, Daphna thought.

"Who is that girl?" Daphna asked, irrationally but undeniably hating her. But then she turned to Quinn and said, "Wait, you know my broth—?"

"Uh oh," Quinn said, but not in response to her question. He was looking past Dexter now. Then he was desperately looking into his book again. His hands were shaking so hard he could hardly hold it.

"*Oh God,*" Daphna gasped when she saw.

Crouching behind one of the parked cars across the street was a man in running clothes holding a handgun. He was using the hood to steady his arm as he aimed.

At Dex.

# CHAPTER TEN
*Disappearing Acts*

Daphna sprinted toward her brother, screaming his name, but her voice was swallowed by the general uproar. She knew the man was waiting for a clear shot through the bodies running past the tree. Crashing through knots of hair-pulling grapplers, she shoved aside anyone and everyone in her path. When she was about ten yards away, Dex finally spotted her. When he saw her face, he blanched.

"Get down!" Daphna screamed. Then she threw herself at him for the second time that morning. She flew into both Dexter and the girl, who seemed to be just standing there in a stupor. All three of them hit the tree and fell to the ground. "Gun!" Daphna choked.

"It's okay," someone said a few dizzied moments later. Quinn. He was there too, but on his feet. Daphna looked up, then desperately over at the shooter.

Who was gone.

Daphna assumed he was hiding, but she spotted something on the hood of the car.

The gun.

"He's crouching down back there!" Dexter warned, comprehending now that he'd have been killed earlier if not for that busybody on her porch. "Stay down!"

But Daphna was pretty sure the man wasn't there anymore. Despite her massive relief, her suspicions boiled over. After extricating herself from the tangle of limbs she was in, she got up, planning to run over to the car, but a group of boys—scary-looking boys—were there now. One of them did some kind of karate kick on the driver's side mirror, which cracked and dangled like a broken arm. A skinny bald boy had the gun now. He immediately shoved it into his pants under his shirt. Had *they* chased the man away?

*No*—

Daphna spun back round. She honed in on

Quinn, who was still holding that book. "Show it to me," she ordered. "Now."

"It's okay," Quinn said. "Things will be fine. Everything will turn out just—"

"We need to get out of here," Dexter interrupted, now on his feet. He helped Nora up. She was trembling so hard he feared she was going to faint.

Daphna ignored her brother, and the girl, whoever she was. *"Give me that book,"* she said to Quinn again.

Reluctantly, Quinn handed it over.

It was pretty substantial. Daphna peeked under the elastic. The cover was black and considerably weathered. It was clearly old, very old. She opened it.

"Daphna," Dex said, wondering who this jerk was with the textbook on the first day of school. Another nerd she'd bonded with already? "We need to get out of here," he insisted, but then he saw Daphna's eyes as they peered at the pages she was looking at.

*Another goddamn book.*

What Daphna saw made her think immediately of The Book of Nonsense. The words covering the pages seemed to be moving, or changing—no, not changing, fading in and out. No, not that either. They were actually rising and sinking like welts on the thick, rippled pages, and that reminded her of The Book of Maps. Whatever this was, it was connected to everything they knew. That much was obvious. Even Dexter wouldn't deny this, if he would bother to look at it. Were they *names? When would this all end?*

Daphna looked up at Quinn. "What's in your other hand?" she demanded.

Quinn gave over the object he was clutching. It was a rock of some sort, curved like the tip of a primitive tool.

Daphna turned it over in her hand, thinking hard. Things seemed about to become clear to her—*some things*—but before her thoughts could crystallize, Quinn said, "Uh oh," again. But then he grabbed the book and rock back from Daphna and told everyone, "Don't worry. I'll handle this."

Branwen and her group of black-and-blued boys had suddenly appeared, and they moved as if they had a plan, fanning out around the tree. Daphna and Nora backed up against the trunk. Quinn and

Dex stayed where they were.

For a moment Dex thought he was back in Gabriel Park, in another time—in another body. But seeing this fool standing there acting tough, butting into business he couldn't possibly even begin to understand, snapped him out of it. "Back off," he said out of the side of his mouth. "This is beyond you. Trust me."

"I got this," Quinn repeated. "It's just like Thermopylae, when the Spartans were massively outnumbered against the—"

"I said back off!"

A portion of the nearby mob seemed to sense something special going on. When they saw the twins, a bloodthirsty cry went up. Someone shouted, "They've got the plague! Wipe them out!"

Nora clutched Daphna's arm, but Daphna shook her off. *Who was this leech?*

Branwen stepped toward Dex with some kind of trophy in her hand, a tall gold-plated cup. One strap of her dress was ripped.

"Where is Wren?" she screamed. She was out of her mind. Dexter saw this plainly in her eyes. But then he saw something even more disturbing in them. It was like the First Tongue was in effect, hypnotizing her—but something much more malevolent. Whatever it was, he saw it in all the kids' eyes.

*Was it in his?*

"We're not afraid of you," Quinn announced, opening his book. "I'm warning you," he added. "I'm warning all of you!"

Dex, all at once overcome with a fury he could neither comprehend nor contain, knocked the book out of Quinn's hands. He was going to fight this kid.

"Hey!" Quinn said.

Branwen reared back with the trophy and came at Dex with it.

Bang! A shot rang out.

Bodies hit the deck all around.

Moments later, both the crowd and Branwen's gang were running away, everyone but Branwen, who remained standing there with the trophy still raised up over her head. It was obvious why. Someone was now there, next to her, someone with a gun—the bald boy. He had the point of it pressed against her cheek.

She turned to him slowly and unleashed the full wattage of her electric smile. The boy, stunned for a moment, shook his head, lowered the gun, and said, "Ah, get outta here."

Branwen walked slowly off, dignity evidently intact.

"Antin?" Dex asked. He'd shaved his head, but it was definitely him.

Antin didn't answer, but he did nod slightly. Did he remember Dex having used Words of Power to try to straighten him out, too? Was this his way of saying thank you, even though it hadn't lasted?

There was no time to find out because someone shouted, "Pigs!"—one of the other boys there, Eyeballs. Before anyone could react, cops, half a dozen or more, appeared seemingly from nowhere and pounced on the gang.

The struggle was chaotic, but brief. It was only moments before they were all face down on the grass, their hands cuffed behind their backs with what looked like plastic zip ties.

Now they were up and getting dragged to a police van parked on the street. Other cops were suddenly on the scene too—lots of them. They'd emerged from a parking lot on the other side of the school and were marching in some kind of phalanx with shields and cans of mace.

Now, at last, everyone bolted the school grounds, in all directions. Daphna scanned the dispersing crowd for signs of Branwen or her posse. She was quite certain they'd not seen the last of them.

*"Where is it?"*

Daphna turned to find Quinn turning in frantic circles, searching the ground. "Where is what?" she asked. "Oh, no—*the book?"*

"Forget it," Dex told them. "We need to get out of here." He was watching Nora, who still appeared unsteady on her feet. He needed to get her away from all this.

"I can't find it!" Quinn shouted. "I was going to pick it up when the gun went off. It should be right here!"

"Find it!" Daphna told him. "That book cannot fall into the wrong hands!"

"A book?" someone else asked.

Daphna turned around to find Mr. G standing right there.

"Don't tell me you're at Wilson now, too," Dex said.

Mr. G seemed not to have heard Dex. "You've lost a dangerous book?" he asked Daphna. "Whose was it?"

"It wasn't anybody's," Daphna told him. She didn't have time for teachers right now, even her favorite, even one who might, in other circumstances, help them.

"Is that it?"

The twins looked to see what Mr. G was pointing to, which seemed to be the cluster of police still in the process of manhandling Antin and his gang into the back of their van. But then they saw two cops standing away from the action, evidently waiting for something—Richards and Madden.

Richards had the book.

It was unmistakable with that bright yellow cover. With the sun on it, the thing was nearly blinding.

"That's it!" Daphna shouted. "Maybe one of those boys took it in the scuffle!" Daphna waved her hands and shouted, but the confusion was still far too great with kids fleeing up and down the sidewalk in front of them.

"No," Quinn said darkly, "the cops took it. They're on the take!"

"On the *take*?" Daphna said. "Why would the police take your book?"

A plain white car skidded to a stop alongside Richards and Madden. Quinn took something out of his pocket, a cell phone. He leaned out from behind the tree and, though kids were still streaming by, began snapping pictures as the car window rolled down. A hand emerged. Richards shook it, then handed the book over.

"Where did it come from?" Mr. G asked the twins. Demanded, really.

Daphna sighed, annoyed he was still there. "Look, Mr. G—"

"I need to know if getting it back is more important than keeping you safe."

"We're fine, really," Daphna promised, exasperated now. "We've dealt with a lot worse than a bunch of—"

"I'm not talking about keeping you safe from mutinous teenagers!" Mr. G shouted, inexplicably out of patience. "I saw the assassin before he ran off!"

Dex and Daphna looked at Mr. G, then at each other, then back at their teacher. Neither responded though. 'Assassin' was a rather specific word. Richards and Madden were still talking to the man in the car. Quinn was still snapping pictures like some kind of international spy. Kids were still running off like birds bursting from a tree with cats in it.

Mr. G's face crunched up. He seemed to be considering something rather difficult. Finally, he wailed, "I'm talking about keeping you safe from the most powerful organization on Earth!"

The twins reacted to this pronouncement with the same expression: They were not shocked. Their eyes simply said, *explain*.

"The Church, damn it!" Mr. G shouted. "The *Church!* You won't survive the day without my help. Now, tell me the truth: You got that book from Heaven, didn't you?"

*"What?"* both Quinn and Nora asked. Quinn came back around the tree with his camera, looking as if he couldn't have heard what he'd thought he'd just heard. Nora, who'd been propped up against the tree, remained there, watching with pale, frightened, but avid eyes.

Daphna saw that Richards, Madden, and whoever was in the car were done talking. The window was rolling up.

*"Was it from Heaven?"* Mr. G screamed, completely undone.

"Yes!" Daphna shouted. "Yes!"

"I KNEW IT!" Mr. G pulled a key out of his pocket and put it in Daphna's hands. "I live right there," he said, pointing to a modest little gray and white bungalow directly across the street. "Go inside. You'll be safe. *Please*, be safe. Don't do anything. Anything at all. Just sit there and wait for me. If there's an emergency, go down to the basement and hide. I'll find you there, and I can get you anywhere in the city, totally undetected. If I can get the book, I can save you. We could do anything! I'll be there as soon as I can to explain. *Please*," he added, seeing the skeptical look on both the twins' faces, "I'm taking a huge risk running off like this. I've been assigned to you your whole lives!"

Without another word, Mr. Guillermo sprinted through what was left of the mob toward the white car, which was already pulling away. He punched at a cell phone he produced from another pocket as he ran for his car, which was parked across the street. He jumped in and screeched off after it.

"What's going on?" Quinn asked, looking frantic. "Why did you tell him my book was from *Heaven?*"

"To get rid of him," Dexter said, observing Nora watch him. "Because he obviously has some serious screws loose."

"But it's gone!" Quinn shouted. "And it's your fault! *You're* not supposed to be an obstacle!"

*"What?"* Dexter knew he was utterly at fault. Daphna's reaction to the pages left little doubt that it was another forbidden book. And it was obvious that Quinn was trying to use it to save them when he'd knocked the thing out his hands. That was how he used to act—before learning to think first. Maybe whatever had gotten into everyone else at school had gotten into him for a moment. But whatever the case, he hated this boy, really hated him. "Why should I care about your stupid book?" Dex demanded, digging the hole deeper.

Daphna missed this exchange because she was watching Mr. G career around the corner. Was she surprised by this turn of events? No. How could she be?

"You have no idea what that book can do!" Quinn raged.

"I don't really care what you think it can do!"

"Dexter," Daphna said, turning back to the boys, trying to stay calm. "That book makes people disappear."

"It *what?"*

Quinn nodded to confirm this, trying his best to calm down as well.

*"Great,"* Dex sighed. Maybe that's why he knocked the book out of Quinn's hands—to keep it out of their lives.

"It's okay," Quinn said, deciding something. "This is only a complication. We'll just have to—"

68

"Let's just figure out how to get it back," Daphna insisted. She wanted to lay into Dex too, for his outrageous, obnoxious, asinine behavior, but she knew that wouldn't help matters right now. He'd hear it from her later though, that was for sure. Not helping was one thing, but actively hindering things? This was going too far.

"Okay," Quinn agreed. "That teacher—did he say he's been watching you your whole lives?"

"Not exactly," said Daphna, slipping Mr. G's key into her pocket while watching the last of the students run from the cops, who were now marching across the athletic field. "He said he was 'assigned to us.' I have no idea what that means, but I can promise you one thing: It doesn't mean helping us. He did help us in some ways, though by accident, maybe. Or maybe not. Anyway, he was my favorite teacher."

"We should go to his house," Quinn said.

"No." Daphna was adamant. "We need to go somewhere to talk first."

"No, really," Quinn insisted. "One way or another, there's always someone who helps. There *has* to be someone who—"

"What are you talking about?" Dex could hardly believe this joker. "I can promise you one thing too," he said. "There is *never* someone who helps."

"I don't trust him." Daphna's tone was final.

"Well," Quinn said, looking distraught at these developments, "I think I got pictures of the guys in the car." He peered at the screen on his phone. "I got the license plate too," he added, "but it's hard to make out."

The police van with Antin and his thugs was finally ready to go. As it pulled away, one of the cops spoke through the speakers on its roof. "By order of the Mayor," he proclaimed, "a curfew is under effect. All youths under eighteen years of age must proceed to and remain in their homes."

The announcement was repeated as the van drove off.

"Jeez," said Daphna when it faded away, "do you think there are riots all over—?"

"I can't go home," someone whimpered.

Nora.

"Who is she?" Quinn demanded.

69

Daphna couldn't agree more. "Yeah—"

"Who are *you*?" Dex snapped at Quinn.

"Forget it," Daphna said. She turned to Quinn and asked, "Can we go to your house? It's closer. We can look at the photos there."

"Sure, but let's hurry. I have to get that book back!"

"Quinn," Daphna said, grabbing his arm as he turned away, "what is that book?"

Nora screamed.

Branwen and four boys were running down the front steps of the school—Branwen with her trophy, the others wielding hockey and lacrosse sticks like swords and lances. They must have been waiting for the cops to clear off with the gang.

"Here!" Dex picked up a bike lying on its side just a few feet away. Bikes were everywhere. Daphna and Quinn each grabbed one as well, and both jumped on.

But Nora did not. She simply stood where she was, frozen. Her eyes were once again unfocused, her lips moving soundlessly.

She looked almost peaceful.

"Let's go!" Daphna screamed. "Let's go! *Let's go!*"

Branwen and the boys were maybe thirty yards away.

Dex waved Nora over. "Come on," he urged. "It's okay. You can ride with me!"

She didn't seem to hear him.

"Leave her!" Daphna insisted, poised on her pedals. "It's *us* they're after!"

When it was clear that Dex didn't know what to do, Daphna peddled close to Nora and slapped her right across the face. Nora's eyes spiraled, but then focused. She ran to Dex, who stood up on his pedals so she could sit on the seat behind him.

Daphna and Quinn took off, pumping for the sidewalk.

Dex took off just behind them, but before he could gain any kind of momentum, something struck him hard in the temple. The blade of a hockey stick.

Dexter saw nothing but stars for a second. Nora screamed when he nearly tipped them both over, but he somehow managed to keep the bike upright.

Mercifully, Dex could see again.
They were off.

# CHAPTER ELEVEN
## *That New Bookshop*

Dex hurtled down the sidewalk fronting the school just behind his sister. It was partly the adrenaline, but Nora didn't seem to weigh much. Branwen shrieked somewhere behind them like some starving predator narrowly missing its last chance at a meal.

Nora was holding on to him like her life depended on it.

Why did he feel so compelled to help this total, and rather pathetic, stranger? It felt like some sort of "assignment" now that Dex thought about it.

And why didn't she just laugh at him or run away when he talked about having been to Heaven? Any normal person would've done that, though she obviously wasn't entirely normal talking about Jesus and Heaven the way she had. There was something off about her, especially with all that muttering to herself, not to mention her outburst in the auditorium. But then, he'd never known a religious person before. *People like her,* Dex thought, *must be especially vulnerable to nutcases like that pastor.*

Dexter didn't know his own mind today, but he knew he wasn't sorry he'd found her.

He pedaled on.

Quinn, who was out in front, veered into the drive separating Wilson from the elementary school. Daphna fell in line right behind him, so Dex followed her. But as they passed the school, doors swung open in several places, and moms with wailing children poured outside. Quinn, Daphna, and Dex all had to stop to avoid running them over.

The thunder crashed again. Immediately after came the snap of wild lightning. The kids flew into an absolute frenzy.

Cringing at the volume of screaming and crying, Dex pedaled after Daphna, who was following Quinn toward the rear of one of the shops on the main road—the same shops they'd stopped in front of after nearly being run over themselves. Dexter's plan was to find out what this new book was all about, deal with it, then get rid of that floppy haired poser as soon as possible. Then he'd help Nora sort out—whatever she needed to sort out. And then maybe he'd get back to his retirement.

He'd forgotten about that.

The main road, which had finally been cleared of the accident, was visible between the last shop and the pharmacy next door. Dozens of kids galloped past in a long, spooked herd. Police vehicles broadcasting the orders for the curfew were just audible from distant streets.

Following Quinn's lead, the twins set their bikes against a wall. Quinn took some keys out of his pocket and began opening the back door of a shop.

"Who *is* this guy, anyway?" Dex asked.

"Quinn," Daphna said. "Who the heck is *she?*"

Nora looked at them both like they were deciding whether to let her live.

"Ah, Nora," Dex said.

Daphna could see liability written all over this girl. "Oh—*kay,*" she said, "but *who*—never mind. Let's just get inside before some housewife tries to bash our brains in with a rolling pin."

Quinn had the door open and was already partially up a flight of steps behind it. Daphna followed him, wondering whether her brother had lost his mind hauling around this useless girl. Dex and Nora brought up the rear.

The entry's walls were plain white plaster, chipped all over. Some of the stairs were cracked as well. At the top was another door with peeling paint. Once they were all fully inside Quinn locked them in the apartment.

The first thing Daphna noticed were the books. The walls were lined with shelves, all of which were filled. Little cards, labels, and tags were affixed under most of them. Daphna spotted valuable old editions of *Peter Pan* and *The Lord of the Rings* quickly enough, *The Odyssey* as well. She felt pretty sure that Quinn had read everything in the room.

The books did not attract Dexter's attention, so while he caught his breath, he looked around the apartment. It was not a very nice one. There was a paltry kitchenette with a sink full of large lemon-colored dishes in the back. A round table sat on scuffed linoleum. It was covered with all kinds of odd shaped tools: knives and little picks, and some spatula-like implements. There were various sized bottles with stoppers, stacks of old looking parchment, and a few empty leather bindings.

A small TV was talking quietly on a counter next to the rusting stove. What wasn't the kitchen was a living room, which contained two futons with a lop-sided wooden end table between them. A box of books sat under it. The carpeting was threadbare, to be generous.

"This is that new bookshop," Dex finally realized when he looked back at his sister drooling over all the books.

"*Oh, God,*" Nora groaned, almost too softly to hear.

Everyone looked over to see her in the kitchen, staring at the TV. She looked as if she were going to throw up.

"What's wrong?" Dex asked.

They all went over to see what she was reacting to. The news was on. Quinn turned up the volume.

"—Repeat, there is no cause for alarm. We would like to emphasize that there is no agreement in the scientific community about the nature of this weather anomaly, nor its implications. All indications thus far are that while the thunder is both extraordinarily loud and widespread, it is not in and of itself dangerous, though earplugs are recommended. It has been determined that the tremors that follow are triggered by the tremendous sound waves generated by the claps. Damage has been minimal. The lightning effect has not been fully analyzed, but it appears to be harmless as well. Nevertheless, because of the severe psychological reactions observed among minors, as a precaution, curfews are in effect in cities world-wide."

"Did he just say '*worldwide*'?" Daphna heard it— she just couldn't believe it.

Nora nodded. "There've been riots in schools today just about everywhere."

Clips of exactly that came on. The four stunned

74

kids watched scenes of children wreaking havoc at schools from Ann Arbor to Sydney.

"I don't believe it," Daphna said.

"Yeah," Quinn said, "it's unbelievable."

"No. I mean, I don't *believe* it. It can't be real. They're—it's all fake—to make us—"

"What? Like in *1984*, where the government makes all the news?"

"Why not?" Daphna said. "The President lied to the entire country on national TV about having a cure before they really did."

"But that was surely to calm people down," Quinn argued. "This will freak people—"

"A ha!" Dex had turned away from the TV to search for something to prove this Quinn jerk was a fraud, and lo and behold he'd just spotted four large boxes on the floor in front of one of the shelving units, four large boxes full of damaged books—*burnt* books if he wasn't mistaken.

Daphna saw what her brother was pointing to. With eyes narrowed, she walked to the boxes and squatted down to inspect a book.

"So, who are you supposed to be, again?" Dex now triumphantly demanded of Quinn.

"Quinn," the phony said, "Quinn Quartich. Ah, those books—"

"As in *Berny* Quartich?"

"My dad, yes."

Dex nodded. Not because he understood what was going on, but because now things at least made some semblance of sense. Potentially.

"These books—" Daphna said, looking up from the soot-encrusted pages of the one she'd picked up.

"Yeah," Quinn said, "my dad bought them from an old lady after her...house burned down. In...Eugene. It happened last—"

"Boy, are you a lousy liar," Dex said, cutting him off. "They were Asterius Rash's. Where else would that many burned books come from around here?"

"I—I—"

Daphna didn't wait for another lie. Her memory caught on something for once. "They *were* names!" she realized. "Antin mentioned something like that—a book of a gazillion names—under the store! Remember, Dex? He picked up a book and said it was just full of names and then tossed it away. It was way too dark to see what was happening on the pages."

Dex did remember.

Now Daphna zeroed in on Quinn, who seemed to shrink a bit. "These *are* from Rash's store," she said, standing back up. "You—" she was starting to fume again—"he said there were vultures sneaking in and taking all the books that were left after the fire. And what's *that?*"

Daphna stomped over to a box sitting under the table between the futons, dragged it out, then snatched up the book sticking out on top.

"Dex, look!"

"The Book of Maps?" Dexter gasped. That wasn't possible.

"It's the book on the Portland tunnels that monk tried to take from our store!" Daphna slammed it back into the box.

*Of course,* Dex realized. The straps on the cover made it look like The Book of Maps. That's why the monk had tried to switch them.

Daphna wheeled on Quinn, who was shrinking even more now, and shrieked, "YOU'VE BEEN ROB- BING OUR STORE TOO!"

# CHAPTER TWELVE
### *Quinn*

"I—I can explain," Quinn stuttered. "This—this is just a typical misunderstanding. You have to let me—"

"No!" Daphna spat. "You're a liar! You're a liar like everyone else in the world! And I'm just a stupid fool like I've always been. You show up out of nowhere today, and I trust you, just like that, because you're cute and read books and you—you—*kissed me!*" she screamed. "I am now, officially, the biggest loser in the history of the world. Let's go." Daphna grabbed her brother's hand.

But Dex yanked it back. He wasn't going to be jerked around like that, like he was one of those squalling little brats outside and Daphna was his mother. And he must have misheard that last part. It sounded like she said this moron had kissed her.

"Don't go! Please!" Quinn begged. "I can explain! You have to let me explain!"

Dexter's refusing to go with her was the last straw, the *real* last straw for Daphna. And she never wanted to lay eyes on Quinn again. She rushed to the door and grabbed the knob. But she hesitated.

That kiss.

Outside of visiting Heaven, that kiss was the most amazing thing that had ever happened to her. For just a moment, but a moment that seemed to stretch into always, it had made her forget about her problems. It had made her forget about herself. The feeling it produced, she realized, was the closest thing she'd ever felt to what it had been like to be up in Heaven.

"Yes," Quinn said, sounding desperate. "Yes, I took them. I'm sorry! I did it for my father!"

"Oh, spare me the—" Daphna started to sneer, but turning back she saw that look in Quinn's eyes again, the look she'd seen at school, that pain. And she knew more about it.

She took her hand off the doorknob.

"I—I was there, in the dark," Quinn explained, "when those boys had you down beneath the store. That awful one, their leader, Antin—I—I think it was the bald boy we just saw up at—He almost shined his light on me. I was there during the fight."

Dex couldn't deny that this was possible. "Antin," he said, recalling that complicated turn of events, "before he pulled that sheet off Emmet's body, he flashed his light around. He thought he heard something."

"That was me," Quinn confirmed. "I'm sorry I didn't help you. It was like *Lord of the Flies!* I left when everyone was gone, but I took some books for my dad."

"But—that was over a year ago," Daphna said, amazed. She took a tentative step back into the room.

"Where is your father, now?" Dex demanded. *So what if he was down there?* "Lord of the *what?*"

"Dex," Daphna said, "his father is gone." She was absolutely certain of it.

Quinn went pale. "How—how did you know?"

"I just do. Your mom too?"

Quinn's face knotted up. Finally, he blurted out, "They're both gone! Gone! And it's all my fault!" He slumped onto the futon and broke down entirely.

Daphna nodded, sadly. They did share something. She'd been right.

"What the heck are you talking about?" Dex had been rather satisfied with the way things were going, but now somehow Daphna's attitude had completely flipped.

Daphna abruptly turned to her brother because things suddenly clicked into place. "It was *him,*" she said, pointing to Quinn, "the one boy you saw on our way to school. He was the one who yelled for us to watch out. And Dex, no one could find the driver who tried to run us over because he *vanished!* Quinn was the boy I saw reading on the bench outside OHSU when I went to the fitness center! He—someone *did* come after me, but whoever it was wasn't there anymore when I turned around!" Daphna was starting to feel faint. "They *have* been trying to kill us, Dexter! All this time!" She turned back to Quinn now, who was trying to pull himself together.

"You—" she said, the tone of her voice softening, "you've been *saving* us." Then, gently, "What do you know about that book?"

"I—I don't know anything," Quinn replied, miserably. "I guess I picked it up with a bunch of others after—after those boys finally crawled out of there, arguing about whether Dexter disappeared or not. But I didn't look at it, at any of them. When I got home, it was just in the box with all the others I got on other days. And it just sat there until about a month or so ago."

"What kind of idiot steals ruined books?" Dex wasn't ready to accept this saving-their-lives thing. And the look on Daphna's face as Quinn spoke was seriously getting under his skin. She couldn't possibly trust this guy, could she? He felt the urge to slap the look off, which would only be fair.

Daphna shook her head at her brother's willful ignorance. "They can still be quite valuable," she said. "They were restoring them." She gestured to all the tools on the kitchen table.

"My dad's business was failing," Quinn explained. "Moving here was kind of our last gasp. My mom wanted him to quit for the last few years. They fought about it all the time. I couldn't blame her, but I couldn't blame him either. It was his passion. He couldn't live without it! I started stealing the books when I heard about the fire. I thought maybe I'd find something rare and valuable that would save his business—and stop the fighting. But Dad figured out where they came from pretty quick and wouldn't touch them, so I started experimenting with restoring the damaged ones myself."

"What about *our* store?" Dex asked. They hadn't even discussed it once with Dr. Fludd.

"I'm all alone," Quinn said. "I broke into the basement the other day and took some to try to sell online real quick. I don't know what else to do for money! I've been feeling like those orphans in *Oliver Twist!*"

"Why don't you stop with the stupid references!" Dex griped. "We're not impressed!"

"Dex," Daphna urged, "let him go on."

"About six weeks ago," Quinn said, looking grateful. "After we moved in. I—when they fight—I—I read.

I read a lot, I guess. I always have. But we used to read together. Everything. We all read everything together. But I found out that working on the books was good too—to block it all out. Even better because it was my own thing. The book I picked that day was the one with the names rising up and down on the pages. I was amazed, and I had to think before I remembered where it came from. I forgot all the books in that shop were about magic. I love magic, especially the idea of magic books. I guess I think all books are magic in a way."

"And?" Dex sighed, nauseated by Daphna's expression at hearing this.

"Sorry," Quinn said. "I—I was sitting there at the table, shocked, and pretty sure I was imagining what was happening on the pages. I called my dad over, but he wouldn't come look, and I got so mad. And my mother started yelling at him for getting me into this profession, and I—I got mad at her, at both of them. I looked down at the page, and I saw their names come up, right next to each other. And—I—I wasn't thinking. Or I guess I thought I was Merlin or something. I picked this up off the table—" Quinn fished the little curved stone out of his pocket. "It's part of an old tool for scraping animal skins to make parchment," he said, holding it up.

"And?" Dex demanded.

"Dex," Daphna said. "You don't have to be so—"

"And!"

"I scraped them off!"

"You scraped what off?"

"Their names! I scraped their names off the page!"

"And they disappeared," Daphna whispered.

"Yes! It's all my fault!"

"But where did they go?" Daphna knew he didn't know, but she had to ask.

"I don't know!" Quinn confirmed. "I want you to tell me!" He turned, desperate, to Dex. "You disappeared down there in the dark under the store," he said, pleading. "That's why I've been looking for you. You disappeared, and you came back! Where did you go?"

Neither twin responded to this at first. Dexter shook his head, thinking Quinn was in for some serious disappointment. Daphna felt a rush of sympathy, but also a sickening pit in her stomach.

"Dex didn't disappear," Daphna finally said, as gently as she could manage. "He was just invisible. I know it sounds crazy—"

Quinn took a second to absorb this, but as he did, he seemed to fizzle. "Invisible?" he asked, as if the word were unfamiliar.

"I'm sorry," Daphna said. And she was, deeply sorry, for both of them. She'd been used—for a good reason, she supposed, and Quinn had saved her life. But she'd been used. He'd gone through her to get to her brother. She'd let her guard down for one second, and this was the incredibly predictable result. "You're not really in my Homeroom, are you?" she asked.

"No," Quinn admitted, though he looked surprised by the question.

Daphna just nodded.

Quinn stood up, took a breath, and began walking around the room. "I waited for something to happen for a few days," he said, "for them to come back, I guess. I stared into the book every minute, but no matter how much I thought about them, I never saw their names again. Eventually, I called the police, but they thought I was pranking them, of course. I hung up when I realized they'd send me off to my horrid aunt, like in *Jane Eyre* or something, but even worse.

"Then I got paranoid thinking I saw cops and creepy people following me everywhere. I knew I had to find my parents myself, like the kids who rescue their father in *A Wrinkle in Time*, but I didn't know where to start. Then I read in the paper that you were at the hospital. I didn't know who else to go to that might possibly help. I went up there, but they wouldn't let me see you. The best I could do was sit outside and hope you came out. And then, when you finally came out, Daphna, I saw someone came after you with a gun. I didn't know what to do! I looked down at my book and saw a name rise up, so I scraped it off."

"And then he was gone."

"Yes. There were a couple of cops there, and—like I said—I've gotten paranoid. I didn't come back for a while, but then I got scared someone else would try to hurt you. But you never came out again. I thought maybe I was too late! Why are people trying to kill you? They told me you were released last night, so I found the doctor's house—"

"Wait—" Daphna interrupted. "That was you this morning on the street, wasn't it? You tried to warn us about the van. Then you erased the driver."

"Yes," Quinn confirmed. "I was following you to school because—"

"Thank you," Daphna said. "Thank you for saving our lives. However many times you did." She *was* thankful. She owed him that.

Quinn smiled a bit through his distress and even seemed to relax slightly. "Do you have any idea what the book is?" he asked, taking hold of Daphna's hands.

Despite herself, Quinn's touch jolted Daphna's heart. She pulled her hands back.

"I—I'll never be able to live with myself if I don't find my parents," Quinn said, too emotional to take in Daphna's reaction. "I feel so—They're my best friends, even if we had problems sometimes. We're supposed to work that all out. We're *going* to work that all out. I know we are. Please, do you have any idea where they might be?"

"No," Daphna said, feeling her heart go weak again. She was impressed with Quinn's dogged optimism, though there was something odd about it. "We do know a few things, though," she said.

"Please, tell me everything," Quinn begged.

"It's kind of a long story."

Dexter snorted. "Yeah," he said, *"The Neverending Story."*

"I'm not exactly sure where to start," Daphna admitted.

"Anywhere," Quinn urged. "Start anywhere."

Daphna glanced around the room, then approached a shelf and removed a book. "Okay," she said. "We'll start with this."

She was holding the Bible.

# CHAPTER THIRTEEN
*Nora*

And so Daphna unspooled the story. She began at the beginning—the *very* beginning— with books. Books were the beginning, books were the middle, and as she spoke, Daphna realized that books would be the end. She explained that Eden was a library rather than a garden. She spoke about Adam, *the* Adam, their poor, misguided father, who read from the forbidden Book of Knowledge, and all the unfortunate consequences that followed for him and Eve, and she supposed, for everyone else who came to live in the world. She explained about the Book of Maps, which poor, bereft Eve had been given so she'd never lose the even more incredible Aleph, which she'd used to track her beloved Adam down through the ages. Daphna told Quinn how it led them all the way to Heaven where they let a hired killer open a locked book that released a fire into the Infinite Library there, a library full of sad angels who seemed to be searching for a missing book.

Daphna told Quinn about their mountainside showdown with the monster, Lilit, the original castoff from Eden. She explained that thanks to Lilit's murder spree, they were the last of the thirty-six Lamed Vavniks, and about how their special ribs were God's insurance policy to guarantee the survival of the human race—how they allowed women who possessed them to conceive children without a man, and how, if buried, they could bring life spontaneously out of the earth. She told him about the Secret Keeper of the Church, and how the whole long, insane story was going to end with them being murdered, probably a few minutes after they left the apartment, if not sooner.

Quinn sat on the futon without making a sound as he listened to it all. Dex could tell that having gone through what he had with that book and his parents, he was prepared to believe every word.

Nora's reactions were not so easy to read. She'd been standing in the kitchen mostly watching the TV. But as Daphna talked, she'd turned to look at Dex every so often. He somehow felt as if she wanted to see how he felt about it all, whether this was all some cosmic joke at her expense, or maybe she was trying to determine that if any of it were true, whether he planned to help her deal with it. Or maybe she was just wondering how to get away from this bunch of nutcases without being sacrificed or something.

"God?" was Quinn's only response when Daphna finally finished. "We're talking about books that belonged to God?" He was whispering for some reason. "Did that book of names come from Eden—or, Heaven, like that teacher said?"

"Anything's possible," Daphna told him. "Our father told us there were many Sacred Books in the Library at Eden, many books he and Eve never touched. I don't think anyone knows what became of them."

Both twins thought about "their" books up there.

"What are we going to do?" Quinn pleaded. "I—I don't know anything about any of this!"

"What about those pictures?" Dex asked.

"Right!" Quinn pulled his phone out of his pocket. "I forgot all about them! They're definitely going to give us a clue!" He tapped the phone, but then screwed up his eyes at it. "I'm really sorry," he said. "My battery just died. But I think if we let it charge for just a few minutes, it'll be enough." He hurried over to the kitchen countertop where a charger was already sticking out of a socket and plugged it into his phone.

An awful silence filled the room as everyone waited for it to charge.

Dex tried to fight off the urge to tell Nora that everything was going to be all right because he knew it wasn't true. She'd turned back to the TV and stared at it, blankly.

Just to break the silence, Daphna turned to Quinn and said, "So, that book. In all the time you looked at it, was it always just names?"

"Yes," Quinn said, "just names."

"How many do you think it had?"

Quinn shrugged. "Who knows? Thousands. Tens

of thousands. Millions even if they change around, I guess. It kind of looked that way."

"Did you recognize any of them?"

"No, but I was wondering if any more were real people, so I started writing them down a few days ago. I never got around to checking, though."

"Could there have been *billions* of names in there?" Dex asked. He'd been watching Nora watch the TV. Did she believe any of this?

"Possibly."

"Like, *seven* billion?"

Daphna looked at her brother. "Do you think it has everyone's name in the world?"

"Why not?"

Daphna now looked back to Quinn. "Do you have the list of names you wrote down? Maybe I can look a few of them up now on my phone."

Quinn nodded, then went over to get a pile of ragged notebook papers sitting on one of the kitchen chairs. But before bringing them back, he checked on his phone. "Good enough," he said, so he brought it over with the pages, which he handed to Daphna.

She only had to read half a dozen names before her eyes lit up. "Hey!" she said. "Penelope Posey! That name was in the paper this morning!" She turned to Dexter now. "The birth announcement! And there are others I've read! Lots!"

"The pictures are coming up," Quinn said looking at his phone, but then Daphna's words seemed to sink in for him. "It *is* everyone in the world?" he asked, looking up at her. "When you're born, you're added in. And when you—" He didn't have to finish the thought. Quinn tossed his phone onto the couch and sat down again, dropping his head into his hands. "That means—" he choked. "That means I—I—" He couldn't say it.

*"Did we kill Wren?"* Daphna whispered, barely able to get the question out. If they'd killed someone, that was it. Game over.

"Heaven!" Quinn was now looking between the twins with wide, beseeching eyes. "You've been there! And you came back! Can we—?" He leapt to his feet and took Daphna's hands once again. Her heart leapt too, despite her cursing it. "Help me!" he begged. "Take me there so I can—"

The thunder crashed outside, making everyone jump. All but Quinn.

"Quinn." Daphna removed her hands from his. Did he not notice that he reached for her only when he was desperate for her help? "The Aleph was destroyed. If there is any possible way to get back, we have no idea what it is."

"Those towers in the news that people are building. The Stairways to Heaven!"

"They're useless," Dex said, and not kindly. "Decoys."

"Are you *sure?*"

"Doesn't matter," Nora said, making everyone turn to her.

"What?" Daphna snapped. "Who are you anyway, and what do you have to do with any of this!"

"Shut up!" Dex shouted.

Daphna looked at him in disbelief.

Nora was pointing at the television, so everyone reluctantly moved to see again. It was still the news. Some sort of disaster. Smoke was pouring out of a collapsed metal structure. Emergency vehicles were all around. People were running through smoke.

"That's one of the towers!" Daphna exclaimed. "What happened?"

"Someone blew it up," Nora said. "Someone blew them *all* up, at pretty much the same time. This is the one in Utah. There might be a war over the ones in the Middle East."

All four kids watched in silence as clips of smoking ruins came on from Jerusalem and Mecca. These were followed by shots of military planes rolling out of hangers.

There was nothing to say, so no one said anything. Finally, Daphna turned the set off.

"Could this be fake too?" Nora asked.

Daphna wasn't interested in discussing that bit of wishful thinking anymore, especially with this helpless girl. Pretty as she was, she seemed to be one of those types who could render themselves invisible by the sheer force of their shyness, the type who'd shatter like glass if you looked at them too hard. The type who didn't know the anything about anything.

"Seriously, who are you?" Daphna asked. Then, turning to her brother, she said, "Who is she, Dexter?"

Then to Nora again, "Why did you scream at that pastor this morning?"

Nora didn't answer, so Dex said, "Nora, this is my sister, Daphna, and Quinn, I guess." Turning back to Daphna, he added, "That crazy pastor was going off about all that fire and brimstone stuff in the halls. She got kind of freaked out and almost got trampled."

"But, Dex—" Daphna said, hoping that in just those two words he heard her telling him that this was hardly the time to look after frightened strays.

The thunder boomed again outside.

No one commented on it, but Nora was shaking like she was freezing cold. Her face, already pale, looked like chalk. Her wild hair seemed almost limp, as if in sympathy with her face. She began to look absent.

"I know all that stuff Daphna said made us sound crazier than that crazy pastor," Dex said, thinking Nora looked a bit crazy herself right now, "but actually, it's all true. It's all completely true."

"*Dex,*" Daphna said again.

"I've spent my whole life waiting for the Rapture," Nora said, coming back into her eyes. "Every day, every hour I've been afraid it would come, so I had to be ready for it. I had to be absolutely perfect, just in case. And I *have* been perfect!" Blood was rushing to her cheeks. "I *have* been perfect! Completely perfect! Until today. *Today!* It was too much today—I don't know why—I hate that thunder so much, and hearing him go on about it was more than I could bear. He says the same thing every day—morning, noon, and night! I snapped, and I wanted to show him I didn't care about being perfect, that I didn't care about the stupid Rapture. That's why I shouted at him, and that's why I pulled the alarm! I'm sorry, Daddy!" she blubbered, falling to her knees. Then she started mumbling something incoherent.

Dex put a hand on Nora's back again. "Pastor Jons—" he said, "he's your *father?* I'm sorry about that stuff I said. I wouldn't've—is that why you thought you were going to Hell?"

*She's as crazy as her dad,* Daphna thought.

"But he was right! He was right all along! I can never face him again."

"*Of course you can,*" Daphna sighed. This girl

was way over the top. "He'll forgive you. There are a lot worse things than interrupting a speech and pulling a stupid fire alarm. Why don't you go home? He's probably worried sick."

"Ah," Dex said again, "he seemed pretty upset. Biblically upset, I guess you could say."

*"He will never speak to me again,"* Nora moaned.

"Nora," Dex said, as encouragingly as he could. He helped her to her feet, unable to bear seeing her crumpled like that. "You heard all that stuff about our ribs, right?"

"You think Jesus was a fake!"

"No, we don't," Dex promised, easing Nora over to sit down on the futon next to Quinn. "Not at all. Or not exactly. It's just that we've learned the stories we know are not—they don't ever seem to be—the whole truth. My point is that what you know about the Rapture or whatever it's called might not be exactly right, either."

The thunder crashed again outside, as if to mock Dexter's feeble claims.

"We need to find out what's really going on," Daphna said, refusing to waste any more time on this girl. She turned to Quinn and said, "Can we look at the pictures?"

"Okay, yeah. Right!" he said, scooping up his phone. "Oh, okay," he said, tapping it to life. "Good." He didn't look good, though. He didn't seem to be holding himself together much better than Nora was. "Good," he repeated. "Here we go. Yeah, so, like I said, I've been kind of paranoid thinking people were following me when I went out, like some bad horror movie. So I took pictures all around in case something happened to me. You know, evidence, I guess."

Daphna had come around behind the couch so she could see over Quinn's shoulder. "What's that one?" she asked.

"It's outside the hospital," Quinn said, enlarging it a bit.

"Hey! Those cops! That's—!"

"Richards and Madden," Dex guessed. He wasn't even looking at the screen. He was keeping an eye on Nora, who seemed lost in thought.

"The cops that took the book?" Quinn asked.

"They've been following you," Dex told him,

knowing he was right. "That's why they were on the scene of the accident so quickly this morning. And that's why they left it so soon. They left when you left. They followed you to school."

"They were waiting for a chance to take the book," Daphna said, watching Quinn scroll slowly through the other pictures. "They must have believed you when you called. Or someone did. And in all the pandemonium school—the book falling on the ground, the gunshot—they saw their opportunity, and they took it."

"Look," Dex said. "I'm sorry I—"

"Just forget it, Dex."

"I knew I shouldn't have called the cops," Quinn groaned. "That's standard stuff!"

Daphna was leaning in to get a closer look at another picture. It was of Richards or Madden— she didn't know which—shaking hands through the window of the white car at school.

"Can you make that one bigger?" she asked. "Maybe we can see who's in the car."

Quinn stretched the image out. The man in the passenger seat was not visible, only his hand shaking the cop's.

But that shake.

"Look, Dex!" Daphna nearly screamed. "Look how they're shaking hands!"

Dex came over and looked at the image. He squinted. He nodded.

"What?" Quinn asked. *"What?"*

Daphna turned to him. "See how they have their thumbs on each other's knuckles? We saw the same thing! The murders—the killings around the world—the other Lamed Vavniks. We saw one of the murder scenes! The cops investigating it—they shook like that!"

"What does it mean?" Quinn asked.

*"He was right,"* Nora moaned. It hadn't seemed that she'd been paying attention to any of this, but she was looking at the image with clear eyes—sad, clear eyes.. "He was right about *everything.*"

"What *now?*" Daphna made no effort to mask her impatience. "Are you going to tell me you know something about this?"

"They're Freemasons."

Dex, Daphna, and Quinn all said, "They're *what?*"

"Freemasons," Nora repeated, grimly. "My father despises them worse than anyone in the world. It's his calling to fight them."

"But who *are* they?" Daphna demanded.

"Only the most infamous secret society in the history of the world."

# CHAPTER FOURTEEN
*Out With it*

No one responded to this at first. Everyone wait-ed for Nora to explain. But all she did was tremble and look sick again.

"Actually," Dex said, "I think he called *me* a Ma-son. I thought he said 'Jason.' Was that what your father meant when he said he was going to tell ev-eryone was responsible for—for everything? In the auditorium?"

Nora nodded.

"Well, he's not right about that," Daphna said, trying not to sound harsh now. "We told you Lilit—that monster—started the plague."

This seemed to help a bit. Nora still looked green, but she seemed to tremble a bit less.

"Who are the Freemasons?" Dex gently prodded. "Do you know anything specific?"

Nora nodded. Then she surprised everyone with a burst of information. "They go back to the Pyramids," she said. "No one knows exactly how they originat-ed, but they have lodges in just about every major city in the world and thousands of members. Mozart was a Mason. So was Ben Franklin and Harry Houd-ini. George Washington was sworn in on a Freema-son Bible. A bunch of the signers of the Declaration of Independence were Masons. President Roosevelt, President Ford, the first President Bush—all Masons.

"Tons of Supreme Court justices were Masons. So were the Wright Brothers, Louis Armstrong, Henry Ford, Mark Twain, Arthur Conan Doyle, and many of the men who started Hollywood. Also Ty Cobb, Benedict Arnold, Paul Revere, Arnold Palmer, Buzz Aldrin, the astronaut, and tons more.

"My father says they have shadow governments poised to take over countries all over the world—when they finally get the chance to, anyway. Supposedly the members don't even know who each other are because they wear masks and disguise their voices. Though obviously it gets out who some of them are."

"Ahhh," Dex said. "Are you serious?" He'd be the last person to doubt the existence of secret mask-wearing organizations, but one with that many members? And members like those? He couldn't help but consider the possibility that Nora was as big a loon as her father was. The looks on Daphna's and Quinn's faces told him they were pretty sure she was.

"The layout of Washington DC," Nora continued, "depicts a Masonic symbol, a—"

"Wait a minute," Quinn interrupted. "You're talking about the group in all the books and movies?"

"Yes," Nora said.

"Then," he challenged, voicing Dexter's thoughts exactly, "if everyone knows about them, how is it some big secret?"

"The *group* isn't a secret," Nora explained. "What they really *want* is the secret. Well, that's only partly a secret. Everyone knows they want the Key to Power, something to let them step out of the shadows and rule openly. But no one knows what that is or how they go about searching for it. That's why all the stories."

Everyone took this in. It was somewhat more reasonable now.

"How do you know all this?" Daphna asked, her tone still mostly skeptical.

"My father is an international expert on the Masons," Nora told her. "*The* international expert. Only," she added, "no one listens to him anymore. They think he's crazy because he says the Masons are responsible for everything bad in the world. He says they've assassinated Presidents and that they blew up the space shuttle. He says they blew up the Twin Towers. It's why our church forced him to retire."

"Is that why Mr. Haslam looked so nervous about him speaking to us?"

Nora nodded. "Yes. Dad promised he wouldn't say anything about the Masons. He was going to, though. He just didn't get the chance. He says they infiltrated our church, and *that's* why they retired him. He wanted to tell everyone that Masons have been all over the neighborhood for weeks. He thinks you two are Masons, or infected by them to spread the plague."

"Sure, why not?" Daphna said.

"But they *have* been around," Quinn confirmed, "since I called the cops. At least two of them are Masons, or in cahoots with Masons, so I wasn't paranoid after all. And neither is your dad."

Everyone processed this for a moment. Then Daphna said, "Does your father know what they want? This Key to Power?"

Nora shook her head. "No, he's never been able to figure it out. He says Stalin was a Mason, and he was after it. And Hitler too."

Dex and Daphna looked at each other, now taking *this* in. As was so often the case, they had the same thought. Dexter expressed it by asking, "Do you know of any other connections between the Masons and the Jews?"

After a moment of thought, Nora nodded. "Well," she said, "my father says the Masons *invented* anti-Semitism, that they invented all forms of bigotry and racism and hate. Oh, and if you draw a Jewish Star using the pyramid as one of the triangles on the back of the dollar bill, the six points touch the letters M-A-S-O-N. I don't know what that means, though. I think my father once said it means they want something from the Jews, and that it's some kind of coded threat."

Daphna pulled a dollar out of her back pocket, grabbed a pen that was resting against the laptop, and drew the star. Though some of what she'd heard so far had given her pause, she wanted to show how silly this oddball was and to get rid of her once and for all. But lo and behold, the star pointed to the letters exactly as Nora said it would. "It's true!" she admitted holding the bill up for Quinn and Dex. "Look—"

"That's—that's amazing," Quinn said. Dex didn't try to look, but he had no doubt it was true.

The skepticism in the room slowly drained away, and was replaced by pure anxiety.

"Do you know anything more?" Daphna asked, her tone now entirely converted.

"No," Nora admitted. "I don't think so. But my father has, well, a lot of books on the Masons. He collects books *by* Masons, too. Both identified and secret."

"We need to get a look at your father's books," Daphna declared. "Do you think he's home? Oh, my gosh! Dr. Fludd! I forgot all about her!" Daphna pulled her phone out and clicked the number. A moment later, she lowered it and said, "That does it. I'm calling OHSU."

"What's going on?" Quinn asked as Daphna searched for the number.

"Not sure," Dex said. "We—"

"Hello, this is Daphna Wax. Yes, yes—may I please talk to Dr. Fludd? She isn't answering her—She what? *Not at all?* Okay, thank you. No, no—just a miscommunication is all." Daphna hung up, looking as ill as Nora.

"What?" Dex asked.

"She never came in to work, Dex!"

"Did something happen to her?" Quinn asked. "Did the assassins—?"

"She left the house in the middle of the night," Daphna explained. "We thought she went to the hospital because she works 24/7. We found a note near the garage this morning, but her car was still—"

And now it was Quinn's turn to look sick. "The black Cadillac SUV?" he croaked.

"Oh, my God." Daphna knew. She already knew.

"What?" Dex asked. *"What?"* But then he got it. "She was coming back in to leave the note! You *killed* her!"

"I—I—" Quinn spluttered.

There was no plan of attack. Dexter just flew at Quinn, bowling into him with a lowered shoulder. Quinn stumbled backwards and fell over the box of books Daphna had pulled out from under the table. The box tumbled over, spilling its contents. Quinn went over too, but he grabbed hold of Dexter. Together they crashed to the floor.

"Dexter!" Daphna screamed. She leapt over and grabbed his arm before his fist could fly. "Dexter! He saved our lives!" But her heart—the same heart that nearly burst when Quinn kissed her—was going cold and sinking like a stone.

"I—I—" Quinn kept stuttering, trying to get out from under Dexter, who was trying to wrench his arm free from Daphna. "I got there after midnight, after I finally got someone at the hospital to tell me you'd gone there and tracked down the address on-line. And I—when I got there, someone got out of the SUV. And they—it was dark. I thought they were trying to break in! I thought it was someone else trying to kill you! It will be okay!"

"Dexter!" Daphna screamed again, pulling on his arm. She wasn't about to pretend there was anything good about the situation, but she could recognize that they didn't know exactly what the situation was. "We don't know for sure she's dead! We don't even know what the book is! We need to find out, and we need to find out as soon as poss—! There's something wrong with Nora!"

Dex stopped struggling and looked. Nora was standing there, gone again inside herself, muttering, looking fully deranged. Ashamed, Dex got off Quinn and approached her. "It's okay," he said, touching her shoulder. "I'm sorry. I'm not really like that."

Slowly, she came back.

"What—what are you doing when you do that?" Dex asked, trying to recover his wind.

"Praying," Nora said.

"Oh."

The thunder boomed outside. Deafening.

"That thunder is doing something to us," Nora said. "It won't let us get along."

Quinn was back on his feet now, but he looked extremely unsteady. "Not all of us," he said, struggling to right his breathing. "I've been noticing. You seem to be okay with Nora, Dex. And me and Daphna are okay."

Now Daphna wanted to punch Quinn, too. Punch and punch and punch him. And kiss—

"I don't know why," Quinn added, "but we must have some kind of conn—"

Dex charged again, but this time Daphna stepped in front of him. "Dexter!" she snapped. "Stop acting like an idiot! Quinn is right! I don't know why, but he is, and there's no point in denying it. We need to look into this Freemansons thing." She paused, trying to get herself back together, bearing up against the fact that yet another chance at a family might be lost. And the thing was, it wasn't that hard this time. Maybe she was getting used to it. No, Daphna knew that wasn't true. It was because she wasn't sure about Dr. Fludd yet. "And we have to get that book back from the cops," she added, "or from whoever they gave it to."

"Mason," Quinn corrected. "Free*mason*."

It took everything Dex had not to smash him in the face.

"Right," Daphna said. "*And* we need to figure out what Mr. G is all about, especially if *he* got the book. There's way too much for all of us to do at once, and—and—" She was reluctantly getting to the hard part of the idea Quinn had just given her. She took a breath, looked her brother in the eye, and then came out with it:

"I think we should split up."

# CHAPTER FIFTEEN
## *Permanently Painful*

"I think Quinn and I should go together," Daphna explained, talking fast so she could get it over with, "maybe to Mr. G's house since he really likes me. You and Nora could go to—" She turned to Nora and asked, "Do you live nearby?"

"Up on Dosch Road," Nora told her, "where the synagogue and church are. We live behind the church."

"Perfect," Daphna replied, then picked up where she'd left off with Dex. "You and Nora could go to her house to find books about Freemasons and Jews, and maybe try the synagogue, too."

Daphna saw the look of disbelief contorting her brother's face while she spoke. She could hardly believe what she was suggesting herself, especially because she wanted never to see Quinn again as long as she lived. It seemed somehow blasphemous even to consider separating, especially since she was the one who'd made them swear never to do that again after the last time. But it also seemed somehow inevitable today.

She saw no other way.

"Dex," Daphna urged, seeing his expression only darkening, "Nora's right. We're not ourselves today. I don't know why we all weren't in that riot earlier with everyone else, but I don't think we avoided it by much. Something tells me we're lucky to have found each other. We can stay in touch by cell," she added, somewhat weakly.

"Why don't you just go in the bedroom and get your kissing over with now!"

"Dexter! That's not what this is about!"

Dex knew he was being monumentally unfair, especially since he'd been the closest of any of them to becoming a full-fledged member of that mob. But he'd been blindsided by all of this. Didn't Daphna say

97

just a few hours ago that she was glad he was with her—*Him!* Of course since that moment he'd been completely useless. Who was he kidding? He'd been useless since Africa. Worse than useless. "Okay," he said, giving in. "Fine. You win." He was a world-class jerk for putting it all on her like that. But there it was.

Daphna swallowed hard, irrationally displeased at her brother's agreement. To hide the flush on her face, she looked out the front window and saw that the street was clear. No one was around at all. Then she turned back to Quinn and Nora and said, "I'm not sure you want to get involved with us." To Quinn, specifically, she added, "I won't lie. What Wren said was true. People who know us tend to die a lot. Honestly, if I were you, I would get as far away from the Wax twins as possible."

Quinn didn't hesitate. "I'd die to get my parents back," he said. "And Dr. Fludd too. We were meant to help each other. I just know it."

Everyone looked at Nora, but all she said was, "Honor your father that your days may be long upon the land which the Lord your God gives to you."

"And—*sooo*," Daphna said, "that means what?"

"It's the fifth commandment," Nora replied. "I've dishonored my father. There aren't many worse sins."

"Nora," Dex said, but she cut him off.

"You don't understand. I prevented my father from warning the community about the Masons, *real* Masons that are actually here. He will only conclude one thing—"

"What?"

"That I'm a Mason too."

For a moment, no one had a response to this.

Then Dex hit on an idea. "If we can get to the bottom of this," he said. "If we can find out what the Masons want with that book—maybe it's the big Key to Power they've been searching for! If we get it back and destroy it, your dad would know you're not one of them, right? I mean, what would honor him more than defeating the Masons and proving him right about all this stuff?"

Cautiously, nervously, Nora nodded. "Yes," she said. "Yes, I think that would please him very much. I'm sure it would."

Dex smiled. Nora looked, if not exactly overflowing with confidence, at least a little bit hopeful. He felt as if he'd just spoken Words of Power.

"But," Nora added, threatening to derail the fragile agreement before it took hold, "can we eat something before we go? I'm starving."

The group was more than happy to accommodate this request, as it seemed no one was eager to charge into battle just yet.

After clearing the table of his book repair tools, Quinn passed around some bowls, then set out a large pot of some kind of stew. It was not only delicious, but incredibly filling. Despite how many servings they all took, the group scarcely seemed to dent in it.

"You could live off this forever," Daphna said, very impressed, even though she didn't want to be.

"Which is a good thing," Quinn said, "because it's pretty much the only thing I know how to make. Luckily, I don't get sick of it."

Everyone ate ravenously for a while longer, lost in their own thoughts. Finally, Daphna said, "It shouldn't be too hard to get to Mr. G's house if it's calm out back, too." Then she added, thinking as she spoke, "If he's there and has the book, well, we'll see what that means. I assume he won't be happy because whatever the book is that he was hoping we brought back from Heaven, that isn't it—no matter how incredible it is."

"The book he wants," Nora said, clearly still savoring her stew, "do you think it's the same one you said the angels are looking for?"

The twins looked at each other. They hadn't thought of that.

"Could be," Dex said, pleased to see Nora getting involved. "Something tells me it is."

"Anyway," Daphna said, feeling pretty sure her brother was right, "if he does get that book of names, maybe we can trade information for it. Or swipe it if we have to."

"And if he's not even there?" Quinn asked.

"Then we search his house until we find out who he really is." Then Daphna added, "I wonder how he thinks he can get us anywhere in the city undetected."

"Maybe he's some kind of undercover cop?"

Quinn guessed.

"What kind of cop goes undercover watching us our whole lives?" Dex said. "That's the stupidest thing I've ever heard."

"Okay, maybe he's a Mason—like the cops I took pictures of. Or the ones you saw at that murder scene."

"Because—" Dex didn't know why because, but it didn't matter as Daphna prudently interrupted.

"I got the impression he meant he could get us out undetected from the basement," she said, "where we might be hiding or trapped. Maybe he has one of those underground garages?"

This seemed unlikely, but then Dex and Daphna turned to each other, matching eyes wide, faces flush with simultaneous insight. They both turned to look at the heap of books still on the floor.

There was the one with the straps.

"Tunnels!" the twins both cried.

But their enthusiasm wilted when they realized they wouldn't be working to find them together.

"That makes sense," Quinn agreed. Though after a moment of reflection, he said, "But I thought the tunnels were downtown, by the waterfront. I read a bit of that book. It says they used to get people drunk and then drop them through trapdoors into the tunnels to sneak them out onto the ships, where they'd be forced to work. 'Shanghaiing,' right? But I didn't read all of it. Let's see." Quinn went and picked up the book, then sat down and started leafing through it.

"That's supposed to be the most comprehensive book on the Shanghai Tunnels," Daphna said, watching Quinn flip through the pages. "I think there were all kinds of crimes going on down there, opium dens and whatnot," she added, thinking she must look just like Quinn did—hunched over, brow furrowed—when she dove into an intriguing book.

Dex wanted to tear the book out of Quinn's hands and go upside his head with it. Instead he watched Nora scarfing the bottomless stew.

"Here's the original map of the whole system." Quinn held the book up. It was crudely drawn, a grid with wavy lines running through it. The grid had to be the downtown streets and the wavy lines, the tunnels running underneath them. And the river was clear enough—a wavy blue line along the edge. "The tunnels do extend a bit from the waterfront," he observed, "but they don't come anywhere near here. Hillsdale isn't even on the map."

"Maybe Mr. G has his own tunnel just to get out of his house," Dex said. "Or maybe he just has some kind of connections to people who can help."

Quinn didn't dispute these possibilities, but said, "Still—maybe we should keep it with us. Do you mind?"

Daphna winced, but nodded, so Quinn tore it out.

"I'd give that to Daphna," Dex advised. "I guarantee she's better with directions than you are."

"Okay, sure." Quinn handed it over.

Thunder crashed, shaking the whole apartment as Daphna folded up the map and tucked it into her back pocket. *"We better get moving,"* she sighed when it stopped.

No one disagreed, but by the intentionally slow way the four of them cleaned up the bowls and glasses and scattered books, it was obvious they still weren't overly anxious to leave the apartment. But, finally, when there was nothing left to stall with, they headed down the stairs and back outside behind the stores.

It was quiet outside now, eerily so. And really, really hot.

Daphna couldn't believe what they were doing, now that they were doing it—even if it had been her suggestion. Were they really separating? After all they'd seen and done together? She was having serious second thoughts.

"It's okay," Dex said, watching his sister's face. He climbed onto his bike and waved Nora over.

But Nora hesitated again. "How—how do you know we're doing the right thing?" she asked.

"I don't know about the right thing," Dex admitted, "only the next thing."

"But—"

"Here's a better question: Aren't you worried my sister's going to slap you silly again if you don't get on this bike?"

Nora got on the bike while Dex tried not to laugh.

"I'm sorry about that," Daphna muttered.

"I never learned," Nora said, getting situated. "I'm so embarrassed. I can't do anything normal kids can do."

"Can you read?" Dex asked her.

"Of course I—"

"Then you got one on me."

Quinn looked perplexed by this exchange, as did Nora. Daphna turned away to hide a smile. When she turned back, the bike was in motion. "Call!" she shouted.

Dex waved to her over Nora's wild hair.

Daphna watched Dex pedal slowly between the shops toward the street out front. The moment her brother was out of sight she knew, in her very bones, that their lives had just changed in some permanently painful way.

# CHAPTER SIXTEEN
*Voices*

Admitting to Daphna he couldn't read had been the greatest relief of Dexter's life, greater even than the relief of constantly averting death and disaster. Yet, somehow, explaining how his eyes took in too much light when it bounced off some surfaces—paper especially—over his shoulder to this total stranger felt almost as good. It didn't feel like setting a burden down this time. It was actually more like lifting something up, something he had the strength to carry.

Dex stopped when he reached the main road, where all was quiet. After a look both ways for cops, he pedaled hard, and seconds later, he and Nora were flying down the hill with wind whipping through their hair. It had turned out to be a beautiful day, freakish thunder and lightning aside. And even if it was crazy hot, it felt good. Nora was squeezing him now for all she was worth. She made no comment on what he'd told her, and he was pretty sure she was praying again, but it didn't matter. He wondered if she were praying that he really could help her.

Dex wasn't going to think about the fact that he just left his sister behind with some creep he didn't trust one bit. She'd *kissed* him? When? *Why*, with everything going on? He thought back to Antin calling her good-looking under the ruins of the bookstore and how he'd been so bent out of shape about that. Then he realized why. That was the moment he'd, on some unconscious level anyway, realized there would be a part of Daphna's life that would never have anything to do with him. And now he understood that the same would be true for her about his life. Maybe it was already.

The thought made Dex momentarily despair, but the sense of speed and the warmth of Nora pressing into his back was so exhilarating that he managed to push it all aside, to forget where he was going and why he was going there.

He forgot everything but speed.

"Turn!" Nora cried.

Dex remembered where he was, worked the breaks in time, and turned up Dosch Road without killing them. Then he pumped furiously up the short distance to the drive on the right that wound up into the church grounds. Instead of attempting that long incline, he reluctantly stopped the bike. He and Nora got off and hid it in some tall weeds. It was strange to realize how close they lived to each other. They were practically neighbors.

"Thank you," Nora said when they were back on the sidewalk. "For what you did for me at school. I could have been killed. You saved my life."

"You're welcome." Dex blushed. "It was nothing. Really."

"And I'm really sorry about your eye—condition."

The pair headed up the drive, walking side-by-side.

"Thanks," Dex replied. "I guess it's not all that— No, it really is all that bad. But thanks. I appreciate—"

Thunder slammed the sky several times just then. Nora grabbed Dexter's hand, but let go quickly when the last flash of lightning faded away.

"It's not against the law to hold hands, you know," Dex said. Did he want to kiss Nora? No, that would be taking advantage of her. She was counting on him to help her.

Nora was blushing now. Her wan face made the red bloom look like fire. "My father," she said, "he says one thing leads to another. It's the smallest cracks in your resolve through which evil enters your life. It's not worth the Lake of Fire."

"Are you serious?" Dex asked, stopping in his tracks. "But then he said, "What's going on?" They'd reached the top of the drive, and he hadn't expected to see the lot full of cars here as well. "I thought—"

"It's overflow from the synagogue," Nora explained. "There won't be anyone around."

"Good," Dex said. "Where's your house again?"

A shadow passed over Nora's face, but she led Dex alongside the large, attractive church with its three sky-scraping crosses, past a little fenced play area, and then behind the facility into a cluster of trees separating the church from the grounds of Dex and Daphna's middle school. Then she stopped.

*"Don't tell me you live in* that?" Dexter gasped, amazed he never knew it was there.

He knew how rude that sounded, but Dex couldn't help himself. In the midst of the trees, surrounded by overgrown weeds and untended brush, was a brick—structure. He guessed you could call it a house, but not only was it in crumbling disrepair, it was absurdly small. A crooked little metal chimney jutted from the crooked, moss-covered roof. Disbelief quickly transformed into sympathy. "I'm—I'm sorry," Dex said. "I didn't mean that."

"We're off the grid," Nora explained, seeing Dex notice the decrepit little well beside the house. "No electricity. No running water. No *windows.* It's the only way he can be sure the Masons can't spy on us. A lady in the church takes pity on me and lets me shower in there. She buys me clothes, too."

All Dex could do was shake his head.

"It's not that my father doesn't care," Nora said. "He just—it's just that nothing in this lifetime matters much to him. It's so short, after all. What comes next is what really counts."

Dex had no response to this.

"Come on," Nora said, looking round. "He's not home. We better hurry."

Nora produced a surprisingly large bunch of keys from her pocket and proceeded to open the front door. This was no easy task as it had six separate locks, each of which required a different key. Once she had it open, she hurried inside, and Dex followed behind her. After relocking the door, Nora walked straight through the main room into what looked like the kitchen, but Dex stayed where he was, transfixed.

Nearly every inch of the walls were covered with crosses hanging on nails, most slightly off kilter. There were hundreds of them, of all sizes and designs. The largest had to be two feet tall, and there were many no bigger than a finger. They appeared to be made of all sorts of materials. Dex could see woods and metals of myriad colors, but also what looked like ivory and jade and glass. The spaces not covered by crosses had tiny shelves jutting out, blocks of wood, it seemed, holding various sized candle stubs. All had gobs of melted wax stuck to them.

"*Hurry, Dex!*" Nora whispered, leaning out from the kitchen.

Dex hurried over to her.

The kitchen was essentially just a hallway lined with warped cabinets and countertops. There was no room for any kind of table. Nora was kneeling down inside a pantry lifting the edge of a large square of linoleum off the floor.

A trapdoor.

For a moment, Dex was back on top of Asterius Rash's bookstore again, looking down through a similar hole, before—everything.

Under the trapdoor was a ladder bolted to a concrete wall.

"His books are down there," Nora said. "At the bottom, there's a flashlight hanging on a nail, just over the last step. Can you—*oh, no*—"

They'd both heard it. Voices, coming from outside.

Nora froze.

"*Nora, go down!*" Dex whispered as loudly as he dared, but she didn't respond.

One of the locks turned on the front door.

"*Nora!*" Dex touched her shoulder, trying to keep her with him.

Another lock turned.

"Okay," Dex said, "I'll go." He hurried down onto the ladder. "I'm sure your dad will be glad to see you."

Nora looked at Dex, then toward the front door as the third lock began to turn. Dex climbed down the ladder, and as he'd hoped, Nora clambered down onto it after him.

The very moment the front door opened, she dropped the trapdoor over them with a smack, leaving them in complete darkness.

# CHAPTER SEVENTEEN
### Hiding Something

Daphna stood watching the corner for a long while after Dex disappeared around it, hoping they were doing the right thing, not just the next thing. Finally, Quinn shook her shoulder. He'd apparently said something.

"What?"

"I just want you to know how sorry I am, about Dr. Fludd. I want you to know that I won't rest until we bring her back with my parents. I know, with your help, with all your incredible experiences, we can fix everything. I knew I'd be able to count on you."

"Let's just get going."

"Okay."

Fortunately, no one was around either of the schools. Daphna and Quinn jogged across the road after reaching the big tree at Wilson, then hurried up to Mr. G's house.

"It doesn't look like his car is here," Daphna observed. "I don't know if there's a Mrs. G or not."

"Good point," Quinn said. "I probably wouldn't have even thought about that."

Ignoring this, Daphna attempted to peek through the front window, but it was covered by thick curtains. *This is a terrible mistake*, she thought. She shouldn't be risking her life with anyone but her brother. She didn't even know Quinn! But it was too late now, and she felt exposed standing there in the relative open, especially now that Quinn wasn't protecting her with that book anymore.

"Let's just go in," Daphna said, heading up onto the porch. She pulled the key out of her pocket and quickly unlocked the door. She and Quinn stepped swiftly into the house, but they closed the door behind them at the same time, causing their hands to touch.

"Sorry," Quinn said.

Daphna didn't reply. Her stupid feelings—her spiking pulse—didn't matter right now.

They were in an entry hall. A long table ran along the wall on the right under framed photos of butterflies.

"Where do we start?" Quinn asked, looking through piles of mail spread out on the table.

Daphna joined him, but nothing seemed out of the ordinary: bills, it looked like. "Let's see what's what," she said, walking down the hall.

The kitchen was straight ahead. Daphna went in and opened the refrigerator, which was empty but for a bunch of Chinese food boxes and a carton of milk. The freezer had a stack of frozen dinners. Quinn, who'd followed her in, opened some cabinets to find them virtually bare as well; cans of soup was about it.

"I'm thinking there's definitely no Mrs. G," he said.

The dirty dishes piled up in the sink confirmed this for Daphna, who'd seen enough. She headed into the living room, so Quinn followed her there.

Three of the walls were lined with cabinets, most of which held books. The wall space between them was filled with more butterfly photos. Daphna went right to a shelf and started scanning. Quinn went to another.

"Big on butterflies, I guess," Quinn said. "He's got a ton of field guides here."

"Huh," said Daphna. The shelves she was looking at were filled with books on all the world's major faiths: Judaism, Christianity, Islam, Buddhism, Hinduism. But also on many lesser-known ones, most of which she'd become at least passingly familiar with through her reading this past year: Confucianism, Sikhism, Baha'ism, Shintoism, Taoism. One book caught her attention because it had a Jewish star on it, but it was called *Kabbalism: Gathering the Divine Sparks*. She took it down and started reading the back.

Quinn was next to her now. "I have to admit I don't know the first thing about any religion," he said. "My parents never talk about it. The only Bibles we ever get are to sell."

Daphna nodded, turning her attention to a cabinet that held, rather than books, fancy wine glasses. They weren't sets, though. In fact, now that she looked closer, none of them were the same. And actually, not all of them were fancy. Most were gold, or gold-plated surely, or silver or crystal, but others were clay or wooden, and some of those rather roughly hewn.

In the center of the room was a large round desk with a laptop and printer in the midst of all sorts of camera equipment.

"I think he takes the butterfly pictures himself," Daphna said, inspecting a long lens attachment.

Quinn tried the drawers, but they were full of office supplies. One was locked; he gave up after pulling on it a few times. He opened the laptop and clicked it to life while Daphna set the lens back down and turned to continue her investigation of the room.

Behind the desk, built into the wall, was a gas fireplace, above which was a painting, though that word seemed a bit generous. It was more like a bunch of black and gray paint dripped and dribbled on a canvas. The only color came from a curvy stripe of blue on the right side and drops of red here and there.

"Can't get into the computer," Quinn said, standing next to her again. Then he said, "Jackson Pollock?"

"Who?"

"He did work like that."

"*I* did work that," Daphna said. "When I was three."

Quinn laughed his funny laugh. "I kinda like it."

The fireplace was glass on both sides, so Daphna squatted down and peered through it. A bedroom was visible on the other side. She walked over to the door that led into it. "C'mon," she said, flushing with anger at Dexter for that childish remark about bedrooms and kissing. "Let's check in here."

The bed was unmade, clothes stuck out of dresser drawers, and a laundry basket overflowed against a wall.

Daphna shook her head. "Are all males slobs?" she asked.

"Ah," Quinn said, but before he could say more, the phone rang on the bedside table. He and Daphna froze, staring at it.

"*Answering machine,*" Daphna said, whispering for some reason.

After four rings, the machine picked up and Mr. G's recording invited the caller to leave a message after the beep. After the beep, Mr. G himself came on.

"Dexter and Daphna!" he shouted. "Are you there? Are you in the house?"

Daphna and Quinn went rigid, as if he could see them standing there. Of course that was silly.

Mr. G waited a moment, then said, "Pick up the phone! If you're in the house, get out! You lied to me! Damn my lousy eyes! The book had a gold *cover* on it! You have no idea what you've done to me! I don't know what you think you're doing, but get out of my house! Look, I can explain everything," he said, easing his tone. "Just leave the key on the kitchen counter and go home. All kids should be home right now. Leave me your number, and I'll give you a call."

Another voice could be heard in the background just then. "You only get one call, buddy."

"Just get out!" Mr. G shouted. "It's—it's not safe in there! Wait! There are two kids in my house. The Wax twins! They've broken in, and they're—"

There was a click, then a dial tone, and then the machine cut out.

"He sounds pretty mad," Quinn said. "Do you think we should go?"

"I think we should find whatever he doesn't want us to see," was Daphna's reply. "And now we know the book he's looking for is yellow, or gold I guess. All the books in Heaven were bright, like golden light. So I guess that makes sense."

Quinn nodded. "What was that about 'one call?'" he asked. "Do you think he's been arrested?"

"Musta been," Daphna said. "Probably trying to get that book back from the cops. But I think they'll be on their way here now. We better hurry."

"Okay."

"Try the closet."

Quinn turned to regard two mirrored doors. They slid apart to reveal a solid wall of clothes on hangers. He pushed some pants and jackets aside and looked behind. "Hey," he said, "how do you like that?" And then he disappeared through the gap he'd made.

Daphna didn't want to go in there with Quinn, so she waited for him to come back out. Only, he didn't come back out. She waited some more, but then got too curious and poked her head through the curtain of clothes. She was expecting to find a little space behind the rack, but not this much. It was a full walk-in closet.

The only reason to block it all off like that was because you didn't want people snooping around back there—because you were hiding something.

Quinn was inspecting the back wall, which had shelves and drawers set against it.

"Stay here for a second, would you?" he said, turning around. "I'm going back to the living room. When you hear me shout, pound on the wall right here. Okay?"

"Ahh," Daphna said, "okay—" She held her breath when Quinn squeezed by her. She watched him drive his way back through the clothes and out of the closet.

A few moments later, she heard him call out, "Go ahead!" Daphna knocked on the wall.

"Harder!" Quinn called, so she knocked harder. "Can you hear *this?*" Now Quinn banged on the wall.

Daphna could hear it, but was confused. It sounded like it was coming from off to her left, which was odd because it seemed like she should be up against the house's outside wall. Quinn obviously wasn't outside. Unless—

From opposite sides of the wall, both snoopers called out, "Secret room!"

# CHAPTER EIGHTEEN
## An Omen

Dex climbed down the ladder as quickly as he dared in the dark. The floor was considerably lower than he thought possible, but soon enough his foot felt solid ground, concrete ground. As he stepped off the ladder, he could hear Nora panicking as she climbed down, but she reached him a few moments later.

Once off the ladder, she hissed, "My father! And someone else! There's no way out!"

"Maybe they won't come down," Dex whispered.

A light clicked on. Nora had the flashlight, an old battered metal one. Dex looked around the room they were in.

Books.

Everywhere, books. Up and down the walls. It was like a bunker of books. The trapdoor had to be twenty feet up.

It creaked.

Nora snapped off the light and pulled Dexter, dragged him, to the far end of the underground library. The trapdoor opened, letting in light from the kitchen, but it only illuminated a third of the space.

Crouched down against some low shelves, Dex willed the dark to keep them hidden if someone came down. He could see now that the room was as large as the house itself and made entirely of concrete. All four walls had simple metal shelves bolted to them, floor to roof. There were gaps between the shelves where other ladders ran up and down the walls, giving access to the books at any location. There had to be thousands of books down there. More!

Great, Dex thought, and we don't even know what we're looking for.

"I apologize for the state you find me in," Jons said, his voice filtering down through the trapdoor from above.

Nora clutched Dexter, cowering against the books behind her.

"To receive an emissary from the Pope himself! I—I am humbled and honored."

"As you know, Pastor Jons," a man replied, "the Church has never shared your—certainty about the depth or breadth of Masonic conspiracies, fashionable as they may sometimes be. But rest assured your vigilance has not gone unnoticed nor unappreciated these many years."

Dex's muscles clenched at the sound of this voice. It was the Secret Keeper of the Church. The man who had Dead Face shoot them in cold blood. The man who'd sent who knew how many other killers to finish the job.

"The Holy Father has many things to worry about," the Secret Keeper continued. "No offense was meant in ignoring you and your important work. Though I'm quite certain that a dedicated man of God like you knows well that proper recognition will be yours, along with all the thanks that count, when Judgment—"

"But they have my daughter!" Jons protested. "Please, we're wasting time here. Help me find that boy, that Wax boy, who has lured her away from me. I will wring his neck for you myself!"

Nora gasped at this, but then covered her mouth. It wasn't exactly pleasant for Dexter either.

"We have ceased efforts on that front," the Secret Keeper replied, "as they have proved futile. Our best assassins were dispatched to eliminate the twins. These are men with no peers in their profession. Do you understand me? They are all missing. As you might imagine, this has us very concerned."

"The Brotherhood is protecting them! I have seen their agents sniffing around for weeks!"

"Regardless, our spies tell us that Masons worldwide have been galvanized by news of something happening here in Portland lately, and specifically today. Threats have been leveled at the leaders of all developed nations, and even at the Pope himself. This is unprecedented."

Now Jons gasped. *"Threats?"*

"Threats to make them 'disappear.' Leaders have been given until two o'clock this afternoon to recognize the Grand Master of the Portland Masons as the Supreme Ruler of one global nation."

"But surely they cannot make good on such outrageous threats?"

"To be sure, many have rejected the threat. But we are not taking it lightly. As you suggested, the Masons may be protecting the twins. As I mentioned, our assassins have *disappeared*."

"This—this is terrible! We—you must prevent this! Why tarry here when—?"

"I came to Portland to investigate the loss of our good men, and I will discover the nature of this threat. Be quite certain, the Masons will suffer the full wrath of the Church before they act against the Holy Father! Even they cannot conceive of the resources at our disposal." He paused a moment, then added, "But I have taken the time to see if you can help the Pope at this delicate juncture. I'm sure that he will wish to thank you personally if you can be of assistance. I would not be surprised if an appointment of some kind wouldn't be in order. I understand you are currently without a congregation..."

There was another pause, after which Jons said, "Tell me, what book do you seek?"

"The Diary of Dr. William Gull."

There was yet another pause, a longer one. Finally, Jons said, "I don't believe I possess that particular title."

"Ah, but I believe you do," the Secret Keeper replied. "You purchased it at an auction thirty-three years ago this month in Geneva, your interest no doubt having been piqued when it was discovered—because of the rumors that Gull, a known Mason, revealed on his deathbed that he somehow exposed the Brotherhood in its pages. This is a long shot, given that we ourselves evaluated the book before you obtained it. We're hoping that modern technology and cutting-edge decryption techniques might reveal something we missed those many years ago."

"Yes, of course," Jons said. "I'm embarrassed to have forgotten about the diary. I, myself, performed a thorough investigation when I first obtained it and found nothing to those rumors. I haven't considered it in decades. But I have no doubt I can find it. However, I was—It's a bit awkward to descend. I injured my back this morning—assaulted by that satanic Wax boy! I'm not quite sure I can manage the—"

"Pastor Jons, it is of the utmost importance that we examine the diary. If necessary, I will go down and retrieve it myself."

"Not at all. Not at all," Jons said. "I shall fetch it forthwith. I do not mean to appear uncooperative. Nothing could be further from my aim. I am fully out-of-sorts with my sinful daughter. It is my pleasure to be of service."

Nora clutched Dex even harder and let out a little yelp of fear, but just then the thunder crashed.

And then it crashed again, rocking the little house.

And then it crashed again.

And again.

Dex and Nora were thrown onto the concrete floor. They could hear things falling upstairs, lots of things.

A book hit Dexter in the head. Then another.

Nora cried out when one struck her in the head. Dex cried out when one hit him in the neck, but both their voices were lost in what was now an avalanche of books.

Dexter managed to roll to Nora, who was curled in the fetal position again. He tented himself over her to absorb the blows, which came one after another, a barrage of punches to the head, the neck, his back, and legs.

The thunder continued to crash, and the books continued to fall, pummeling Dexter.

"Hold on!" he urged Nora, but he doubted she could hear anything, even right under him like that.

It felt like he was being beaten with a baseball bat. The blows kept raining down; he was sure they would both be killed.

But then it stopped.

It was quiet. Dex was battered and bruised, but alive. Nora was under him, whimpering, but very much alive, too.

They'd been buried by the books.

"An omen," Jons said above the trapdoor. "A most ominous one."

"A damnable delay," the Secret Keeper snapped. His voice was terse now, severe. "Find the book and bring it to me at once. In the end, it may be of little import."

The floors creaked as the pair moved back through the kitchen.

Dexter held his breath. It was hard to breathe under the books, and they were heavy.

It sounded like the front door opened, then closed. He dared to let out a sigh of relief.

But now footsteps came back toward the kitchen.

Nora found Dexter's hand and squeezed it, desperately.

The trapdoor creaked. *He's closing it!* Dex thought. *He's not coming down!*

But it stopped.

It creaked again and smacked down.

*Open or closed?*

The answer came with a pained groan, and then the sound of feet on the ladder.

# CHAPTER NINETEEN
### *Every Single Day*

Quinn burst back into the closet.

"Great job!" Daphna exclaimed. "It's just like—!"

"The Hardy Boys!"

Daphna grinned. "I was going to say Nancy Drew. They were always finding secret passageways and rooms. I love those books!"

"Me too!"

The pair smiled at each other, but then Daphna turned away. "One of these shelves must swing open," she said. There were three separate units. Daphna attacked the first, sweeping off shoes, shirts, ties, and everything else that might be covering up a clue. When it was cleared, she moved to the second. Quinn took on the third, but neither of them found anything like—whatever it was they were looking for. A knob? A switch?

The lower portion of the units held dresser drawers, so they emptied them next. But neither found any way to open any kind of door.

*"There's got to be a way,"* Daphna sighed when there was nothing left to remove.

"Hmmm," said Quinn. "Ever read Sherlock Holmes?"

"Of course," Daphna said, offended, "every story."

Quinn smiled again. "My dad almost got his hands on a First Edition of *Enter Sherlock Holmes,*" he said. "For five bucks."

"You're kidding me."

"No, marbled endpapers and gilt pages and everything. He found it at an estate sale but didn't have the heart not to tell the old widow what she was selling."

"That'd've been worth a fortune! And you needed money! Wow," Daphna said, extremely impressed, "your dad sounds like he was a really good—I mean, he sounds like he *is* a really—Oh, gosh, I'm sorry."

"It's okay," Quinn said, shaking off the despairing look that had crept over his features. "Let's think like Holmes for a second. What do you notice about the shelves? Describe them for me."

"Describe them?"

"Yeah."

"Well, there are three units, all white, each with four shelves resting on—Hey! Let's take them out."

So Daphna and Quinn removed the shelves.

"What are those?" Daphna pointed to the little plastic discs now exposed on the back of each unit. They'd been covered by the back edges of the shelves.

Quinn approached the middle unit and popped one out. Behind it was a screw.

*"Oh,"* Daphna sighed. "They cover up the screws that hold it on the wall. If you set the shelves at different places, they'd show, and it would look ugly."

"There's an extra one here," Quinn pointed out. It was true. There were two behind each shelf in all the units, but three on the middle shelf of the first. The one in the center was larger than the others. It was about the size of a—

Daphna attacked it.

The little plug popped right out into her hand.

She and Quinn looked at what was behind it.

A keyhole.

Daphna and Quinn turned to each other with the same victorious smiles and said, at the same time, "Elementary, my dear, Watson!"

They burst out laughing.

Then they stopped.

Their eyes locked.

Daphna's heart battered her ribs as the moment stretched and stretched, straight out into infinity.

She wanted this to happen, but she didn't want herself to want it.

She had no idea what to do. Except maybe faint. Fainting was her best option.

But before she could manage, they were kissing.

Quinn was kissing Daphna again, but this time Daphna was kissing him back.

But just before the world tipped off its axis again, Daphna shoved him away. She jammed her eyes shut for a moment, willing her head to clear.

"Daphna," Quinn said, "I—I'm sorry. I—"

"I'm already helping you!" Daphna wailed. "Okay?"

"What—what do you mean? I thought—it seemed like you—"

"You did it on purpose! I know you did it on purpose!"

"What? I did *what* on purpose?"

"You erased her so we would have to help you!"

"*Dr. Fludd?*" Quinn gasped. "You think I—I would never do anything like that! What kind of person do you think I am?"

"How am I supposed to know? Maybe the kind of person who was desperate for my brother's help and knew how easily someone like you could get someone like me to help someone like you!"

"*What?*" Quinn was incredulous now. "What do you mean someone like me and someone like you? And why would I come up with something so elaborate and unlikely—?"

"BECAUSE THAT'S WHAT PEOPLE DO IN THIS WORLD! THEY *USE* YOU! THEY DISCOVER YOUR WEAK-NESSES AND THEY LIE AND CHEAT AND SCHEME AND PLOT AND DESTROY EVERYTHING YOU CARE AND DREAM ABOUT!"

Quinn looked as if he were considering all kinds of responses to this, but what he finally said was, "The first time I saw you was in my father's shop. You were there with your dad. You were nine. It was April Fools' Day, and I was going to play a prank on you, some-thing brilliant like sneaking up and saying 'Boo!' or pulling your hair. You were wearing white shorts with white stripes down the sides and a white shirt and one of those visors. It was white too. You even had white tennis shoes. You looked like an angel."

Daphna shook her head as if to ward this off. "I don't remember dressing like that," she challenged. "I'm sure I'd remember dressing like that!"

Quinn ignored this. "I forgot all about scaring you as I watched you move around the shop," he con-tinued. "I'd never seen a kid act like that in the store. They usually wrecked the place. But you were totally into the books, lost in your own world. You took them off and put them back onto shelves like they were made of glass. You had no idea I was following you in and out of the aisles, falling over stacks of books. You had no idea I was falling head over heels in love with you."

A strangled sob escaped Daphna's throat.

"Love at first sight?" she wailed. *"At age nine?* You expect me to believe in something like that in this world!"

*"I* believe in it," Quinn said. "You and I were meant to meet again this way, to—"

"Quinn," Daphna said, exasperated, "why do you always talk like that?"

"Like what?"

"Like things are supposed to happen the way they do."

"I—I don't know. I guess sometimes I really think they do."

"Well, let me tell you something," Daphna snapped. "God isn't writing the script. Mysteries don't exist just to entertain you. Tragedies don't happen so you can build your character!"

"But—"

"Did my mother have to die to teach me the value of appreciating the people in my life while they're still there? What about *her* life? Did Evelyn rot away from the plague so I could find a boyfriend to teach me about Destiny and True Love? Only children think the world revolves around them, Quinn. I may be a lot of things, but I'm not a child. I was evicted from Storybook Land a long time ago."

"You—you're right," Quinn conceded. "I'm sorry. I—I guess I read too much. I don't refer to books all the time to impress people. I do it because it's all I know. But I kissed you because I've been dreaming about kissing you since the moment you left my father's store that day."

"Living in a dream world—" Daphna shouted, "it—it isn't living!"

Quinn had no reply for this. He looked utterly defeated, and now Daphna felt ashamed. She felt like she'd just done a very bad thing.

"No," she said, deciding just to forget about his supposedly being in love with her. "I'm sorry. I'm not right about being so upbeat. Being confident and optimistic is a *good* thing, no matter the reason. Expecting happy endings makes them more likely to happen, I'm sure. You've helped me already by being so positive. Please, don't stop."

"Okay," Quinn said, but he did not meet Daphna's eyes. "You don't trust me," he said. "I understand."

"I don't trust anyone. No one but Dexter, and now something's happened to us."

"Daphna, no—we'll all get back together as soon as we can."

This seemed like the proper line of thought to pursue, and more importantly, to act upon. Daphna took Mr. G's key out of her pocket and put it into the keyhole. Then she looked at Quinn, at his damnably handsome face.

He nodded, so she turned the key.

The entire shelving unit opened into the closet revealing a dark room behind it.

"Yes!" Quinn exclaimed, but he did not try to hug Daphna. Instead, he went right into the room, feeling around on the wall for a light switch.

Daphna hesitated, but when the light came on she stepped inside.

Into a room full of filing cabinets.

"This is weird," Daphna said. "It's like everything is happening over and over again."

"What do you mean?"

"Never mind—Hey, that's just a few days after my birthday."

Quinn approached the cabinet Daphna was pointing to. It had a label on the top drawer, a fourteen year old date. He opened the drawer and pulled out the first file.

Daphna hung back, sure that whatever was in there wasn't something she wanted to see.

"There's a copy of your birth certificate in here," Quinn said. "Yours and your brother's. At least I think that's what it is. It's in Hebrew maybe? Except for your names. There's a picture of you—at least I assume it's you."

Daphna hurried over. Yes, that's what it looked like, an Israeli birth certificate with their names on it. Clipped to it were two photos, one of her and one of Dex. Dex was in their father's arms. Daphna was in their mother's—their mother! They were in a hospital.

Daphna pulled a piece of paper with typing on it out of a file, a brief note that read: "Have reached the children. Nothing unusual to report." There was a stamp above reading, 'Copy.'

Bewildered, Daphna turned the folder over. There was a date on the tab—the same date on the cabinet. The drawer was still open, and now she saw that it was stuffed with files, all dated in order. She grabbed the next one and found photos of her and Dex in their cribs.

Frantic now, Daphna rifled through more files until she found one with a report longer than a few lines. She pulled it out and read: "Twins' mother did not return from cave expedition. Presumed dead. Father injured. Move to America being planned. Will follow." One further in the cabinet said, "Father functional with brain injury/memory impairment. Mother not dead but living with family disguised as caretaker: reasons unclear."

Daphna shoved the file back into the drawer, then slammed it shut. She turned to take in the full effect of all these cabinets—these drawers that apparently contained a chronicle of her life. She opened the top drawer in the next cabinet and found a file with pictures of her and Dex in their Multnomah Village house. They looked about two.

'Nothing unusual to report.'

Flipping through random files now, Daphna saw picture after picture of her and Dex, most of which featured their mother as well. It was as if all her lost photographs had materialized here, even the ones she could only imagine. This trove should have felt like a goldmine, but instead it disgusted her. It was a violation she could scarcely conceive. It felt as if someone had quite literally stolen her memories.

Daphna counted the cabinets. There were fifteen. She moved to the next to last and opened it. After fingering through the files inside, she pulled one out. There were photos of her and Dex in the Clearing, in the rain, with seven elderly people lying dead in the leaves. The report read, "Twins not killed in events of the day, but you can be assured that I was ready should they have been. As previously reported, the book in question is not the one we seek."

"I—I can't believe this," Daphna stuttered. *"Every*

*single day?"*

Quinn had a drawer open in the last cabinet. "This is yesterday," he said. "Or last night. There's a picture of you and Dexter coming out of the hosp—"

Thunder slammed the world just then. The house reacted like it had been kicked. Then more booming claps followed, slamming and slamming and slamming the house, threatening to knock it down. The filing cabinets toppled and crashed to the floor, spilling their contents like piñatas. It was a wonder none of them struck Daphna or Quinn, both of whom sank to the floor in the midst of it all, huddling together.

When the thunder finally ceased, they found themselves surrounded by what looked like felled metal trees. Folders and photos were strewn about like leaves covering a forest floor.

Neither spoke for a few moments, but finally Daphna said, "I lost all my own pictures. All my albums were destroyed." Then, without a warning, she jumped up and scrambled over the mess and back into the closet. After crashing through the wall of clothes, she ran back into the living room. She needed to get out of there, to get some fresh air, though she was sure what she'd find outside would be some fresh horror instead. She settled for throwing open the drapes to let the sun shine on her face.

Fortunately, no one was around. Daphna just stood there looking at the sky, trying not to think about pictures, about her inadequate memories, about Quinn and kissing and destiny, about abandoning Dexter *again*, about Heaven and Earth and Just Desserts.

She tried to let her eyes unfocus but was distracted by an image of that ridiculous painting behind her reflected on the window glass. She looked at all the squiggles superimposed over the school and thought about the paths that pastor said they better choose. A quote came to mind: *The road to Hell is paved with good intentions.* She was probably on that road, headed straight for the Lake of Fire. But how could she be blamed if it was the only road open to her?

Quinn was there, standing behind her.

"All that camera equipment is obviously not just for butterflies," Daphna said without taking her eyes off the two images in the glass. Now it sort of looked like worms attacking the school. They'd attack her that way, when she was finally dead and buried, all but her precious rib, she supposed. "The butterfly thing is probably just his cover," she added. "I guess I know why he's been at every school we've gone to now."

"But," Quinn said, "with all those things you told me about, almost getting killed all those times? He just watched? What if you died?"

"He *wants* us to die," Daphna realized, finally turning around. "He knows we're Lamed Vavniks somehow. I think he believes we can come back from Heaven after we die."

"And bring back the book he wants. That why he wrote he was ready if you got killed."

"Exactly! I think Nora was right. They want the same book the angels are looking for—some kind of lost book from Heaven, or in Heaven."

"But why just watch you and Dex?"

"It can't be just us." Daphna was sure of this. "It would have to be all of us. Mr. G said he was 'assigned' to us. That means he has a boss. That means he works for an organization, an organization able to identify the Thirty-six and spy on them every minute of their lives."

"But he left you guys to go after the book."

"Right. Because if that's the book he's searching for, then it wouldn't matter if we die. But that's why he told us not to do anything but sit here and not get killed—just in case."

"Any idea what this organization could be?"

"Well," Daphna said after thinking it over a moment, "it's not the Church if he was trying to protect us from them. And it's not Masons or he wouldn't be down at the police station trying to get your book back from them."

"Wow," Quinn marveled. "I can't imagine who it—But wait, if they're watching all of the Thirty-six and waiting for them to die—didn't you say you were actually at the murder scene of one—?"

"Oh, my gosh!"

"What?"

"That murder scene—when Dex and I were there. In the hotel room—there were two cops, and someone taking pictures! We figured it was a reporter. The cops were Masons, but the photographer—I know there are always people taking pictures at crime scenes, but he could have been the person 'assigned' to that poor man. That means he was probably there when he was actually killed!" Daphna was suddenly steaming. "If they're watching us, then they watched *all* the others get murdered one by one and did nothing about it!"

"Why not kill you themselves?"

"I guess if they believe in Heaven, they probably don't want to sacrifice their chances of winding up there by committing murder. Though I can't imagine watching people get murdered without doing anything about it wouldn't keep you out."

"Seems like it should."

"I guess there's a room full of files for Evelyn's life somewhere," Daphna said. "Which would mean they had to know she was Eve, or at least that she seemed to be living forever. *Who are these people? You know what?*" she said. "I don't care. They clearly don't interfere." She grabbed the drapes to drag them closed. "Let's go down to the—Is it *ninety-nine* degrees?"

There was a thermometer stuck on a plunger to the front window. Daphna leaned closer to see if she'd read it right. She had.

"Daphna!" Quinn cried.

There was no point in darting away. There was no point in lamenting the stupidity of opening the drapes in the first place, let alone of standing there so long.

Branwen was standing right across the street with five boys. She was sporting a new outfit—jean shorts and a sleeveless chiffon top. She looked fully refreshed, and fully insane. Her stunning eyes were positively crazed, and they were locked on Daphna's.

# CHAPTER TWENTY
## *Spines*

Sweat dripped from Dexter's hair down his temple and into the corner of his eye, but he dared not move to wipe it. It was ghastly hot under the pile and difficult to breathe. Nora, he realized, was still under him. He could hear her praying. Their faces, it seemed, were mashed, cheek-to-cheek. Their hearts pounded together, hard enough, he was certain, to shake the entire pile of books right off of them.

Dex tried to calm himself by taking long, slow breaths. He tried to remember where he was and what circumstances required his immediate attention, but the ability to think had utterly deserted him.

The pile moved. It pressed down on him a bit, and this finally brought him back to his senses. Jons was walking on the books, evidently very slowly. Was he looking for this diary? He couldn't possibly expect to fish it out. He probably couldn't even see very much of the—" *Oh, no, Dex thought. The flashlight.*

"Emerge, Mason," Jons said, not very far from their sweltering spot, "or I will drop a match in this hole and send you to the place you surely serve."

"No, Daddy! No!" Nora shook herself out from under Dexter. Books slid into the hole she created as she pushed and clawed her way up to the surface.

Dex was still buried, so he stayed put. But, no, he couldn't let her face this alone. He forced his way up as well, shedding books like scales, and in a few moments both he and Nora stood atop the pile, facing Pastor Jons, whose jowls shook with a rage he couldn't seem to put into words.

"Please, Daddy, let me explain!" Nora begged.

*"Explain?"* Jons howled. "Explain what, you weak-willed little harlot? Explain how you allowed yourself to be seduced by this—this—!"

Jons ceased his rant, and it took only a moment for Dex to see why. The pastor was looking down, his eyes wide to popping, at a particular book sitting on the heaping pile. Nora saw it too.

It looked pretty much like most of the other books, cream-colored old leather, but it was obvious what it must be. The book was just lying there equidistant from the three of them. Jons took a step toward it, but stopped and clutched his lower back, wincing in pain.

Nora stepped forward on the shifting pile and picked it up. "I am not a Mason," she said. "Dexter is not Mason. He's just—"

"YOU WILL OBEY YOUR FATHER, CHILD! GIVE ME THAT BOOK!"

Nora didn't reply this time. She seemed incapable of deciding what to do.

"Please," Dex said to her, "he can't stop us both. He can hardly move! Let's take the book out of here. We'll figure out what's going on and fix things. We'll fix everything. She hasn't dishonored you," he told her father.

"Has he told you fantastic stories?" the pastor asked, ignoring Dexter. His voice was low and wicked. "Did he show you magic? You must confess everything."

Dexter could almost literally see Nora's will crumbling. "Please," Dex implored, "you have to trust—"

"*GIVE ME THAT BOOK*," Jons boomed, "*OR RISK DAMNING YOUR SOUL FOREVER!*"

"You—you mean," Nora stuttered, broken, "it's not too late?"

"No, child," Jons promised, his voice soft and soothing now. "It is never too late to repent so that you may regain the good graces of God. It is never too late to be forgiven, but you must make proper amends with me *right now.*"

Nora stood still, just holding the book, turned into herself. "Do you forgive me?" she asked.

"I do, child. I do. Repent and give me the book right now. And then I will absolve you of your sins. You must do it *right now.*"

Dex tensed. He knew what was coming, and when Nora held the book out to her father, he lunged for it.

"No!" she cried.

Nora had a surprisingly strong grip. Dex got his

hands on the book, but could not pull it away. The two grappled in a tug-of-war.

"Unhand that book!" Jons commanded, but he did not interfere.

The corner of the binding was cutting into Dex's palm, and he could feel that it was loose to begin with. He didn't have a hold on any actual pages, which made him fear the cover was going to rip right off.

And his heart was not in the struggle.

Nora was fighting for her soul, so Dex decided to give it to her.

But before he let go, there was a ripping sound, and then Dexter and Nora fell in opposite directions onto the books.

From his back, Dex watched Jons hobble over to his daughter, bend down painfully, and snatch the block of pages from her. Then, grunting and moaning, he limped to the ladder with it in his hand. Dex found only the cover in his own.

"Daddy!" Nora begged. "Absolve me! Before it's too late!"

Jons paused at the bottom of the ladder. His face was fully lit by light from the kitchen.

"Later," he said. "If there's time." Then he hauled himself onto the ladder and grunted his way up into the house.

"Daddy, please!"

Dex didn't give chase. Instead, he crawled over to Nora, who was sobbing. *"Are you okay?"* he whispered when the front door slammed upstairs. Jons had left his daughter there, the life of her immortal soul hanging in the balance, with a Mason.

"I don't understand," Nora choked, sitting up. "I don't understand."

"It's okay," Dex told her. What else was there to say? "He's desperate to help the Pope. It's not every day the Pope asks for a favor. He'll come to his senses. It's going to be okay."

Nora abruptly stopped crying and looked at Dex with full, round eyes. "You're—you're defending him?"

"I—" Dex said, unsure how to explain. But then the answer produced itself: "I'm defending you." He had a nearly overwhelming urge to kiss Nora just then, but he fought it off.

"I'm sorry," Nora said, looking down. "I'm sorry about the book. I'm sorry I didn't trust you."

"It's fine," Dex promised. "I understand. I'd have done the same thing if I were you. And you were just obeying the commandments, right? How can that be bad? Let's get out of here. Can you make it up the ladder?"

"Yes," Nora said, pulling herself together. "I'm fine." She got up and headed right for it. Dex was about to toss the book's cover away when Nora said, "Don't! Maybe there's some useful information on it."

"Right!"

Dex followed Nora up the ladder and into the kitchen, then gave her the cover to examine.

Nora turned it sideways and read the spine: "*The Diary of Sir William Gull.* Ever heard of him?"

"No," Dex said. "Anything on the back?"

Nora looked at the back. There was nothing printed on it at all.

"What's that?"

"What?"

Dex approached and took the cover. "Look," he said, bending it over backward. Some kind of paper, just a strip it seemed, was jutting out of what appeared to be a sleeve or slot inside the spine cover. Nora's eyes went wide as he slipped it out. It was long, as long as the spine itself.

"This must be the secret! *Ha!*" Dex said, feeling as if justice, for once, had been served. "Can you read it?"

It was a half sheet of paper, old and yellowed and folded over itself like a fan. Dex handed it to Nora, who took it to the main room, which was now buried ankle-deep in fallen candles and crosses. She waded through to a small desk, where she sat and smoothed the paper flat. Dex stood and listened as she read aloud:

**Monday, 1 October, 1888**
**I shambled through the fog last night like some kind of wounded wraith, chilled by the sound of my own boots clacking along the cracked cobblestones. The darkness was otherwise mute. Perhaps it feared having its tongue ripped out at the roots like the rest**

of us. An intolerable insult to be given such an assignment at my age—and in my condition! I could easily have suffered another stroke! With no more crusty old Dr. Gull to order about, who would do their dirty work?

But I'd be lying if I said I didn't derive a certain satisfaction at the sight of all the shuttered tenement windows, bolted to the last against the nightmare claiming dominion over London's nights, a nightmare in which unsuspecting women get murdered—worse, mutilated—in the streets. They've named it, too, this nightmare: Jack the Ripper. Wonderful, that name. Terrifying and wonderful! And there I was, their nightmare in the flesh, struggling just to walk without falling on my face. I considered abandoning the errand, but I dared not defy the Brotherhood.

At one forty-five I heard the Constable's men shouting in Mitre Square, so I knew they'd found the second body, the Eddowes woman. It had been dumped there after its visit to my slab, minus a kidney and most of its uterus. I'm quite certain this "investigation" is a waste of time—stuff and nonsense all of it—and no doubt it will bring someone of prominence to ruin.

Still, corpses are hard to come by for study, so even Jewish bodies will do. How they identify these low women, who evidently do not know their own race, is beyond me, but like so much, it is none of my business. I can only assume they do not wish this connection between them to be discerned, at least not by the authorities.

Speaking of the authorities, the shouting grew louder. I had to act quickly, before the opportunity was lost. Sweating as I wheezed along, I nearly wiped my face with the bloody fabric clenched in my fist, the piece I'd torn from the woman's apron and dipped in her blood. I am becoming an absent-minded fool!

I turned on Goulston Street, chose a random stairwell, and tossed the fragment of cloth onto it. Then I produced a stub of white chalk from my pocket. I suspect the message will never make the papers. If it does, it will no doubt be recorded incorrectly. But it doesn't matter. Nothing carries more weight than a mysterious secret, and secrets are never kept by outsiders. It's the crucial difference between the Brotherhood and everyone else. And this is why I will have to destroy this entry, lest I jeopardize what little time I have left of this life. No, I will conceal it! One day someone will discover it, and I will defy them in all their arrogance from my grave! My tongue will be long gone, but my backbone will endure! And now I know just where to hide it…

With a steady hand that still does my bidding despite the ravages of age and disease, I scrawled the phrase on the doorjamb over the bloody cloth:

*The Jews are the men that will not be blamed for nothing.*

Obscure enough to spread far and wide, I'm sure, but clear enough to its intended audience: Give up the book or we will not stop persecuting you. We will not stop <u>killing</u> you until we discover your secret and expose it to the world.

Hurried footfalls sounded along with the clamoring voices, so I dropped the chalk back into my pocket and moved off as quickly as I could.

Despite my infirmity, by the time the men arrived, the murk of the night had reduced me to naught but shadow. I fear it won't be long before history does the same.

"Ah—wow," Dex said when Nora looked up at him. "Did we just learn who Jack the Ripper was—a broken-down old doctor?"

"I—I think so," Nora agreed.

"That piece of paper must be worth a fortune."

"Those murders last year, all around the world," Nora said, "the ones you and Daphna said were really that monster killing all the—um—"

"The Thirty-six is the easier name to remember," Dex said.

Nora nodded gratefully. "My dad told me the paper said people thought it was some sicko group everyone was calling—"

"Jack the Tripper!"

"Right." Nora looked frightened, but she also had a faint glimmer in her eye of something Dex recognized as resolve—the kind that came simply from starting to figure things out. "So," she added, "those killings more than a hundred years ago are connected to—all this?"

Dex had to think about it, but not for long.

"Yes," he said. "I guess the Masons—they must be the Brotherhood mentioned in there— I guess they found some women who didn't know they were Jewish, women it seemed no one would care too much about, and killed them and cut them up. They pretended a serial killer was murdering them so no one would know what was really going on."

"But, why? Did they think they were part of the Thirty-six?"

"I don't think so, or not exactly. They couldn't have thought these random women in that one area of London were all Lamed Vavniks. And this Gull guy didn't seem to know what he was looking for, not specifically, anyway. They obviously didn't know about the extra ribs, but I think they suspected there was some secret difference some Jews have—or all Jews, maybe—and they could use the discovery to force them to give over some book."

"And Quinn's book—with all the names?"

"Could be it," Dex said. *"Must* be it. We've got to figure out what it is. Are you okay?" Dex could see how fragile Nora still looked. "I'm really sorry your dad—"

"Is God *really* gone?"

This caught Dex up short. No one had made any comment at Quinn's apartment when Daphna described God's decision to remove himself from the world to provide mankind with genuine free will.

"Ah, yes," he told her, wishing he could say something—anything—else. "He didn't tell Adam and Eve where he was going, but He's somewhere. I'm sure He hears your prayers."

"Are—are you sure?"

"Yes. I'm absolutely sure. And He sees everything." Dex chose not to mention the Eye, the Great Eye he'd glimpsed in the Aleph. Even remembering it was too much.

"Okay," Nora said, bucking up. "We'll solve all this, and my father will have to understand."

"And then he'll be asking *you* for forgiveness."

Nora smiled. "So," she said, standing up, "let's just do what Daphna suggested."

"What's that?"

"Go next door and ask the Jews what secret book they've been hiding from the world."

# CHAPTER TWENTY-ONE
## Definitley It

"What should we do?" Quinn spun around, scanning the room.

"Basement!" Daphna yelled, finally tearing herself away from the horrifying but hypnotic pull of Branwen's lunatic eyes. Those eyes weren't entirely her own anymore—that was obvious.

"But we don't know if he's got a tunnel down there or not," Quinn protested. "We could get cornered!"

Daphna shot a wild look around the room. She didn't know what to do, where to go. Branwen and her flunkies were there now, banging on the door. Daphna's brain felt like that painting of scrambled lines, hopelessly tangled thoughts, a thousand paths leading no—"That's it!" she realized, fumbling the page from the book of Portland tunnels out of her back pocket. She unfolded it and held it shakily up in front of the painting over the fireplace. The squiggles on the page matched some of the squiggles on the painting—the black ones that touched the blue streaks.

Which were the river.

They were banging on the front window now.

Daphna leapt to the hearth, tore the frame off the wall and smashed it on the mantel.

"The basement!" she shouted, pulling the map out.

"This way!" Quinn called, catching on. He bolted for the kitchen.

There were two doors. The back door had a semi-circular window revealing a little deck and garden outside. Just as Daphna reached it, a boy's face appeared in the glass, his expression deformed by the desire for violence. Daphna screamed as he jerked on the knob. Quinn, rushing past her, tore open the second door just as something shattered a window in the front of the house.

"We're going to kill you!" Branwen screeched through it. "Do you hear me! We're going to *kill* you!"

Daphna rushed down the steps Quinn had revealed. He slammed the door behind him after letting her pass, leaving them in the dark. *"Light!"* he howled. "I need light!" But he evidently found a switch because some exposed bulbs lit up dimly around the basement.

Now glass shattered in the kitchen.

"Can you lock it?" Daphna called up to Quinn after nearly taking a header down the steps.

"There's no lock!"

"Is there a rope or a cord?"

The wall along the steps was covered with hooks that held various tools. Quinn scanned them for second, then started fumbling with his belt. He ripped it out of his jeans, cinched it over the doorknob, then worked one the holes over an empty hook.

"Good idea!"

"Best I can do!" Quinn said, rushing down the steps.

Someone rattled the door, then yanked on it. It didn't open. They pounded on it.

"We're coming down there!" Branwen railed before the rattling resumed. The door opened the slightest bit this time. "You'll never see the light of day again!"

Daphna knew they didn't have much time. She folded the map and shoved it into her pocket, then whirled round, scanning the dusty, unfinished basement for anything that could hide a tunnel entrance. There was a water heater, a furnace, more filing cabinets, two old couches. Everything was coated with dust.

"You're dead!" Branwen screamed through the crack that was now exposed at the door." Then she saw what was keeping it shut. "It's a belt! Get a knife! Get a knife!"

"It's got to be a door in the floor, right?" Daphna was almost pleading.

She and Quinn ran around, scanning. There were no carpets to pull up. The floor was all exposed concrete. Neither saw any kind of panels in it.

"Honey, we're home!" Branwen called through

134

the increasingly large space at the door.

*"Where is it!"* Daphna wailed.

The basement door crashed open. Branwen let loose an exultant howl, but a moment later a man's harsh voice hollered, "Police! Freeze!"

After a moment of panicked silence, Daphna and Quinn—frozen where they stood—heard movement. Then, "Now, punks! Drop the knife and put your hands up on the wall over your heads! I said DO IT NOW!"

"They're down there!" Branwen protested. "We have to get them! We have to kill the witch!"

An argument ensued. Daphna looked at Quinn, who nodded. They resumed their search, scanning for clues as quickly and quietly as they could. Daphna was sweating profusely, despite the cold down there.

"Downstairs! She's—!"

"Drop the knife! Do it now!"

Daphna pointed to a tall, hulking object in a dark corner, set against a wall. The bulb hanging over it had burned out, so it was mostly obscured by shadow. She and Quinn hurried over into the darkness where it stood.

It was a wardrobe, as covered in dust as everything else was down there.

Except for its handle, which clearly had a handprint on it.

"No way," Quinn said too loudly. "That's it. That's definitely it." He tried the door, but it was locked. He touched the keyhole embedded in the handle, then turned to Daphna.

Daphna fumbled Mr. G's key out of her pocket. Her hands were shaking, but she inserted it directly into the lock.

The key turned!

Quinn eased the creaky door open.

Jackets. Lots of jackets. They seemed to fill the entire space inside.

But they knew this trick.

A horrific thunderclap crashed outside, shaking the house. Daphna and Quinn both grabbed the wardrobe to avoid falling.

Then the thunder crashed again, and again.

"Get back here!" a cop demanded when it finally ended.

"That witch is down there!" Branwen raged. "I'm telling you! She killed my best friends!"

"Get back here!"

Pounding footsteps sounded on the stairs.

Quinn and Daphna forced their way into the wardrobe. Daphna closed it the moment she could and was relieved to hear the lock click when the door latched. Quinn was behind her, already groping around at the back. There wasn't enough room for Daphna to help, so she stayed where she was, trembling and sweating against the door.

A struggle was taking place in the basement now. Things were being knocked over. "She's down here!" Branwen screamed. "She's down here! Don't touch me! My parents will sue you! They'll have your badges!"

"*Daphna,*" Quinn whispered, his voice muffled by all the coats, "*I can't find any kind of door back here. It's just—No wait, something's leaning against the back. Feels like a long piece of wood.*"

"*Get it out of the way!*"

Quinn grunted, then shoved something through the coats. It was almost as tall as Daphna, and it ensnared her arm with some kind of wire attached to it. Daphna panicked for a moment, but yanked herself free.

"*The back wall,*" Quinn whispered. "*It's metal. And it's freezing cold.*"

"*The tunnel! There's got to be a latch! Feel around!*"

Something hit the wardrobe, inches from Daphna's face. She couldn't help crying out.

"There! You heard that!" Branwen was evidently trying to open the door now. "In here! She must be hiding in here! I'm not leaving until—until we get them!" Now Branwen was kicking the door. "I'm not leaving until that Wax witch gets what she deserves!"

Daphna turned around as best as she could, breathing in moldy fabric. "*Hurry!*" she urged.

"*I'm trying! I can't see! It's just a wall!*"

"*Use your phone!*"

"*Oh!*"

"The Wax twins? They really are here?"

"Daphna! And her boyfriend!"

A dim light came on in the wardrobe.

"Well, well, well," a cop said, "he wasn't lying, then. Tell you what—we're gonna cut you a break, all of you. Go on and get out. Go home. We'll take it from here."

"No! She's—!"

Daphna heard gasps, loud and clear, right through the door, right through the coats.

"How dare you point that thing at me!"

"If I were you, I'd get going before there's an unfortunate accident."

There was a long pause, then the sound of feet on the steps again.

"You'll regret this!" Branwen called, but then it was quiet.

Then, a cop's voice: "That you, Daphne? And the boy with the book?" The handle rattled a bit. "You guys playing kissy-face in the dark? Hope you made good use of your tongues!" Hearty laughter followed this.

Daphna held her breath. Did she know that voice? Quinn continued to search the back wall, breathing frantically.

"Come on out of there," another cop said, pulling hard on the handle. These were those same cops! "We have some folks who'd like to talk to you about that book you gave them. No big deal."

Daphna ignored this, willing Quinn to find something.

A cop kicked the wardrobe door. Hard. It splintered a bit.

Daphna screamed.

Another kick. This one caused a loud crack.

Daphna jammed her body back through the coats to get away from the boot she was sure would break through the door. She bashed into Quinn, but he somehow gave way, as if there was more room back there than she'd imagined.

Another kick.

The door broke apart, but Daphna was falling into cold air.

# CHAPTER TWENTY-TWO
## *No Right Moment*

"It must be over a hundred degrees," Nora said. They were outside now, near the well.

Dex had to agree. He was already a sweaty mess from the heat under all those books, and it was almost as bad outside. This was not normal. "We should rip that up," Dex said.

"I guess you're right." Nora looked down at the brittle old diary entry in her hand. "I can barely stand to touch it," she said. "It feels evil, even if it is worth a fortune."

"I'll do it," Dex offered. "Destroying valuable texts is one of my specialties."

Nora handed it to him, and he proceeded to shred the page, the page that would have settled the dispute over Jack the Ripper's identity once and for all, not to mention put his retirement issues to rest. But that thought didn't occur to him until the deed was done.

Dex dropped the shreds into the well. He and Nora watched them fall.

"Uh oh," Nora said. "I think some of them landed in the bucket. It's usually up," she explained, turning the crank mounted on the side of the well to raise it. "It's my job to keep it at the top. Father would have been angry."

When the bucket reached them, Dex and Nora were surprised to see more than just fragments of Gull's entry inside.

Along with them was the rest of the diary.

"That's weird," Dex said, lifting it out. "Do you think your dad tossed it because he knew it was useless without the cover?"

"If he knew where the secret was," Nora replied, "he would definitely not have left the cover with us."

Dex thought a moment, then said, "He didn't really seem like he wanted to find the book to begin with."

"I don't think he trusted that man. I don't think he believed he had anything to do with the Pope, talking about assassins and killing you and Daphna. I know my dad. He wouldn't really try to hurt you. He must have assumed the man was a Mason and didn't want him coming back for the book. He's told me many times to use the well if I have to get rid of something in a hurry. That's why I'm always to have the bucket up."

"You're probably right," said Dex. "But that guy is definitely who he says he is. Though I don't think anyone else in the Church knows what he does—even the Pope."

Dexter tossed the book and fragments into the well and watched them fall until he heard the block of pages splash.

Just then a thunderclap crashed. If Dex's head was in a pot and someone slammed the lid on it, the effect couldn't have been any more jarring.

Both Dex and Nora covered their ears and looked up to watch the lightning. It snapped, zigzagging overhead, then started to fade, a bit like the vapor trail of an airplane.

Only it didn't fade away completely this time. The faintest white lines stayed scratched across the sky, like the crazy crisscrossing marks ice skates leave on the ice when a crowd clears off.

Something was happening up there, but it was hard to see clearly what it was. Impossible, actually, because the sky seemed to blur around the lines.

"I'm scared," Nora said, staring up at them. "I'm scared of that thunder, but I'm even more scared of that lightning now. What's it doing? It looks like heat rising up off a road when it's hot—hot like this."

"That *is* heat," Dex said.

"Do you think so? From the lightning being so hot? It's electricity, right?"

"That's not lightning." Dex shook his head. It should have been obvious from the start.

"What do you mean?"

"Those lines—" he said, "they're not electricity."

"What are they then?"

"Cracks."

"*Cracks?* In the sky? You—you don't mean in

Heaven, do you?"

"Yes," Dexter said. "The walls of Heaven must be cracking from the heat—from the fire. Anyway, the heat is leaking out. We better get a move on."

Dex headed down the drive leading down and around to the synagogue, but Nora remained fixed where she was, staring up at the ripples of heat coming down from above.

"Nora," he said gently, coming back, worried that this was going to be too much for her.

Nora didn't start praying. Instead, she looked at him, clearly all there in her eyes. Why were her eyes clear? Why were his?

"I just wanted to say thank you again," she said, "for understanding. For not leaving me back there like maybe you should have. You've done so much for me in just, I guess, a few hours."

"It's okay, really," Dex said. But he was pleased. So pleased.

The pair made their way back past the play area and down around to the little paved way that linked the church and synagogue parking lots. They walked through all the cars, hunching a bit to avoid being seen, but there was no one out there. When they got around behind the building where the entry courtyard was, they stopped and squatted behind a van.

"What exactly is our plan?" Nora asked. "I don't think we can just walk right in and not get in trouble with the curfew and all."

"Good question." Dex wished that Daphna were there to offer a suggestion. He hoped she was okay. He'd have to call as soon as they had a minute. Maybe he should have called already. No, he should call right now.

"Dex." Nora was pointing at something, the courtyard gate.

People were suddenly flooding out through it. At the same time, a long line of cars started moving into the lot. Horns honked.

"What's going on?"

"They have two services," Nora explained. "The first one must have just ended. And look, there are lots of kids."

And so there were, of all ages. The younger ones were getting dragged by their hands. The older ones seemed to be arguing with each other. All the adults looked highly agitated.

"They must be allowed to come for the religious event!" Dex said, getting to his feet. "Let's go."

Nora stood up and the pair walked swiftly into the crowd coming out.

"Hey!" someone shouted as they squeezed past the first few people going the opposite direction.

"Can't you wait!" someone else demanded.

But no one stopped them.

"What should we do?" Nora asked. "Find the rabbi?" They were wedging their way into a rather peaceful courtyard made up of pavers inscribed with people's names.

"I guess," Dex said. "But we better hurry before the service starts. Let's get inside."

It was no easy task getting in through the crowds leaving the main entrance, but once they managed it, Dex and Nora found themselves in a foyer facing three sets of wooden doors. People were flowing out through all three. There appeared to be many rows of benches behind them.

They forced their way through again, irritating just about everyone they brushed by.

Dex saw a man collecting prayer books, so he approached him. "Um," he said, "is the rabbi around?"

The man, a full-bellied guy wearing a green and yellow Oregon Ducks tie with a matching skullcap, looked put out by the question. "Resting between services," he said.

"We really need to see him."

"Who doesn't today?" the man snarled. "And it's mostly because of kids like you! The first service was a disaster! Go home and give the guy a break!"

"Okay, okay," Dex said, backing away. But he'd seen the man glance across the sanctuary toward the raised platform on which the ark resided. The towering glass cabinet was fronted by glass etched with colorful geometric patterns. It was topped by a little replica of the Ten Commandments. Dex knew it housed the Torah.

The rabbi was obviously not in there. Tall chairs sat on either side of it, only they were all empty. But there was a door, a little door he now saw, in what looked like a short hall next to the platform.

"Thanks, anyway," Dex said, taking Nora by the hand.

The room was filling up now as people streamed in for the second service, so there was plenty of cover for the pair as Dex led the way to the little door. The walls of the hall it was in were covered with dark little plaques engraved with what looked like names and dates—names were everywhere, it seemed. Dex squinted at one, assuming they were commemorations for deceased congregants, but Nora nudged him.

The door was right there. Dex turned and looked at it, then scanned the crowd. He could hear angry talk about the outrageous thunder and heat and the even more outrageous children. He was waiting for the right moment.

But there was no right moment, so Dex just grabbed the knob, which, thankfully, turned.

He opened the door just enough for Nora to slip inside.

After one more quick check to make sure they'd not been seen, Dex slipped in behind her.

# CHAPTER TWENTY-THREE
## *Going Underground*

Daphna landed on Quinn, then rolled onto a dirt floor. Quinn didn't seem any worse for the wear. He immediately jumped up, and she watched him reach up to close the door they'd fallen through.

A tunnel! They were in a tunnel!

The hidden door clicked under Quinn's hand and became invisible, blending in with the wall of earth into which it was set.

Quinn let out a huge sigh and stepped back. "There was a little button," he said, picking up his phone, which had fallen but was still casting a bit of light on some kind of beam running up along the wall. "It was way up in the corner."

Daphna got up, took her phone out, and waved it around. The beam was part of a roof support. Branches of the tunnel ran off in several directions, and it looked like similar supports were spaced every so often in all of them. But it was too dark to be sure.

"Look at this," Quinn said. He was aiming his phone now at the beam at about eye-level.

Daphna moved to see what he was looking at. There was something scratched into the wood there. Upon close inspection, she saw that it was quite clearly a butterfly.

"Maybe it's a marker for your teacher's house," Quinn guessed, "since he's into butterflies. Like an address."

"Yes," Daphna agreed. "That must be what it—"

There was a clang that made the pair jump. One of the cops had kicked the wardrobe's metal door.

Daphna and Quinn remembered their panic. They waved their phones around, trying to identify the most promising tunnel.

The door was struck again, with tremendous force. The clang echoed in the dark. The door buckled a bit, but did not give way.

"Look!" Quinn said, rushing into a tunnel running off to his left.

Daphna followed. In the meager light produced by their phones, she saw a motorized scooter—in fact, a whole line of scooters, all leaning against the wall.

They heard one more clang, and then the sound of the door falling into the tunnel. They heard the cops jump down.

"Get back here, Daphne!" one of them yelled.

Quinn grabbed the closest scooter. "I can drive these!" he said, stepping on to it.

Daphna leapt on the deck behind him and threw her arms around his chest. Quinn got it started and turned a headlight on, sending a beam of light up the tunnel.

They were moving.

Quinn let out a whoop as they picked up speed. Daphna had to tighten her grip, shocked at how fast the thing could go.

Two more motors started up behind them.

Daphna looked back. "They're coming!" she screamed into Quinn's ear.

Quinn turned left so suddenly that Daphna nearly lost her grip on him. She swung out off the deck on one foot and only saved herself from falling by grabbing his shirt.

Quinn slowed down so she could get readjusted. "Sorry!" he said. "I'll call out the turns so you can lean into them with me!"

The cops roared by, missing the turn Quinn had taken, but one yelled to his partner to stop.

Quinn had just gotten the scooter moving again when the cops came round the corner. "Faster!" Daphna cried. As they sped into the darkness of the new tunnel, she kept her eyes on their pursuers. The support beams whizzed past her head in a blur.

They were flying, but not fast enough. The cops were right behind them.

"Faster!"

"Left!"

Daphna leaned, though not quite at the same time Quinn did. They made the turn, but barely avoided falling off together. Quinn skidded, but kept them upright by slowing down. Then he gave it gas again.

The cops were there, right round the same corner.

"Stop right now!" one of them demanded.

"Faster!" It was all Daphna could say. The cops were right on their tail.

"Left!"

Daphna nearly fell off again.

"We're too heavy!" Quinn shouted.

The cops were *still* behind them.

"Right!"

This time they made the turn fairly quickly. It was awkward—they fishtailed a bit—but Quinn didn't have to slow down.

The cops stayed right behind them, the two of them, side-by-side.

"Left!"

Quinn and Daphna whipped around the turn. No wobbles or skids.

"Right!"

"Left!"

The turns came easily now. Daphna had given up looking back and just clutched Quinn with her cheek pressed between his shoulder blades. She could feel his chest muscles tighten at the exact moment he began to execute a turn. She could allow his motion to dictate hers.

"Left!

"Right!"

"Right!"

Daphna was starting to feel as if she and Quinn were making the decisions to turn together now, and it reminded her of having the ability to share thoughts with Dexter after returning from Heaven.

"Left!"

"Left!"

"Right!"

Daphna closed her eyes and felt the separation between her and Quinn start to dissolve.

*Dex,* she thought. *Please be okay. If you're not, I'll never forgive myself.*

The scooter hit a jarring bump just then, and because Daphna's thoughts were elsewhere, her grip on Quinn was not what it should have been. She tumbled off the back of the scooter and hit the ground hard on her back.

The air burst from her lungs.

She expected to be run over by the cops, who she'd somehow forgotten were behind her. But they weren't there.

"What happened?" Quinn was there, helping her up.

"I'm okay, Dex," Daphna gasped. Her ears were ringing, and she was winded and dazed. And crying. "Don't leave me."

Somehow she was back on the scooter again, holding on to Quinn. They were moving, but very soon there was a sputtering sound.

And then they stopped.

Slowly, Daphna regained her senses. They were at a corner. Quinn turned and put a finger to his lips. *"Out of gas,"* he whispered, turning the headlight off. Once they'd stepped off, he laid the scooter on the ground in the middle of the tunnel.

Daphna nodded. She wiped her tears in the dirt-smelling dark, listening, trying to think of what to do next. The sound of the cops' motors echoed somewhere in the maze of tunnels.

Maybe they'd lost them.

Daphna didn't think so. She could think clearly now, so she hurried around the corner and pulled her phone out.

*"Don't!"* Quinn whispered when she lit it up and started tapping.

*"We need to find a way out!"* Daphna whispered back, waving the phone up and down the nearest support beam. *"Put yours in airplane mode so no one can track us!"*

Quinn did so as fast as he could. Then he hurried to the beam across the way, shining his phone's flashlight at it. *"What are we looking for?"*

*"Anything!"*

Daphna didn't see any kind of symbol on her beam, so she moved down to the next one. Nothing. Quinn did the same, shaking his head after sweeping the light.

The motors sounded from somewhere nearby. Then a light shone past the corner.

They were getting closer.

Daphna and Quinn hurried to the next set of beams.

Nothing.

It was hard to see anything clearly with her hand shaking. Daphna dropped the phone, snatched it up, and moved down another beam.

The motors were getting louder.

*"We better just run,"* Daphna concluded. *"We don't have—"*

"Here!"

Daphna rushed over to see the beam Quinn had his light on. Yes, there it was: another butterfly.

The motors were now very, very loud.

"That way!" one of the cops yelled.

Quinn reached up and began feeling around the dirt wall next to the beam. Daphna did the same. She couldn't help glancing over at the corner, where the light reaching it was clearly getting stronger.

"Can't find anything!" Quinn complained.

"Hurry!"

"Found it!"

Daphna could see the thin line of the door's edge where Quinn had wedged his fingers.

They heard the crash. A cry. The cops had hit their scooter.

Quinn was doing everything he could to pry the door open, but it wouldn't budge.

Daphna reached up and pushed on the dirt-covered door. There was a click, and it popped open.

Footsteps sounded. Running feet.

One of the cops was coming.

"Stop right now!"

Quinn clambered up into the dark space behind the door. Once in, he turned and reached out for Daphna, then hauled her up, too.

They closed the door as quietly as they could.

Then they held their breath and listened.

Feet pounded past.

They exhaled.

Daphna turned and realized that once again she was buried in coats.

*"Should we go into this house?"* Quinn whispered.

*"I guess we have to,"* Daphna sighed. *"If it's not locked."*

Neither was eager to find out, but after taking a moment to gather themselves, they pushed forward to the front of the wardrobe—this one seemed a bit larger—and pressed their ears to the wooden door.

Neither heard anything, so together, they gently pushed on it.

The door swung open.

# CHAPTER TWENTY-FOUR
### *The Book of Names*

So much for his powers of observation. Dex had led them not into the rabbi's office, but rather into a cleaning closet. But to his surprise, the room was not empty. Inside, he and Nora found a twitchy little man in a homemade robber's mask made from a ski cap with poorly cut holes for his eyes and mouth.

"Don't hurt me!" the man yelped. "Don't touch me! Don't hurt me!" He backed away from Dex and Nora, knocking solvents and sprays off a shelf. He grabbed a mop out of the bucket it was standing in and held it out to fend them off.

"Who—what?" was all Dex could manage.

"Keep back, filthy Jews!"

*"What?"*

"Just keep away! Or I'll—I'll—tear your horns off!"

"Our *what?*"

"It's one of the oldest anti-Semitic lies," Nora explained as she inched toward the door. "He's in some kind of hate group. He's a hater. They sometimes come to our church, too. My dad would say he's a Mason. Let's get out of here."

"No," Dex said, "this jerk isn't going to talk to us that way." He looked the man in the jumpy eyes and said, "What are you doing here?"

The hater, still backed up against the shelves, still looking horrified, simply snarled. But then he said, "I want to hear what you've done to the children. I want to hear what you're doing to the weather. I'm going to find out your plan."

"These kind of people are dangerous, Dex," Nora warned, seeing him rolling his eyes. "We don't have time for—"

An amplified voice from the sanctuary interrupted her.

"Welcome, everyone. L'shana Tovah. Welcome on this rather difficult beginning to a new year." The voice echoed loudly in the closet.

"That must be the rabbi," Dex said, turning toward the door. The masked man cocked his head to listen, but made sure not to take his eyes off Dexter. He continued to hold the mop out like a lance.

"Needless to say," the rabbi continued, "an ill wind is blowing through our nation today, through our world it seems. But I urge you to remain calm, to—"

"Tell us what's going on!" someone shouted from the congregation. "Tell us what's wrong with our kids!"

"Tell us what's wrong with the weather!" someone else demanded. "Does it have to do with those towers? Who blew them up? Is there going to be a war in the Middle East?"

"Hey," Dex said to the hater, "why do you think Jews have horns?" That remark had gotten him thinking. The man looked at him with angry blue eyes behind his mask, but then looked away.

"Please," the rabbi urged the grumbling crowd, "let us take this opportunity to look inward on this solemn Day of Judgment. Let us resolve on this great day to rededicate ourselves to making our worlds, our inner and outer worlds, as perfect as possible."

"I'm talking to you," Dex said.

"*Silence!*" the hater hissed. "He's going to reveal the plan!"

"Despite the tower constructed in Jerusalem by fanatics," the rabbi continued, "these so called 'Stairways to Heaven' were never of interest to us. The afterlife is not a Jewish concern. It will be what it will be. What *is* a Jewish concern is life *here,* life *now.* Our people strive to live righteously, not for potential rewards in Heaven, but for the real rewards living such lives provide for us here on Earth."

"I said, I'm talking to you!"

"*Everyone knows Jews ain't human! The horns prove it!*"

"Over the next ten days we have the gift of time," the rabbi said, "time for Tefila, prayer; time for Tzedakah, charity; and perhaps most important, time for Tshuva, repentance for sins against God and each other."

"Cutting them off or hiding them under those Jew hats don't prove nothing!"

"I remind you that God cannot and will not forgive you for sins against your fellow man. You must seek that out on your own."

"You're animals," the hater spat.

"That does it." The pent-up rage Dex had somehow managed to keep at bay—mostly at bay, anyway—since he'd left the house that morning, erupted out of him. He charged the hater and ripped the mop right out of his hands.

A moment later he was beating him with it.

The man cowered under the blows.

"Dex, don't!"

But Dexter only increased the violence of his attack. The guy wasn't even fighting back, which infuriated him even more.

Dex was using the wrong end. He turned the mop around and whacked the jerk with the handle.

"Owww!"

"That's better!"

"You must understand how to repent properly," the rabbi said, "how to seek and gain real forgiveness, because today we speak of God—"

"*Owww!*"

"Dex, please!"

"—as if He consults a book, a sacred but fearsome book."

The mop froze over Dexter's head. He turned to listen.

"In this Book is the name of all living people. But beginning on this Holy day and for the next ten days, the accountable members of our community—that is those of us thirteen years of age and older—hope to earn the right to have our names sealed in it. For those whose names are not in this Book ten days from now will not be among us next year at this time. And while of course we don't take this literally, we take the *idea* of this fearsome book very, very seriously. I refer to, of course, The Book of the Living."

Dex, still frozen with the mop over his head, turned to look at Nora. Both their eyes had dialed wide. The hater bolted past him and through the door. Dex saw this happening, but made no attempt to stop it. "That's it!" he said, tossing the mop aside. "That's what it is! The Book of the Living! It's *real!* I have to call Daphna!"

Dexter pried the phone out of his pocket and

told it to call his sister. It rang twice, but then the call dropped.

"Filthy animals!" the hater screamed from the sanctuary.

"How dare you!" someone hollered back.

Dex shoved the phone back into his pocket. He and Nora hurried out of the closet just in time to see a group of four angry congregants pounce on the hater.

"Please!" the rabbi admonished. "This is not necessary! Please take your seats!"

The angry congregants, four men in suits and ties, fought over the hater, yanking his limbs in four directions.

"Don't touch me!" he wailed. "Don't touch me!"

The rest of the congregation was on its feet now, shouting a thousand things.

In the midst of the hullabaloo, which included the rabbi clamoring for calm, a single supremely horrified voice broke through. It came from a woman, her face aflush and streaked with tears. She'd burst into the sanctuary through the middle set of doors. The crowd parted for her as she sprinted, screaming bloody-murder, all the way up to the stage and right to the rabbi, who she unceremoniously shouldered aside for his microphone.

"The news! The news!" she wailed into it. "It's on the news!"

This was enough to silence the entire congregation. The men fighting over the hater let him drop to the floor, after which he scuttled away like a rat.

"The news!" she repeated with her eyes popping out. Then she finally got specific. "They said the ozone layer is dissolving! *We're all going to die!*"

# CHAPTER TWENTY-FIVE
### For Just a Few Minutes

Daphna and Quinn were in a basement very much like Mr. G's. It was unfinished, crowded with disused furniture, and smothered in dust. Two scooters sat inside against a wall. Fortunately, no one was there.

There was no other exit in the basement, other than a flight of stairs leading up to a closed door. Daphna dusted herself off as she tiptoed up to it. Quinn followed, doing the same.

Neither could hear anything, so Daphna carefully turned the knob. She opened the door just a crack.

Voices.

"I imagine this minor artist is no longer a priority for us, but what is your advice, Mr. Brown?"

"I agree that we have much more pressing concerns, Mr. Grey," someone replied. Mr. Brown, it seemed. "But we must not neglect the issue entirely. I understand the painting has been dealt with?"

"Guillermo assures me that he has personally taken care of it," said a third person, a woman. "We'll reach an agreement with the artist to forget about it forever. If he reneges, he'll lose a fortune—for starters."

"Excellent, Ms. White," said Mr. Brown.

Daphna turned to Quinn, thinking about the paintings at the Jesus exhibit she'd mentioned to Dexter just that morning. Was that what they were talking about? None of it seemed to have made any kind of impression on Quinn, who continued listening intently.

"We apologize for Guillermo," another person said. "He has, up to now, performed his duties well. The twins never knew he was watching them, and he never before interfered in their lives, even during several dire situations."

"Be that as it may, Mr. Black," replied Mr. Brown,

"the larger situation demands our immediate attention. For it is far past dire. What has so easily overcome children will soon affect adults. Our time is short. What is emanating from above is nothing the world has ever known, except perhaps in its darkest dreams."

"And the Masons," someone said. "Should we attempt to neutralize this book—this weapon—they've obtained?"

"It would be wise to discover the nature of this threat, Ms. Green. It behooves us to make sure it in no way jeopardizes *our* quest. The Masons have never had the confidence to expose themselves so boldly by leveling such direct threats. But we must focus on ending *all* these threats. And to do so, we must end our search once and for all."

"What do you propose?"

"We must find the twins and learn the truth about where they've been. Our man at the Vatican swears they passed through some sort of portal."

This was met by oohs and ahs.

"We must possess this portal," Mr. Brown added. "But if it is lost, then we have no choice: We must send someone to the Realm, for that is surely where the Book must be."

"But no one knows anything about the Realm!" someone protested. "*No one!* And there is no proper subject! It would require some sort of—*hybrid!* And none of us have ever even considered—!"

"Dr. Lewis has a theory—" Mr. Brown said.

"No," a woman declared. "We must at last risk everything by attempting to enter the well."

"Suicide, Ms. Gold."

"I see no other choice."

There was a pause, after which Mr. Brown said, "If we are to take this final, surely doomed step, we must exhaust all other possibilities. I must first be permitted, with all possible speed, to—"

The thunder exploded outside, shaking the house. Something shattered somewhere, but no one commented on it. No one said anything. An impasse had apparently been reached. It was silent.

Until Daphna's phone rang.

Daphna, who'd been distracted by the faint memory of a man at the Vatican yelling stop just before she and Dex were hauled, bleeding to death,

154

into the Aleph's spangled light, frantically squeezed at the phone in her pocket. She managed to silence it before the third ring. But it was way too late.

"The basement!" someone shouted.

Quinn and Daphna were already leaping down the steps. Quinn reached the wardrobe first, which they wisely hadn't closed. He held the door open for Daphna, but she didn't get in.

*"Come on,"* Quinn whispered. *"I'm sure the cops are long gone!"*

"No," Daphna told him. "We're trying to find out who these people are, right? So, let's ask them."

*"But they may be dangerous!"*

"You heard them. I was right. Mr. Guillermo wasn't allowed to interfere with us. They only watch."

"Daphna Wax," someone said, causing Daphna and Quinn to whirl around. "I imagine this fortuitous turn of events is the result of Guillermo's overzealousness this morning."

The debate about staying or leaving was now moot, because Daphna and Quinn found themselves facing a collection of six mostly ordinary looking people in slacks and sweaters, three men and three women. Somehow, they'd come down the steps without being heard. The group seemed middle-aged, but everyone looked rather fit and trim, and unusually tall.

A man with weirdly youthful hair swept over his forehead was the one who'd spoken. He wore a button-up wool sweater over a black turtleneck. "We've been to Heaven," Daphna told him, getting right to the point. "My brother and I. But we can't get back. We had a book that took us there."

*"A golden book?"* Turtleneck asked. From his voice, it was clear he was Mr. Brown. His question was followed by an audible holding-of-the-breath in the room.

"No," Daphna said, "a small silver book full of colorful light. But it was destroyed there. We can't get back."

Mr. Brown took this in for a moment. Everyone seemed to be digesting the information. There was murmuring all around. The group seemed both disappointed and thrilled.

"Are there books, there, in Heaven?" asked Mr.

Brown. "Other books?" His face was neutral, and he asked the question rather casually, but it was clear that he was beyond anxious to hear the answer. The others were too.

"Yes," Daphna said. "It's full of books, an endless amount of books. It's a Library. One book is missing, and all the angels are looking for it. Is that what you're looking for? By the way," Daphna added, trying to mimic Mr. Brown's composed tone, "a book—with a key in it—it was opened—and flames came out. And now Heaven is on fire."

Mr. Brown's nonchalant composure cracked.

He nearly choked. Everyone did.

"Do you see?" he asked, turning to the group. "Do you see! We have no time!" The group nodded. "Then I have your consent?"

No one spoke, but it was obvious that positions had shifted.

"I alone will pursue this," Mr. Brown declared. "If I do not succeed this very day, we will storm the well."

Heads nodded gravely all around.

Daphna's phone rang again. She eyed Mr. Brown and then the others, but no one seemed poised to stop her from answering it. She took the phone out and looked at the display.

"Dex!" Daphna nearly screamed. "Are you safe? What's happening?"

"Jack the Ripper!" Dex nearly screamed back, confusing Daphna. But then he explained about the famous murders and how they were really a cover up for the Mason's real search.

"Horns," Daphna said when he was done. "Yes, I see. They could actually be about the same size and shape as the ribs."

"And we know what the book is," Dex said. And then he told her what happened at the synagogue and that the book of names was, in fact, The Book of the Living. "And, Daphna," he said when he'd finished, "the rabbi said that if your name isn't in the book ten days from now, you won't live through the year! But if your name's already out of it, how is that supposed to happen? We need to get the book and figure out how to put names back in!"

"Dex, are you safe?" Daphna asked, both too amazed and too terrified by this news to respond to it.

She checked on the group of strange suburbanites. They were still watching her with disturbing intensity, but only watching. "Okay, listen," she told her brother when he promised he wasn't in danger. "Mr. G is part of a group looking for this other book, this golden book—the missing book from Heaven, I think. We're with them now. And I think this book can fix, well, anything and everything, including putting names back in Quinn's book. It can even fix what's happening up in Heaven. They think it's in some kind of realm, one of them does anyway, the one in charge." Daphna looked at Mr. Brown as she said this. He was looking right back at her, but his eyes didn't give away what he was thinking. "And he seems to know a way to get there," she added. "What?"

Daphna listened while her brother explained how the Masons were planning to use the book to vanish world leaders at two o'clock—and that he and Nora were going to get it back before they could.

"That's in less than three hours!" Daphna gasped. "Where do you think they have it? The cops did tell us the Masons want to talk to us about the book. How are you going to—?"

"You just gave me an idea." Dex told her.

"Okay, but please, Dexter, please be careful! Call me if there's any—Okay, okay. Be safe!"

Daphna had wanted to tell Dex about the mysterious painting someone had been, or was going to be, threatened about, but she didn't want to risk alienating these people right now.

"What happened?" Quinn asked when she put the phone away.

Daphna looked at him and said, "I know where your parents are."

*"What?! Where?"*

"The book you found. It's called The Book of the Living. It—"

Daphna saw her audience turn to one another in mild but genuine surprise.

"Do you know about it?" Daphna asked Mr. Brown. "The Masons are going to vanish world leaders with it at two o'clock."

"We must act swiftly," Mr. Brown told his group.

*"Where are my parents?"* Quinn begged. He was nearly out of his skin.

"I'm sorry," Daphna said, taking Quinn's hands. She ignored the electricity she felt when their skin touched. "We were right about the book," she told him. "You must have your name in it to, well, live. It's a book with the names of everyone who's living. Your parents—they're in Heaven, I guess. And I think we have ten days to get their names back in it before they're stuck there forever."

Quinn went weak in the knees. "But if we—" he stammered, "if Dex and Nora get it back—maybe we can write their names back in. Maybe that would bring them back!"

Daphna looked to Mr. Brown to see what he had to say about this.

"Possibly," he said. "But I'm sorry to say the likelihood of your brother getting the book back, resourceful as he may be, is nil. The Masons are one of the most notoriously vicious organizations ever to exist, and they have been seeking that book for a very, very long time."

Now Daphna was the one having trouble staying upright.

"This book you want," Quinn said to Mr. Brown, "this golden book—if we find it, could we bring them back with it?"

"Indeed," Mr. Brown confirmed, "for the power that Book contains knows no bounds."

"What is it?" Daphna asked. Whatever it was, she would find it and put an end to all of their problems once and for all. Mr. Brown did not immediately respond, so she said, "I told you about The Book of the Living. I didn't have to do that."

Mr. Brown looked at the others, who all nodded. "The book we are searching for," he said, "is called the Sefer Yetzirah."

"That's Hebrew?"

"Yes, it means The Book of Creation. It's one of history's oldest manuscripts. It contains instructions on how to combine the twenty-two Hebrew letters and the ten primordial numbers to manipulate the very fabric of the universe. It gives one the power to create. Did you know the word 'grammar' derives from a word that meant 'magic'?"

"I saw a book in Heaven," Daphna said. "It had letters inside, moving around. English, though."

Mr. Brown only nodded at this. "You saw what you could understand."

"Can we get to this realm of yours quickly?" Daphna asked.

Mr. Brown nodded again.

"Good. Let's go."

"How risky is it?" Quinn asked before Daphna started heading for the steps. "What do we have to do?"

Mr. Brown hesitated a moment, then said, "I'm going to take you to a clinic downtown, to a brilliant doctor we know. He will reduce any risks in the procedure to the absolute minimum."

"Fine," Quinn said. "But what's he going to do?"

"For just a few minutes, he's going to kill you."

# CHAPTER TWENTY-SIX
### Take Us To Your Leader

"We need to get arrested," Dex said, putting his phone away. He and Nora had managed to get out of the synagogue in one piece, though barely. They were in the parking lot now. It was even hotter. The sky was one sweeping blur.

"Arrested?" Nora said, sounding frightened by the very idea.

"Daphna says the Masons want to talk to us. She and Quinn might know where the golden book is—in some kind of realm. I'm sure it's incredibly dangerous, and I don't even want to think about it."

Nora didn't seem to have heard any of this. She was doing that praying thing again. Her eyes were closed, and her lips were moving rapidly as she inhaled and exhaled deeply.

Finally, she opened her eyes.

"That helps, you, huh?" Dex asked.

"When I feel pain or fear coming up," Nora explained. "Or anger. I wanted to smash things just now, like everyone else."

"And that makes it go away?"

"Yes—Why do we need to get arrested?"

"The Secret Keeper, the guy from the Pope—he told your dad that some leaders rejected the two o'clock threat to disappear them."

"What does that mean?"

"It means they probably don't believe the Masons can do it. Why would they? I wouldn't."

"I guess I wouldn't either."

"Well, maybe this theory is dumb, but in the movies, the bad guys always show they mean business when they're making a big threat."

"You mean with some kind of demonstration?"

"Exactly. They've had the book all day. They've made the threat. If they really wanted the world to take them seriously, wouldn't it make sense to make someone disappear already? Someone really big, probably."

Nora contemplated this a moment. "They don't know how?" she guessed.

"They must not know they have to scrape the names off, or how. Or they're just being cautious until they know exactly what they're doing. Daphna says they're looking for us. I'm betting they want to know what we know about it."

"But getting arrested won't keep us safe from them. Some cops are Masons too."

"That's what I'm counting on. We're going to get that book back."

Nora looked afraid, but resolved. "Okay," she said. "So, how do you get arrested? What do we have to do?"

"Let's find out."

A police car was just coming up into the lot, no doubt responding to the near riot of people still fleeing the synagogue. Dex jumped up and down and waved his arms at it.

The cruiser wound its way through what was left of the crowd and pulled right up alongside them.

A window rolled down.

"Greeting Officers Richards and Madden," Dex said, leaning in.

The two cops looked at each other.

"How'd you know our names?" Madden asked. He had a bandage on his head, and his arm was in a sling.

"We go way back," Dex told him. "Anyway, we know all about that book you guys finally found. So take us to your leader."

# CHAPTER TWENTY-SEVEN
## The Classic Deception

Quinn followed Mr. Brown upstairs and through the little house while the rest of the group leapt into some kind of frenetic action, rushing off in different directions. Daphna followed Quinn, feeling guilty about how much pain he was carrying around. She'd lost so many loved ones, but she'd never accidentally *killed* any of them, or wiped them off the face of the Earth, anyway.

But his ridiculous story about her white outfit and falling in love with her as a child? It was really bugging her. But it didn't matter. She'd do everything she could to help him get his parents back. Maybe doing a good deed under these kind of circumstances would help make up for some of the damage *she'd* done.

Yes, she'd help Quinn. And then she'd say goodbye to him.

Quinn turned around as he walked and tilted his head at her.

They were passing through a series of rooms, and it was obvious what he wanted her to see. There were bookshelves everywhere, but not a single book on any of them.

*They're waiting for the right one,* Daphna somehow knew. But her thoughts drifted again. What would Dexter do if he knew she was planning to let Mr. Brown kill her? He'd *kill* her, that's what. But Brown couldn't really mean *kill* her, kill her. Because if you kill someone temporarily, then you didn't really kill them. At least she didn't think so.

Anyway, she didn't trust this Mr. Brown character, that was for sure. It was because their agendas aligned so nicely that she was willing to go along, at least until she got a better idea of what he had in mind. And what was the realm he was sending them to if not Heaven? Ultimately, she didn't care, as long as she got her hands on this Book of Creation, which seemed to be the answer to all her problems.

She was going to find it, and she was going to use it to make things right, above and below. Simple as that.

Quinn cleared his throat. They were approaching the front door, but now he was tilting his head toward an office next to it. Daphna got a glimpse inside, though all she saw was a gorgeous wooden desk stacked with books. She couldn't identify them, but it was clear they all had the name Brown on them.

"Are you an author?" Quinn asked as Mr. Brown opened the front door.

"Me?" Mr. Brown said, chuckling as the trio stepped outside. "I guess you could say that. Mindless fluff to entertain the masses. Nothing you'd be remotely—"

It was unnaturally hot outside. Incredibly, unnaturally, stop-you-in-your-tracks-and-sear-your-lungs hot. Scores of people were out on the sweltering street anyway, pointing fearfully up at the sky. The lightning, which seemed already to have struck, lingered somehow. It looked almost like it had scratched itself into the surface of the sky.

"Must be well over a hundred now," Mr. Brown remarked, following the pointed fingers as best he could under a hand tented over his eyes. "Remarkable," he added. "They look almost like scars."

"Those aren't scars," Daphna said. *How dense could she be?*

"No?"

"They're cracks."

Mr. Brown paled a bit. "Good lord," he said. "This may render the Mason's threat child's play. All the more reason to make haste."

He hurried to his car, a grey sedan, and opened the back door. Daphna climbed in, noticing now that though she and Quinn had traveled fairly far underground, they were still in Southwest Portland. Quinn, looking ill but resolute, climbed in behind her.

Moments later, they were racing through the streets, or trying to. People were out everywhere it seemed, and many of them were milling about right on the streets. Hundreds. Maybe more. Mr. Brown had to keep hitting the brakes to weave around anxious sky-gazers. The air of panic was almost as palpable as the heat. Explosions were coming, and not only from the sky. Daphna could feel it, and she could see that Quinn could as well.

"So," she said to Mr. Brown to distract them, "will you tell us why you've been watching my brother and me? You were watching all the Lamed Vavniks, right?"

"That's right."

"Because you've been hoping one of us would die and come back from Heaven with the book you've been looking for."

"That's also right. We make it our business to be there at the time of your deaths to inform you of the possible existence of the book in Heaven and the potential for you to bring it back to Earth. As absurd as not just telling you all early on might seem, consider what it has meant to your lives to know you are among the Righteous Ones. It is best you do not know until the end."

Daphna had no quarrel with this. She wished she didn't know. Oh, how she wished she didn't know. Though she didn't think for a second they weren't told for their own sakes. "I know our ribs can create life on their own, while we're alive," she said. "In female Lamed Vavniks. And I know all our ribs can spawn life from the earth when we're dead and buried. But, how exactly can they bring us back from Heaven?"

"We believe the life force in your ribs is so powerful that, even if all your other bodily functions have terminated, they can be, to put it simply, re-started. That is, if circumstances allow. For example, if at the time of death your vital organs have not been destroyed."

Daphna was too amazed to respond. She just looked at Quinn, who said, "But you never really thought the book was in Heaven."

"Personally, no," Mr. Brown confirmed.

"Then why are we killing ourselves?"

Daphna wondered if Quinn was really planning to go through with this. *Was she?*

"What is this 'realm' supposed to be?" she asked when Mr. Brown did not immediately reply.

Mr. Brown glanced in the rearview mirror at both Daphna and Quinn, then said, "It is my opinion that the book was somehow lost in Purgatory, the realm a soul passes through between this world and the next, and *that* is why it has never been found."

"Can you not get there from Heaven?" Daphna asked, suddenly hopeful. She'd heard of Purgatory. This seemed promising.

"That is correct," Mr. Brown confirmed. "Angels have no access to Purgatory. If the book was somehow lost there, it could remain hidden forever."

"So your plan is to send us into Purgatory," Quinn surmised, "but bring us back before we make it to Heaven?"

"Precisely."

"How do you know all this?" Daphna asked.

"Theories," was Mr. Brown's only reply. "But Dr. Lewis is a genius, I assure you. He is at the absolute cutting edge of his field."

They'd reached a highway ramp. Mr. Brown merged into traffic. There was a lot of traffic.

Daphna didn't have anything more to say, and it seemed Quinn didn't either. They looked out their windows.

Mr. Brown flipped on the radio.

"—Remind you that there is no agreement that the effects observed in the sky are evidence of ozone depletion. There is absolutely no cause for—"

Mr. Brown changed the station.

"Parents sedating their own children! Locking them in closets and—!"

He changed it again.

"Tensions over the destruction of the towers are reaching a boiling point in the Middle East. There is a genuine chance of—"

Mr. Brown turned the radio off.

Daphna feared she was not going to have the courage to face whatever it was that Dr. Lewis had in store for her, so she focused on the prize again, this Book of Creation, and its apparently unlimited promise. Then she thought about the book in Heaven that had drawn her to it, that blank book she'd not mentioned to a soul. And she thought once again about the letters flowing through the one next to it: A's and D's and G's. There was another letter, she remembered, but she wasn't sure what it was. And maybe it wasn't a G she'd seen. Maybe it was a P. Was it somehow spelling someone's name? Could her book somehow be the story of her life? Is that why the pages were blank—since it wasn't fully written yet?

Daphna realized Quinn was talking again. They were moving quickly now, heading toward downtown Portland.

"The Masons do indeed date back to Ancient Egyptian times," Mr. Brown said, evidently in response to a question Quinn had asked. "If you've read the Bible, you know about the rather famous conflict between the Egyptians and the Hebrews, though conflict isn't really a fair word for oppression.

"Anyway, as you may know, the Hebrews, despite being enslaved, proved victorious, due, according to the Bible, to the direct intervention of their God. The Egyptian civilization eventually perished while the Hebrews went on to flourish. The Masons—"

"Didn't believe it was due to the direct intervention of the Hebrew's God," Daphna guessed.

"Correct," said Mr. Brown. "Not 'direct' anyway. They became determined to discover and usurp the power of the Jews, a power they claim the Jews eventually used to secretly gain control of the world."

"But that's exactly what the Masons want to do," Quinn objected.

"Of course," Mr. Brown replied. "It's the classic deception: Accuse your enemy of that which you are guilty of yourself."

"But the Jews never had the book, did they?"

"We have long regarded The Book of the Living as apocryphal, but the Masons have always believed it to be real. You may know that the Ten Plagues were what finally persuaded the Egyptian Pharaoh to release the Hebrew slaves. But it was the final plague that really did the trick: death of the firstborn sons. The Masons claim this was the *only* plague, and the Egyptian firstborn sons—"

"Disappeared," Daphna said.

Mr. Brown nodded. "They believe the book is the real reason the Jews have not only survived but thrived down through the millennia while so many other peoples have come and gone. And the Brotherhood has done everything they could think of to get it from them. I mean *everything*. The expulsion from Spain in 1492? Ferdinand and Isabella were secret Masons. Before that, in the 1200's, the Jews were expelled from England for refusing to give up the book. Though The Book of the Living was never our concern, we eventually concluded that it could not possibly exist, or at the very least that the Jews did not have it. This was after World War II."

*"The Holocaust?"* Daphna gasped. *"That's right!* Nora said Hitler was a Mason!"

There was silence in the car for a while as this sank in. Finally, Daphna said, "Some people think Jews have horns."

"Ignorant people," Mr. Brown replied.

"But, the history of that—"

"Yes, it relates to you and your brother directly."

"Their ribs?" Quinn asked.

"As I mentioned, the Masons tried everything they could think of to wrest this book away from the 'Elders of Zion,' as they called the non-existent world Jewish leadership they believed to be in possession of the book. The legend of the Thirty-six is no secret among the learned," he explained. "There was a time the Masons thought they could find them by identifying some kind of anatomical anomaly, or at least to throw a scare into the 'Elders' that they would someday find them—and thus blackmail them into handing over the book. Fortunately, they failed."

"Jack the Ripper," Daphna said.

"What?" Quinn looked hopelessly confused.

"Dex told me. All that mutilation. They were look-ing for—I guess they didn't really know what they were looking for."

"The Masons have made numerous attempts over the centuries to identify the Lamed Vavniks," Mr. Brown explained. "Fortunately, they lack the skills we possess in that department. But at long last, it seems they've won their prize. I might mention, by the way," he added almost off-handedly, "the Thirty-six haven't always been Jewish."

"That seems only right," Daphna said. "It's not like Adam and Eve had a religion. And the book has ev-eryone in the world in it, not just Jewish people. But that—maybe you can help with another question."

"I'm happy to try."

"If The Book of the Living has everyone in the world in it, then that means it has liars and thieves and killers—"

"Most of whom surely don't repent."

"Exactly. And they aren't all dropping dead the next year, I'm pretty sure. So, I'm wondering if maybe this thing about needing to have your name sealed after the ten days isn't really true."

"As you well know," Mr. Brown said after a momentary pause, "there exist some very powerful books. When those books fall into the hands of human beings, they are often used to further human ends. Despite what I expect your experience shows, those ends are not always evil."

Now it was Daphna who was confused.

"I think he's saying that you do have to have your name in the book to live," Quinn told her, "but when the Jews got hold of it way back when, or maybe just when they heard of it, they made up the idea of having to repent every year to stay in it. I guess to help people get along."

"So it has nothing to do with how you live?"

"I'm afraid not," said Mr. Brown, sensing Daphna's disappointment.

"It's just like the Lamed Vavniks—the Thirty-six!" she complained. "We're also called The Righteous Ones, but I don't think there's anything especially righteous about us at all!" She pressed back into the seat, sweating again at the thought of the Lake of Fire.

"Righteousness," Mr. Brown said, "in my experience is only ever a choice."

Daphna did not reply to this. She was too upset. She looked out her window, trying to keep herself together.

"But the ten days?" Quinn asked.

"That day, ten days from now, was not likely chosen at random," Mr. Brown said. "I would expect that the book, like any good census, renews itself every year. My guess is that names are constantly added as people are born, but the names of the deceased only vanish on that day."

"So *not* being listed on that day means you can't be alive?" Now it was Quinn having trouble holding it together. "You can't be added back later?"

"That would be my understanding. The page, so to speak, would have turned."

"Can you be added back, if you were somehow erased, *before* then?"

"I don't see why not, assuming your body has not been destroyed."

"You *are* part of the Church, aren't you?" Daphna asked, turning to Quinn and squeezing his hand. The look they exchanged was clear. Either Dex would get back The Book of the Living and they'd add his parents' names to it, or they'd get Mr. Brown's golden book and bring everyone home that way. One way or another, they'd bring their loved ones home. "They know who the Lamed Vavniks are," she added. "And that's how you have a man at the Vatican."

"We are most certainly not part of the Church," said Mr. Brown, and rather emphatically. Then he said, "Ah, good, we're just about here." They were on Park Street, nearing the Portland State University campus.

"There's the Art Museum!" Daphna exclaimed, having just spotted it. She pressed her face to the window.

Mr. Brown looked at her in the mirror, apparently surprised by her feeling the need to point this out.

But then Quinn shouted, "Look!" He pointed at a police car stopped directly in front of the museum. Dex and Nora were in the back seat.

"Stop! *Stop the car!*" Daphna jerked wildly on the door handle.

Mr. Brown pulled over two blocks past the museum. He turned off the engine but did not unlock the doors.

"Wait!" Quinn urged while Daphna struggled wildly to lift the recessed door lock. "We know some of the cops are Masons—one of them has a bandaged head—he could even be the one who crashed in the tunnel. You told Dex they were looking for him. He might have—"

"Gotten himself arrested," Daphna realized, sitting back again. "But the museum—"

"They're still using the museum," said Mr. Brown. But he wasn't talking to Daphna or Quinn. He was on his cell phone. He clicked it, then put it into his pocket. Then he turned around and said, "The museum used to be Portland's Masonic Temple. We haven't known where their leaders have been meeting for years, but it must still be there. How clever of them to keep using it. Often the first place people ought to look is the last they do."

"We need to help!" Daphna insisted. "The Book of the Living might—"

"—be of no help at all," Mr. Brown said. "The only thing we can be certain of is a terrible struggle should we try to wrest it from the Masons. If your brother manages the feat, wonderful. In the meantime, we will have complete privacy to conduct the journey."

Through the rear window, Daphna saw Dex and Nora get out of the squad car. The cop with the bandage got out with them. He also had his arm in a sling. The three of them walked up to the glass front doors of the museum, and after the cop unlocked them, went inside.

Daphna took in a long, deep breath and let it out. Then she turned back around.

"If you really want to help your brother," said Mr. Brown. "If you really want to stop the evil spewing from the sky before it settles upon us all, you must help me find the book I seek."

"Alright already," Daphna said. "Let's stop flapping our gums and go get the damn thing."

# CHAPTER TWENTY-EIGHT
### *Jesus 2.0*

Dexter tried to reassure Nora as they walked toward the red brick façade of the Portland Art Museum, but she was praying yet again and therefore deaf to his words. It was just as well, because he knew they were empty. It was now absurdly, ridiculously hot. He had never been anywhere this hot.

Dex had no idea what he was going to do, or what they were walking into. They climbed the front steps and approached the center set of glass entry doors.

Above the front doors hung a huge banner proclaiming, "Jesus 2.0." It said the exhibition opened today, but no one seemed to be inside.

Madden, who'd left Richards in the car, tried the door with his free hand. It was locked. There was definitely no exhibition opening today. It must have been cancelled. But then Madden took out a key ring, shook out a particular key, and opened the door with it.

"Follow," he said, locking the door after ushering them in. He didn't seem especially happy to be dealing with Dexter this time around. Nor had his partner. After Richards made a call on his cell, neither spoke a word on the drive from Hillsdale.

They were in a kind of vestibule or waiting area with a ticket booth and some chairs arranged around a statue.

Madden led the way through another set of glass doors into the first gallery, a high-ceilinged hall filled with portraits of Jesus. The artists had given him just about every possible look. He was Caucasian, Black, Chinese, and Native American, for starters. His outfit and hair varied even more. He had dreadlocks; he was bald; he was wearing a turban; he had long blonde hair; he wore a dress.

"This is all so—" Nora said. "I don't know what this

is all so."

Dex agreed.

Beyond that they passed through a narrow gallery full of images of Nativity scenes. There were sculptures, paintings, and multimedia displays. One of them depicted the Three Wise Men as the Three Stooges, another as the Three Little Pigs. Dex saw some kind of three-dimensional projection in the corner of the Three Wise Men giving baby Jesus cell phones, tablet computers, and noise-cancelling headphones.

"I don't see the point of this," Nora said. "It seems so—wrong."

Dex didn't know what to think about it. It seemed mostly silly, as silly as Virgil Durante's museum of horrors. Why was he always being led into museums?

Next they entered The Last Supper room. It was a large rectangular hall with three flat leather benches in a line at its center. The walls were packed with paintings, nearly floor to ceiling all around.

"Sit and wait," Madden said.

Dex and Nora took a seat on the middle bench.

"What happened to your arm?" Dex asked.

"Your goddamned sister, that's what."

"Oh." *Go Daphna,* Dex thought, wishing he could get the details.

"Take some time to think about telling them what you know," Madden snapped. Then he added, "Take some time to think about all the things you don't want to happen to you if you refuse."

"We're sorry about the bicycles," Nora said. "And for being out during the curfew."

"What?"

"Ah—nothing," Dex said.

Madden didn't seem interested, anyway. "Do you have cell phones?" he asked.

"Ah," Dex said again, "no."

"Come here."

Dex and Nora looked at each other.

"Now."

Nora got up and hurried over.

With his free hand, Madden patted her down.

Nora turned red from ear to ear.

"Now you."

Dex went over and submitted to the pat down, which seemed unnecessarily harsh.

172

When Madden was satisfied, he simply turned and left, locking the door they'd come through behind him.

"Dex, what about your phone?" Nora asked when the door clicked shut.

Dex sat back down on the bench next to Nora and pulled the phone out from between two of the cushions.

"I put it there when he was searching you," he explained. Dex put it back in his pocket.

"What if they search us again?"

Dex hadn't thought of that.

"Maybe we should leave it hidden here. If there's an emergency, we'll know where to run to get it."

"Okay." Dex tucked the phone back between the cushions. "We'll get it on the way out," he added, trying to sound certain that they'd be coming back out.

Dex didn't know what to say next, so he looked around the room for a minute, waiting.

But nothing happened.

"You lied to a policeman," Nora said.

Dex looked at her, amazed. "A policeman sending us to a bunch of psychos bent on taking over the world."

"I know—I know," Nora said, looking embarrassed. "It's just that—I couldn't do it, even if—I mean, isn't lying, well, *lying*? Does God care what your reasons are for doing something bad?"

*"Nora,"* Dex sighed, "you sound like Daphna used to. Wait—is that also why you wouldn't get on the bike? Because it wasn't ours?"

Nora nodded.

"Look," Dex said, shaking his head, "the world isn't black and white. If God stuck around maybe it could've been, but it's hard to know what's right and wrong sometimes. If there's one thing I've learned, it's that life is complicated. That's probably the only thing I've learned. You might have to do something that feels wrong if we expect to get that book back, not to mention out of here in one piece."

Nora nodded. She looked like she was seriously considering his words, which pleased Dexter tremendously. He looked around the hall again, this time actually taking in what he saw.

Like the others, it was all about alternative versions. These renderings varied as much or even more than what they'd seen so far. The only thing they had in common was that they all featured Jesus and his disciples at a meal.

Dex saw the one Daphna had mentioned, the one in a fast food restaurant, where everyone was eating burgers. Jesus stood, holding up a shake, as if to propose a toast with it. In another he was actually holding up a piece of toast. In another they were all in a school cafeteria, having a food fight with slices of pizza and soggy grilled cheeses.

Most were more conventional than those were, though the style of the room and the types of foods and tableware were all very different. Most, like the one at the Vatican, had Jesus sitting in the center of the table with his disciples on either side. Dex recalled he was holding a glass of wine in that one. The disciples all looked horrified. Some here did as well, but many had very different expressions, from sneers to hysterical laughing. One had them all drunk and another asleep. In a few, Jesus was standing—actually on the table in one. Some of the tables were laden with Chinese food boxes, others giant legs of lamb. There were plates and goblets and glasses and mugs. One had sippy cups. Everyone was wearing bibs in that one.

Dex's mind raced to come up with ways to get The Book of the Living as he looked around. He was certain it was there, in the museum, somewhere, and it was fairly likely he'd wind up seeing it. But under what circumstances, he had no idea. It was impossible to formulate a plan unless you knew exactly what you were planning for. Dex was also certain the Masons didn't know how to use the book, but how could he take advantage of that fact? He needed help! He should call Daphna.

Nora was praying again. Her eyes were closed.

"Nora!" Dex snapped. "You can't pray your life away!"

She opened her eyes, stunned.

"I'm—I'm sorry," Dex said, ashamed of the outburst. "I think your praying is great. I think it's great that you can deal with bad situations by leaving them. But you can't really help—help me, help us, *here, now*—if you're not really here."

"You're right," Nora admitted, her eyes downcast. "I know I hide inside. I've been hiding inside all my life."

Something made Dex want to kiss her again just then. But he didn't dare.

"I'm so scared," Nora said. "Why are they making us sit here like this?"

"They want us to get as nervous as possible," Dex guessed, thinking it was working pretty well. "You know, like how the cops make people sit in the interrogation rooms forever while they—never mind. They just want to break you."

"One's missing."

Dex looked to see what Nora was pointing to.

There, right in the middle of the main wall, which was otherwise packed with paintings spaced no more than a few inches apart, was an empty space, a long horizontal strip of bare wall, perhaps five feet long. There were a series of hooks there, holding nothing.

"My sister told me once about some study that showed people will stare at that space longer than any of the actual paintings in here."

"Why is that?" Nora asked, staring at the space.

"I don't know. Maybe people are just more interested in what's not there than what is. Or maybe it's because everyone always thinks there's something better out there than what they've got right in front of them."

"For some people, that includes the entire world," Nora said. Then she closed her eyes, and withdrew into herself again. But this time a tear dripped from her right eye and ran down her pale cheek.

Dexter desperately wanted to brush her hair aside and wipe it away.

"I've always felt that way about my father," Nora admitted. "I've always wished he was someone else. I've always dishonored him." Then she opened her eyes and said, "Can I ask you something?"

"Yes, sure."

"At school, in the hall. You were going to start smashing things with that backpack."

"I—Yes, I guess I was."

"Why didn't you?"

"Because I saw how scared you were, and I knew I had to help you."

"You needed to be someone's hero—is that it?"

"No. I don't know. Maybe," Dex said. "Yes, a little. But mostly I was feeling like there was really no point to trying so hard and risking so much all the time if the world wasn't going to give me credit for it. It didn't seem living like that was worth it. But since I met you I don't seem to care so much anymore."

"I have something to confess," Nora said.

"You do?"

"I've done something bad, so bad."

"Nora—"

"I tripped you, in the hall. And then I grabbed your legs—on the floor—on purpose."

"You what?"

"I knew who you were. I recognized you from the news when I ran out of the auditorium. My father had been warning me about you for over a year."

"I—I don't understand."

"You may not think living the life you've had was worth it, but I've never lived any kind of life at all. I wanted you to take me with you, away from my father forever. I believed you were a Mason, and I wanted to go with you, and I didn't care where you took me. I wanted to be evil if that's what it took to feel alive. I used you."

Dex looked blankly at Nora for a long few seconds.

Then he laughed. He couldn't help himself. He laughed hard.

"What? Why are you laughing?"

"I've been used worse," Dex said. "It's okay. Really."

"Really?" Nora smiled now through another falling tear. "I know you're not evil."

"Sorry to disappoint you."

"You can kiss me now."

"Wha—what?" *How did she know?*

"I said you can kiss me now."

"I—I can?"

"I'm not going to die in here without ever having been kissed."

"You shouldn't be here," Dex said, at last realizing what should have been obvious before they ever got

176

in the car with Richards and Madden. "You should go, or hide, while you still have the—"

"Now. Please. Kiss me now."

Nora closed her eyes, but this time she didn't disappear. She was right there.

Dex, trembling, closed his eyes and leaned toward her.

"Come with me," a voice commanded.

Both Dex and Nora jolted, pulling back just before their lips met.

It was an inhuman voice, like a robot's.

Someone was in the gallery, someone in a hooded black robe and bright blue mask. There was something designed over the mask's left eye: a bent ruler, some kind of compass, and the letter G. He had stepped out from behind a painting that swung open like a door.

The figure waved Dex and Nora forward.

"Come with me," he repeated in that creepy electric voice.

"It's okay," Dex said. "He's got a voice distorter." He rose and offered Nora his hand. She shifted uncomfortably on the bench for a moment, but she accepted the offer of help getting to her feet.

Then, after letting out two deep and very nervous breaths, Dex and Nora followed the masked figure into the darkness behind the secret door.

# CHAPTER TWENTY-NINE
## Pam Reynolds

Instead of restarting the car, Mr. Brown surprised Daphna and Quinn by opening his door and getting out. They were apparently at their destination. Being so close to the museum was immensely comforting to Daphna. After climbing out, she and Quinn followed him through a set of glass doors under an awning—into some kind of health clinic.

"Where is everyone?" Daphna asked after stepping inside. She was doing everything she could, focusing all her energy on not thinking about her brother. He could handle—one of the most notoriously vicious organizations ever to exist.

*Please God*, Daphna prayed. Then she stopped.

The place, which was arranged in a circle, was as silent as a tomb. There was a chiropractor, a nutritionist, a naturopath, and an acupuncturist, each with a closed door to their separate, evidently equally abandoned facilities.

"This way," said Mr. Brown. He led them through the middle of the circle, to the far end, to a door that had no identification on it. Across from the door was a glass-walled yoga studio.

It turned out the place wasn't entirely deserted. Someone was inside the studio sitting cross-legged on a blue mat, a man in an orange robe. He looked deep in meditation.

Mr. Brown reached for the knob on the unmarked door, but didn't open it. Instead, without turning around, he said, "There was a woman, a number of years ago, named Pam Reynolds. She had a massive aneurysm in her brain. That's part of an artery that has ballooned. It could not be safely removed using standard surgical procedures, so her doctor tried something radical, a procedure called, 'Standstill.'"

"What's that?" Quinn asked, though he sounded like he didn't really want to know.

178

Daphna heard this. She was interested in the answer, but somehow not as much as she was interested in the meditating man. She couldn't take her eyes off him sitting there so serenely. He seemed so peaceful, as if nothing in the outside world was of the slightest relevance to his state of mind. For some reason she thought of her blank book up in Heaven.

Mr. Brown remained facing the door. It was as if he couldn't bear to share this story face-to-face.

"During the operation," he explained, "Ms. Reynolds' body was lowered to sixty degrees, her breathing and heartbeat were stopped, and the blood was drained from her head. She was, effectively, *dead* while they successfully removed the aneurysm. She was then revived. She recovered fully."

"*That's what you want to do to us?*" Quinn yelped.

Daphna heard all this as well, but she forced herself to stay focused on the meditating man. He looked old, but somehow youthful at the same time. His eyes were closed, his breathing slow. She tried to channel his calm so her bladder wouldn't empty at the prospect of what she was getting herself into.

"But here's the point of the story," Mr. Brown said. "This case represents the best documented event of its kind because of the controlled circumstances in which it took place. After recovering, the patient reported that—"

"She was pulled toward a light," Quinn said.

Mr. Brown turned around. Daphna did as well.

Quinn was reading his phone. "It's true," he confirmed. "At least according to Wikipedia."

Then he read, "'As she got closer, the light became very bright. She began to discern figures in the light, including her grandmother, an uncle, other deceased relatives, and people unknown to her.' It says eventually her uncle pushed her back to her body."

"We believe," said Mr. Brown, "that she was passing through Purgatory during that time." He paused to look between Daphna's and Quinn's paling faces. "Right, then," he added. "Any questions?"

*hold your tongue*
Dex and Nora followed the masked figure down a flight of stairs, a rather long flight of stairs. They were obviously going underground. At the bottom was a

fancy carved door with the same symbol that was on the blue mask. The figure knocked in some complicated way, after which the door was opened by an identically robed and blue-masked figure.

They were ushered into a large chamber tiled in blue and white diamonds, arranged in checkerboard style. A dozen blue theater-style chairs were set up along opposite walls, and in every one of them sat a robed figure wearing the same blue mask. Dexter swallowed a giant lump in his throat, and he could see Nora do the same. It felt like they'd walked into an alien tribunal, one that was sure to judge them harshly.

A raised platform sat in the rear, carpeted in blue and supporting what looked like a throne. On the throne sat one more figure, robed like the others, but wearing a red mask.

In the center of the chamber was a large square carpet. It was black, but filling it was a gray circle, and inside the circle was a five-pointed star. Each point was a different color. Symbols adorned each point. In the center of the star sat a podium, on top of which rested what had to be The Book of the Living, now without its protective yellow cover. Dex congratulated himself on getting them to the book.

*Now what,* he thought.

In front of the podium was what looked like a high-backed wooden bench of some kind. The legs were framed and it faced the throne, so it wasn't clear whether anyone was sitting in it.

Both Dexter and Nora instinctively turned to look at the door they'd come through. It had been closed. Two hulking Blue Masks stood in front of it, arms crossed on their bulging chests.

Nora turned back around and began to pray.

"This is not the boy who discovered the book," said the man on the throne. His voice was also distorted. It was low and vibrated in an awful way.

"The boy is one of the Wax twins," someone said. More mechanical words. It was impossible to tell who'd uttered them. The masked figures in the chairs all around sat immobile, inscrutable.

"And the girl?"

"We do not know. But they were both there when we obtained the book."

"Check her name."

A Blue Mask rose from a chair and approached the podium. He leaned over The Book of the Living, then said, "Eleanor Jons."

"She is of no use to us," Red Mask decreed. "Send her away."

There was a long pause as the group considered this. Finally, a voice said, "If she is close to the boy, she may know what he—"

"Hold," said Red Mask. "'*Jons.*' She is the daughter of that meddlesome pastor. She is here to spy."

"Then she should die," a voice declared.

Dex looked at Nora. It was clear she wasn't hearing this, and he was glad for that.

"The time for trifles is over!" Red Mask boomed. "We dread no man! No nation! No power on Earth! Tell me you two: What do you know about how to properly remove a name from our Book?"

"Consider your words wisely," another voice added. "For they may be the last you ever speak." Two Blue Masks rose on either side of the room and approached the bench facing the throne. Each took an end and, together, they spun it around on hidden wheels.

Dexter gasped.

It wasn't a bench. It was a torture device.

A man was in one of the bench's two seats, his arms and legs strapped down, his head held in an apparatus attached to an armrest that supported his chin like those contraptions eye doctors use during examinations. It had gears and knobs all over it. The man's mouth was forced open by some kind of pincer and a clamp gripped his tongue, pulling it out of his mouth unnaturally far. His eyes bulged. His face was covered in sweat and tears.

"That's the rabbi!" Dex cried.

Nora fainted dead away.

"Nora!"

Before Dex had a chance to help her, the door giants seized him by the arms and dragged him toward the bench's empty seat.

# CHAPTER THIRTY
*One More Way*

Behind the door lay a gleaming white operating room. There was an operating table on a hydraulic lift under a large round lamp, larger than but not unlike the kind dentists use. Behind the table was a massive steel machine with attachments all over it: retractable arms, monitors, storage compartments, tubes, dials, and gauges. An IV cart and several rolling trays with silver tools sat next to it. A cart next to them held four large tanks topped with more gauges and tubes.

Another large machine sat across the room, two connected machines it seemed. The shorter one looked like a chest freezer, the kind you get ice cream out of at corner stores. It was attached to a taller unit that looked like a dryer with colored buttons on its door.

A bank of monitors blinked along the back wall, just behind a couch and a very large desk. A sink sat next to the door, flanked by a shelf full of towels and supply boxes.

Daphna processed this all very slowly, so it took a moment to dawn on her that a man was at the sink washing his hands, a rather elderly man in a lab coat with a shock of haywire hair. He straightened up and said, "Excellent, let's get started," in a soft, almost feminine voice.

"This is Dr. George Lewis," said Mr. Brown.

But Daphna was looking at the operating table again—the *single* operating table. As was Quinn. Daphna could tell it was dawning on him too that Mr. Brown never intended to send them both. He'd allowed them to think they'd be going together, but she realized now he'd never said as much.

"I'll do it," Quinn said.

When Mr. Brown turned to him, Quinn added, "Daphna's been to Heaven, but she doesn't know anything about Purgatory, or The Book of Creation.

She's been through way too much as it is."

"Quinn," Daphna said, "it should be me. My rib—"

"Needs to be protected at all costs! What if it doesn't work? What if you get stuck there?"

This gave Daphna pause, but she nonetheless retorted, "There's still Dexter's!"

Quinn looked at Mr. Brown. "Does it have to be one of them?"

"We believe our best chance of success would be to send one of the Righteous Ones—"

*"There!"*

"But because we have never attempted this before, it might be prudent to try it with a typical human first."

*"There!"* Quinn shot back.

"But Quinn," Daphna pleaded, "it's much less of a risk for me. If something goes wrong—if I die—my rib can bring me back."

"Though, according to our best guess," Dr. Lewis said, "you would only live again for up to six weeks."

*"What?"* Daphna wailed. No one told her that!

"That's it then!" Quinn declared. "There's no reason for you to go unless you absolutely have to. I'm doing it."

"No!"

"They need a guinea pig, Daphna! And it's my parents who are up there. The guilt is killing me! It's eating me up like the worst possible disease! But that's not the only reason I want to go."

Dr. Lewis, who'd been watching this in silence from the sink, tapped his watch and looked at Mr. Brown, who put his hand up to request patience.

"I *want* to go," Quinn promised, "because, if I fail, I'll be with them. I know you don't love me, Daphna, and so I have nothing to keep me here. But that's not all, either."

*"Please,"* Daphna begged. *"Please don't—"*

"You have Dexter. He loves you and needs you. I want to do this for you. I want you to see that people can be trusted. I want you to know that one day you'll find someone else out there who you'll believe really does want only the best for you. Daphna, you don't have to do everything all of the time."

Daphna looked at Quinn blankly for a moment. Then she turned to Dr. Lewis and asked, "Do you know if the Righteous Ones actually have to be more righteous? Or is it just the rib?"

Dr. Lewis seemed surprised by the question. After a moment, he said, "I believe it is, as you say, 'just the rib.'"

Daphna looked between Mr. Brown and Quinn, then said, "Hold on. Give me two minutes, okay?" Before either could react, she hurried out of the room. The surprised pair hurried after her.

Daphna pushed open the door of the yoga studio and approached the man in the orange robe. He was still sitting in the same position on his mat, still deep in meditation. Daphna glanced up and saw Quinn and Mr. Brown watching her through the glass wall. She sat down and crossed her legs.

"Do you believe in life after death?" she asked. Something told her formal introductions, or even basic manners, were simply not necessary just now. Up close, the man's age was still indeterminate. 50? 80? He had white hair but perfectly smooth skin.

"A more useful question," he said without opening his eyes, "might be, 'Is there life *before* death?'"

"But Heaven—"

"'Heaven' and 'Hell' are words of little use to me. There is Heaven here, on Earth, for those who live. There is Hell too, for those who can't or won't."

"But, everyone *lives,* don't they?"

"To draw breath, to have a beating heart—" the man replied, "this is to be alive. But to *live* is something else altogether."

Daphna had to think about this.

"How long have you practiced?" the man asked. He took deep, slow breaths in through his nose and down, it seemed, into his belly.

"Um," said Daphna. "Practiced?"

"Meditation."

"Oh, I've never—"

The man opened his eyes and looked at her with surprise. His eyes were chocolate brown.

"Interesting," he said.

"Why?"

"You are not throwing bricks through windows or turning over cars."

"No," Daphna confirmed. "My friends and I, we seem—"

"Do any of them practice meditation?"

"No, I don't think so. You're so—peaceful. Would meditation help kids—people—resist this—what's happening?"

"Only what we call the False Self can fall prey to what some call the Evil Urge," the man explained. "This is the Self that isn't truly us, the Self created by accidents like where and when we are born and who our parents are. Meditation is a means by which one temporarily takes leave of this False Self. Upon return, the practitioner sees the so-called 'Self' for what it is: borrowed clothes. And she is thus much less susceptible to unproductive urges of all kinds."

"But how have I—?"

"There are other means of shedding the False Self. One effective technique, if done properly, if done selflessly, is prayer."

*"Nora,"* Daphna whispered.

"Another is via the practice of compassion, or any other feeling that leads one to place the needs of others above one's own."

"Dex has been doing that with Nora," Daphna said. "And that's it for me, too: I'll risk anything for— the people I'm trying to help. And Quinn is trying to save his parents." She thought a moment, then added, "but Quinn seems even more immune. I mean, he doesn't love his parents any more than I love my—"

"There is one more way," the man said.

"What is it?"

"One's False Self diminishes in direct proportion to the degree that one is in love, true, romantic love."

"But he's *not* in love with me!" Daphna protested. "He only wanted me to think—Even just now, he's pretending it's for me."

"You don't trust him?"

"I don't trust anyone."

"Ahh. You will discover that people are people only through other people. Despite the obvious risks, if one does not trust, one cannot fully live."

The man nodded, closed his eyes, and returned to his meditation.

The conversation was over.

Daphna bowed her head. It seemed like she'd just been taught critical things, yet she still didn't know what to do. How could she risk leaving Dexter alone?

How could she even consider doing that to him? How could she risk making him the last Lamed Vavnik on Earth? How could she do that to the world? Could a more selfish act be conceivable? But how could she let Quinn do this for her when it was more likely she would succeed? He needed to get his parents back, but she needed to get Dr. Fludd back. And she needed to put an end to the fire raging in Heaven. And to set the world below back in order. And Dex might need her to save him! And Quinn could die!

Daphna looked up to share her frustration with Mr. Brown and Quinn.

But they were gone.

"No!" Daphna cried, scrambling to her feet. She ran back into the hall and crashed through the door of the operating room.

When she saw Quinn laid out on the table, she screamed.

# CHAPTER THIRTY-ONE
## *The Bench*

"I'm going to ask you one more time," Red Mask growled from his throne. "How do you properly remove a name from this book? We are loath to damage the pages in any way until we know the Book's full power."

Dexter did not bother struggling with the straps fastening his arms and legs to the chair. He was simultaneously trying not to look at the rabbi on his left and to see if Nora was still on the floor. She seemed to be in her usual fetal position.

He cursed himself for the arrogance of coming with no plan, for the unforgivable stupidity of bringing Nora here even if he'd had one. He didn't know what to say, so he said what he felt like saying: "I guess that's for me to know and you to find out."

"As you wish," Red Mask said. He nodded, and the two giants swung a second metal contraption around to Dexter's face. They forced his head onto the chinrest and fastened a strap around his forehead.

Dex clenched his teeth as hard as he could, but one of them punched him in the stomach. He gasped for air, and when his mouth opened, a clamp on a hinge swung into it, grasping his tongue.

"The rabbi here is still considering his words," Red Mask said. "Why don't you do the same? In the meantime, perhaps we can loosen your tongue a bit."

He nodded again, and one of the giants twisted a knob.

The clamp retracted a bit.

Dexter screamed.

# CHAPTER THIRTY-TWO
## *Standstill*

"Do not interfere," Mr. Brown said, grabbing Daphna roughly by the arm. "Or you will jeopardize his life."

Quinn was unconscious, draped under blue cloth. An IV ran to his arm. Two other tubes ran from his chest and thigh to the large steel cart with all the monitors and attachments. Yet another tube was down his throat.

Daphna wavered on her feet, but Mr. Brown steadied her. He slid a chair behind her and helped her sit down. Then he sat down in a chair next to her.

"Remain calm, young lady," said Dr. Lewis while he affixed electrodes to Quinn's head. "This is a delicate operation. The boy has been given complete instructions on what to do on the other side. Now sit there calmly while I finish the prepping."

"Oh, God," Daphna groaned. This was her fault for being indecisive. She was now going to have to answer for this, too. *"Oh, God. Oh, God. Oh, God."*

She tried the breathing thing again and did better this time. It helped a bit, especially when she managed to take air all the way into her stomach through her throat.

Daphna lost track of time for a while.

When she came back, Daphna saw Quinn's eyes had been taped shut. Dr. Lewis was inserting something into his ears. She turned away, looking for anything to distract her, and something did, something odd and out-of-place on the giant desk at the far end of the room. Sitting next to the computer was a colorful sculpture made of—gumdrops?

Daphna got up and approached the desk. She recognized the double helix now. It was a model of DNA. She'd done a similar project when she was in elementary school. Dr. Lewis must have grandchildren. The thought struck her as odd.

Daphna took the model back with her to her seat.

"We have three ways of determining brain death," Dr. Lewis said when Daphna sat back down, as though someone had asked. "One: a cessation of functioning in the cerebral cortex, as indicated by a flatline on the EEG here." He pointed to a monitor. "Two: lack of brain stem response to auditory stimuli—hence the speakers in the boy's ears. They will emit clicks. And three: a lack of blood flowing through the brain, which we'll take care of soon enough.

"Now, this device here—" Dr. Lewis pointed to the large contraption hooked into Quinn—"is a heart-lung machine. It will provide circulation and oxygenation while the heart is stopped. It is cooling the blood as we speak."

"Here, now," he continued, sounding as if he were simply explaining how equipment worked rather than how he was killing a human being. "The boy's temperature has reached 75 degrees. The ECG—" He pointed to another monitor—"indicates cardiac malfunction."

Daphna leapt to her feet. "Please stop this!" she begged. The gumdrop model fell to the floor. "I'll do it! I'll go!"

"Daphna," warned Mr. Brown, standing up in case she did something stupid, "you risk his life with this behavior."

Daphna forced herself to sit back down. She tried to take in long, deep breaths, but couldn't control them. She gulped for air like a drowning victim.

Dr. Lewis was giving Quinn a shot now. "A massive dose of potassium chloride," he said.

A moment later, he pointed to the EEG: a flatline. Then he pointed to another monitor and said, "Brain stem response to the speakers is growing weaker. There," he added a moment later. "It's gone."

Next Dr. Lewis turned off the heart-lung machine. Then he reached below the table and pushed a button, raising Quinn's head. "To drain the blood," he said.

Once Quinn was partially upright, Dr. Lewis stepped back from the table and looked at Mr. Brown. He gave a satisfied smile and said, "Success! The boy is dead."

"Bring him back!" Daphna demanded, again on her feet, but Dr. Lewis looked only at Mr. Brown.

"Bring him back! Time is disconnected up there! You can bring him back *now!*"

Mr. Brown looked at his doctor with no expression at all. He said nothing for an excruciatingly long few moments, but then finally nodded. Dr. Lewis switched on the heart-lung machine. The readouts on all the monitors immediately jumped back to life.

"That's good, right?" Daphna asked. "He's going to be okay?"

"It will take a few minutes for his blood to warm up," Dr. Lewis said. "Have patience."

Quinn's eyes began to flutter.

Daphna, Mr. Brown, and Dr. Lewis all rushed to the operating table.

The moment they reached it, Quinn's eyes burst open. He let out an awful strangled sort of squawk as he reached up to dislodge the tube in his throat. Then he began to thrash, threatening to loose the others still in his chest and thigh.

"Hold him!" Dr. Lewis barked.

Everyone held down Quinn's shoulders and arms.

"His legs! Hold his legs!"

Daphna lurched to Quinn's feet and clutched his ankles.

"Fire!" Quinn rasped. His voice was awful, ragged like Asterius Rash's used to be. "The fire!"

"The Book!" Mr. Brown shouted in Quinn's ear. "Did you get the Book?"

"Fire!" Quinn shrieked, trying now to tear the tape off of his eyes. "Books on fire! Everywhere! The Dragon is burning the books! Trying to get out!"

"He's still there!" Mr. Brown yelled, throwing himself over Quinn's flailing body. "Do it now!"

Dr. Lewis let go of Quinn. Calmly, he took a needle out of a long silver box sitting on one of the carts. It was already full of a clear liquid.

Daphna smelled something sweet, a hint of licorice and lemon—*tarragon?*

"What is *that?*" she begged. *"What are you doing?"*

"It will help," was all Dr. Lewis said. He injected Quinn in the arm.

Quinn seized violently. Now the tubes jerked out

190

of his body and his blood began to spill. Then he collapsed, and the monitors went berserk.

Daphna backed away from the operating table as Dr. Lewis spun round, frantically reinserting the tubes. Then he grabbed those paddles she'd only seen on TV and shocked Quinn with them. Mr. Brown had also backed away. He sat down again, breathing hard.

The crazy beeping machines settled down.

"Is—is he okay?" Daphna asked, crying now. If Quinn—

"Is he back?" Mr. Brown asked. *"Is he coming back?"*

"Coma, I fear," said Dr. Lewis. He didn't sound panicked at all, which was both disturbing and reassuring.

*"Coma?"* Daphna whined. "He's in a—?" She moved to take Quinn's hand, but felt her foot squish something—those gumdrops. She reached down and pried the hunk off her shoe, but instead of tossing it away, she looked at it.

Then she looked at it closer.

Each gumdrop had a letter on it. There were four in her clump: A, T, C, and G.

Daphna squatted down and sorted through the others scattered on the floor. They were all A's, T's, C's and G's.

She got up, white as a sheet, her mind spinning.

Mr. Brown looked at her.

Suddenly, Daphna understood. She knew exactly why she'd been attracted to a single Book in the Light, why she knew in her very soul that it was hers.

It *was* hers.

"Quinn didn't go to Purgatory," she said, her voice hitching, "he went to Heaven. The Books in Heaven—they contain the formulas for our DNA. We come from those Books, and we return to them when we die. Those Books contain people's souls—*and they're burning!*"

Daphna didn't have time to observe how this was received because her phone rang. She ripped it out of her pocket.

It was a one-word text message from her brother.

The word was 'Help.'

# CHAPTER THIRTY-THREE
## *Fraying*

Dexter had never been in so much pain. He'd never known so much pain was possible. He couldn't hear. He couldn't see. He couldn't think.

The entire universe was pain.

His tongue, his mouth—his whole *head*—they felt like they were going to shred. It was a thousand times worse than being shot. Dex felt his consciousness fraying until, finally—and mercifully—it snapped.

*in trouble*

"It may simply be the inferior life-force of the typical human," said Dr. Lewis while he worked dials and knobs on Quinn's machines.

"Then perhaps the twins," Mr. Brown suggested.

"If this boy does not return, I'm quite certain we'll succeed with one of them. Wonderful that there are two."

Daphna wasn't listening. She rushed over to the operating table, leaned over, and kissed Quinn on the lips. He was still disarranged under all the draping he'd tossed about, so despite her panic, she tried to make him more comfortable. When she tucked his right arm under, she found something in his hand—some kind of folded paper. As quickly as she could, she stuffed it into her pocket.

Mr. Brown stood up and said, "Let's do it now."

It took a moment for Daphna to hear this. "What?" she said when it got through. "No. I have to leave. I have to leave right now."

"You said you wanted to go!" Mr. Brown shouted, his youthful face turning hard. "You, yourself, said you had the better chance of succeeding, and you don't believe your friend even made it to Purgatory. So now is your chance. We have no time! We have to send you!"

Daphna turned to Dr. Lewis. "Take care of him,"

she demanded. Then she turned to Mr. Brown and said, "I have to go. My brother needs me."

*"We* need you!" Mr. Brown screamed. He seemed to have lost control of himself entirely. *"You* have to find that book!"

He rushed at Daphna and grabbed her by the shoulders. When she tried to squirm away, he flung her to the floor like she was stuffed with straw. He stood over her, his face contorted, his fists clenched.

Daphna knew she hadn't a chance in the world of fighting her way out.

"Quinn brought something back," she said. "A note. It's in his hand under the covers."

When Mr. Brown and Dr. Lewis attacked poor Quinn, Daphna got to her feet and sprinted for the door. "Take care of him!" she begged, bursting back into the commons. She ran past the yoga studio without a glance. But after lurching outside, she pulled up short.

The rioting had begun.

The streets were packed with people smashing windows and looting stores. Fortunately, no one seemed to notice or care about Daphna Wax's arrival on the scene. She turned momentarily back to the wellness center. Mr. Brown was evidently not pursuing her, which was a relief. She hoped that was a good sign for Quinn and that no one out here would venture back to that little room.

It was hotter than Daphna thought possible. The cracks in the sky were spreading, emanating crimson waves in all directions. A digital sign on a bank across the street said it was 112 degrees.

Daphna took a deep breath in through her nose and drew it down her throat, then set off running toward the museum, taking care to avoid the looters, who remained focused on looting.

No one paid her any mind.

Just a few seconds later, she was there, standing at the museum's front doors.

All was quiet.

All was locked, as well.

Daphna looked around for an idea, but nothing presented itself. Then she looked up, and the moment she did, black-robed figures, a dozen or so, leapt off the roof. They flew toward the street for a few dizzy, surreal moments, but then swung back, attached to cords she hadn't noticed, and crashed through the windows running along the upper floor.

A slamming door made Daphna spin round to the street. A half dozen more figures in black were leaping out of one of those stretch-limo SUV's. It was bright white. They ran up the steps right past her with a metal battering ram, which they used to crash through the museum's front doors.

Were they wearing *swords?*

The whole thing lasted only a few seconds. Daphna looked back at the SUV, trying to understand how it all could have happened so quickly.

Her heart seized.

The man in the passenger seat was looking right at her with sad eyes. That curtain of white hair encircling his bald head was unmistakable:

It was the Secret Keeper of the Church.

Daphna turned and rushed into the museum.

# CHAPTER THIRTY-FOUR
## What You Want to Know

Someone approached Dexter's chair and leaned over him, which brought his mind back to life, to agony. But now the clamp freed his tongue. Dex closed his mouth and cried. The rabbi's tongue was freed as well. He let out a terrible groan.

"Now," said Blue Mask from his throne with that god-awful voice. "I will ask you both one more time. If you do not tell me what I need to know, you will never tell anyone anything ever again."

"I know nothing of this book!" the rabbi raged, though his words were almost incomprehensible. "We have never believed it to be a literal thing!"

"I see," Red Mask said. "What do you have to say, Mr. Wax?"

Dexter wasn't sure he could speak, but he didn't get the chance.

"I'll tell you," someone said. Nora. She was there, beside Dexter now. "Don't hurt them any more. I'll tell you what you want to know."

"Nora," Dex managed to croak. She wasn't strong enough for this. It was his fault. *What in God's name was he thinking bringing her here?*

"Scraped," she said. "The names have to be scraped off the pages."

"It will not damage the pages?"

"No."

"Is a special tool required?"

"I—I don't think so."

"Bring me the Book."

A Blue Mask rose from his chair, then collected it from the podium, along with a frighteningly large and vicious looking dagger with five gleaming blades. Beside the expected one at its tip, two more came out at angles, and then two more straight out below those. He walked over to the throne and handed both the book and dagger over.

Red Mask opened the book on his lap and considered the pages before him a moment. Then he looked up. "Who shall be our test subject?" he asked. "Oh, wait. I think I know." And then he laughed. "My brothers," he said, holding the frightening dagger aloft, "say a little prayer for the Holy Fath—"

Just then the door behind Dexter crashed to the floor.

Blue Masks all around the room leapt to their feet, expertly producing swords with red and gold handles from behind their chairs.

Dex couldn't turn to see what was happening behind him, but he saw a silver streak fly past his head. It buried itself in the chest of a Blue Mask, the first to charge. He crumpled to the floor with blood pouring through a hand clutched to his heart.

Mayhem ensued as sword-wielding men robed in black rushed past him and clashed with the Masons. More blades plunged into more chests. Men all around the room screamed and fell dead where they'd been struck. Dex saw two men kill each other at the same moment, skewering one another with their swords.

Dex realized he could see Nora in his peripheral vision, still next to him, unmoving. He could hear her praying.

*"Let me out!"* he hissed, but it was no use. He jerked in his restraints, but that was useless too.

A Blue Mask was struggling with a man in black just in front of him now, their swords clanging. The man in black seemed to get the upper hand, but just before he delivered a fatal blow, he vanished.

Dex looked up to see Red Mask, still sitting on his throne, scraping furiously at a page in The Book of the Living. And now Dex saw that men in black were disappearing all around the room.

*"Oh, my god, Dex!"* someone whispered right in his ear.

Daphna!

Daphna almost fainted when she saw her brother in this—*thing*. She struggled with the straps while swords clashed all around her, praying none of them found her. Dex's head was free! Next she worked on his arms and legs.

When he was loose, she set to freeing the man in

the other chair, whoever he was. They had to get out of there before they were killed. It was a bloodbath!

"Nora!" Dex leapt up, wincing at the pain in his tongue and jaw. He looked to shake her into awareness, but saw her eyes were open, and that she was looking fearfully around the room. Dex did as well, realizing that it had gone quiet. Daphna was just realizing the same thing.

A few men in black lay in puddles of blood, but the rest were simply not there anymore. A dozen or so Blue Masks lay dead around the room as well. The others were back in their chairs, sitting upright and motionless, as if nothing had happened at all.

With no warning, the rabbi reached down and pulled a sword out of the body of a Blue Mask. Then, baying like a rabid dog, he charged the throne.

Red Mask moved only his hand.

And then the rabbi was gone.

"And now," Red Mask said, pointing his five-pointed dagger directly at the horrified twins. "Your turn."

"No!" Nora screamed.

Red Mask set the edge of the blade on the book and slid it slowly across the page.

# CHAPTER THIRTY-FIVE
## *Dripping Daggers*

The remaining Blue Masks leapt back to their feet, drawing their swords again. Red Mask lifted his dagger and turned his attention to the doorway. Dex spun round to see what everyone was reacting to.

Five people were walking into the chamber, three women and two men. They weren't masked or in black. Rather, they wore slacks and sweaters. They were all dusting their shoulders.

"The Colors!" Daphna cheered. She didn't know what else to call them. They were all there, all but Mr. Brown. The group was unarmed, but looked supremely unafraid.

"We have no conflict with you," Ms. White announced. "We are here for the twins."

Daphna almost cried out for them to take The Book of the Living, but she resisted. They probably just wanted to get them to safety first.

The Blue Masks were moving slowly forward, but Red Mask put up a hand to stay them.

"There is no need for further violence," Ms. Gold declared, looking round. Then to Red Mask she added, "You have your prize."

"But—!" Daphna said, though nothing more. She understood that they were *only* there for her and Dex. Mr. Brown had sent them.

"Indeed I do," said Red Mask in his metal voice. "And who might you be?"

"We are none of your concern," said Ms. Green.

"Is that a fact?" Red Mask looked down into The Book of the Living, placing the edge of his dagger's main blade back down on the page.

Daphna cringed, expecting the group to start vanishing one by one, but Red Mask did not scrape off a name. Rather, he only stared at the page. After what seemed like forever, he looked up and scanned all five of the Colors' faces, then looked back down again.

The Colors simply stood and waited.

Red Mask continued staring. He stared so long that the twins had time to look at each other.

Finally, he looked up again and said, in a voice that sounded mostly amused, "Your names do not appear. How remarkable. But you'll find we're not entirely surprised."

Again, the twins looked at each other.

*"Who are they?"* Dex whispered. It seemed absurd that this mild-mannered bunch of professor-types, weirdly tall as they were, could threaten a room full of men with swords—not to mention The Book of the Living—but he was long past judging books by their covers.

*"They're Mr. G's bosses,"* Daphna whispered, *"the ones looking for the golden book—It's called* The Book of Creation."

*"But who are they?"*

*"I don't know."*

"Kill them," Red Mask said.

The five Colors, standing in the center of the chamber, turned to face the Blue Masks, who approached them now from three sides with swords drawn. The Colors did not draw back in the least, nor show the slightest trace of fear.

The twins drew back. Dexter pulled Nora with him. She was once again completely absent to the proceedings.

"I'm afraid you don't know what you're dealing with here," said Ms. White, turning back toward the throne. "It would be best for you to let us take the twins. Otherwise," she added, "very soon there may be no one for you to rule."

"We have no interest in harming you," added Mr. Black.

Red Mask nodded, after which all the Blue Masks set their swords on the floor.

Dex and Daphna exchanged hopeful glances now. Were they surrendering? But then the Blue Masks reached under their robes and pulled out small daggers. These looked much less menacing than the swords they'd just put down, but strangely, they all dripped with some kind of liquid.

"Darkness," Ms. White told Red Mask, "is descending, as you surely—"

One of the Blue Masks leapt at her. She made no effort to evade him or the dripping dagger he plunged into her heart.

Ms. White fell to her knees, clutching at the dagger's handle, her face contorted with shock. She screamed something like, "Keres!"

There was a burst of light, and then she was gone.

Daphna's eyes went wide. The air smelled like— *tarragon.*

This was clearly not what the Colors expected. Appalled, the twins watched the others leap away, though leap scarcely described their movement. They leapt completely over the Blue Masks, as if thrown by trampolines. Ms. Green landed on the wall, then ran across it toward the doorway, hissing. She bared a mouthful of frightening teeth and attacked the guard who was blocking the exit by simply driving him into the floor. There was a sickening crunch as the man's bones were crushed, but she'd fallen on his dagger. There was another scream and another burst of light.

Ms. Green was gone now too.

What followed was awful to behold. Ms. Gold, Mr. Grey, and Mr. Black attacked the Blue Masks with a feral rage, snarling and spitting like wild animals, leaping to avoid daggers and crushing any body part they could get hold of. They got hold off many, snapping necks and spines like twigs. But in the scrum, Ms. Gold and Mr. Grey were both stabbed. With two bursts of light, they were gone.

The twins looked around for Mr. Black. He was on the floor, face down next to the podium, writhing in pain. There was only one Blue Mask left alive, and he stood over the body.

"Let him go!" Daphna pleaded with the man. "We'll stay with you! Let him go!"

"I scraped him," the last Blue Mask panted, holding his dripping dagger up.

"Show us his back," Red Mask said, still ensconced on his throne. He seemed not to have moved at all.

The Blue Mask leaned down, but Mr. Black jumped to his feet and crushed his throat. But the scrape had been enough.

There was one last burst of light.

# CHAPTER THIRTY-SIX
## *The Mask*

"I would like to know what else you've learned about this book," Red Mask said in his horrid android voice. He had still not moved, and he sounded not the least bit put out by the fact that the chamber was now empty but for the four of them and a slew of dead bodies. "If you can provide me with information I deem valuable," he said, "I will consider letting you live."

"You don't want to erase us," Dexter warned. "Trust me. We go, *you* go. *Everyone* goes."

Evidently unimpressed, Red Mask turned his attention to Nora.

"You, girl," he said, "may leave. Tell your father his worst fears have come to fruition. Tell him to spread the word."

"We're not lying," Daphna insisted. Her heart was threatening to implode in her chest. "It's a long story. Our ribs—there were thirty—"

"Go!" Red Mask ordered Nora. "Right now!"

Nora did not go. Dexter assumed she hadn't heard, that she still wasn't mentally present, but he saw now that her eyes were open and clear. She was staring directly at Red Mask.

With no warning, she began walking toward his throne.

"Nora, don't!" Dex warned, but she ignored him.

*"What's she doing?"* Daphna whispered.

*"I'm warning you,"* Red Mask hissed. He set his dagger on the page.

But Nora did not stop approaching.

"I'M WARNING YOU!"

She was right in front of Red Mask now, but rather than scrape her name off the page, he clutched the book to his chest as if to prevent her from taking it away from him.

Dex and Daphna looked on, confused and

afraid.

Instead of reaching for the book, Nora reached for the red mask and simply pulled it off its owner's face.

The twins could not believe their eyes.

"Why, Daddy?" Nora asked. *"Why?"*

"I tried to spare you this!" Pastor Jons raged at his daughter. "He shoved Nora back, but cried out in pain as he did so.

"His back!" Dexter realized. "That's why he never got up!" Finally over the shock, he ran to help. Daphna was right behind him.

Jons had the Book open on his lap again, but before he could get the edge of his dagger to the page, Nora lunged at him and grabbed his arm.

The injured pastor yowled in pain as he struggled with his daughter. "Damn you!" he roared.

Nora wrenched his arm off the book, but he wrenched it back.

Dex and Daphna reached the throne, but before they could decide how to help, the pastor's arm, with Nora still gripping it, swept crazily over the page.

An instant later, both Nora and her father were gone.

# CHAPTER THIRTY-SEVEN
## Of Course

*"Noooo!"* Dex wailed, spinning round, scanning the room as if Nora had suddenly decided to play hide-and-seek among the corpses on the floor. *"Please, no!"*

"Oh, God, Dex," Daphna said. "I'm sorry. I'm so sorry! *But wait!* It sounded like Mr. Brown thought if we wrote someone's name back in, we might be able to bring them back!"

"Let's do it then!" Dexter snatched up The Book of the Living, which was sitting harmlessly on the throne. Now he looked frantically around for something to write with.

"But wait!" Daphna said again. "We need to talk this through." She took the book from her brother and opened it between them. "It's okay," she promised, seeing his panic. "We have ten days to figure out how to do it right. Everything's going to be okay. And if we can't figure it out, that will be okay too, because we're going to find The Book of Creation—It can do anything! *Anything!* It's going to fix everything for everybody, no matter how bad things get." She didn't want to say how bad things had gotten—not yet.

*Yes,* Dex thought, looking at the names rising and sinking on the page like slow breaths, *they'd be swift, but not hasty. They'd do it right. Everything was going to be okay. Nora was going to be okay.*

"Well, well, well," someone said.

Jolted, Daphna dropped the book.

"We meet, as they say, once again."

The twins spun round to see The Secret Keeper standing calmly on the fallen door. He was, of course, pointing a gun at them.

"This is The Book of the Living," Dex said, snatching the book up from the floor. He grabbed the pastor's giant dagger, too. "Your name is here," he added, opening it up. "I'll scrape it off if you don't drop that gun."

"You've been looking for a way to Heaven," Daphna added. "We're going to send you there if you don't put the gun on the floor and back away. Do it now!"

"The Book of the Living?" the Secret Keeper replied, quickly surveying the macabre scene in the chamber. "So that's what they found." Then he looked pointedly back at Daphna and said, "Swords make much less noise, but I'd trust this old man's ability to pull the trigger before your brother can manage to erase me. I understand you have some vision problems, Dexter? Look at him squinting at the thing like it's a mile away. Shall we have a test? By the way, what is my name?"

Dex stared as hard as he could at the letters rising up of the page, willing them to come clear.

Daphna hung her head.

"Close the book," the Secret Keeper ordered, taking a few steps into the chamber. "Now."

Sighing bitterly, Dex closed it.

"Good. Very good. Now put it down."

Reluctantly, Dex set the book on the throne.

"Now, back away."

When the twins did as they were told, the Secret Keeper approached the throne. Rather than pick the book up, he flipped it open with his gun. A quick glance at the exposed pages was enough to make his pupils dilate. He flipped it closed again.

"What will you do with it?" Daphna asked. "Kill more people?"

The Secret Keeper regarded Daphna a moment, then said, "You misunderstand my job completely."

"Is that so?" Daphna wanted to make him talk so she could think of how to get the book away from him. She knew Dexter was thinking about it too, though he was just staring at the book.

"My job is to help people believe," the Secret Keeper explained. "I seek any and all means toward that end. This book," he added, pointing the gun at it, "this book that contains life itself—God has delivered it to us so that we can at last enforce His will on Earth."

"But he didn't deliver it to you!" Daphna insisted. "And that's exactly what He doesn't want!"

"Then why, my child, do I have it?"

Daphna couldn't think of a response to that.

But Dexter could.

"You don't!" he shouted, leaping forward, swinging the dagger he never put down. But he did not leap at the Secret Keeper, who was consequently more surprised than defensive. Before he could properly react, Dexter had driven the elaborate blade—all five razor sharp blades—deep into The Book of the Living. Then he leapt back and away from it.

The Secret Keeper, his curtain of hair flying, rushed to the book. Pointing the gun at the twins with one hand, he moved to rip the blade out of it with the other—but he stopped before attempting to do so. "No!" he roared, looking closer at it. "You fool!"

"Run!" Dex cried, grabbing his sister's hand.

Baffled, she bolted with him for the door.

Bullets whizzed past the twins' heads as they flew out of the chamber and down the hall.

Daphna let go of Dex's hand and ran in front, hunched over, scrutinizing the floor.

"What are you doing?" Dex asked, nearly running her over from behind.

"Dirt!" she explained, quickly turning left into a dimly lit passageway. "The Colors were wiping it off their clothes!"

Dex followed as Daphna led them down several narrow hallways and into and out of a series of storage rooms. She finally stopped in an entirely unfinished space. The walls were stone. The floor was dirt.

"There!" Daphna said.

On the far wall was the mouth of a tunnel ringed with large rocks.

The twins could still hear the Secret Keeper howling as they sprinted into it.

# CHAPTER THIRTY-EIGHT
## *One More Thing*

As Daphna had been hoping, scooters were lined up against the tunnel wall.

"Yes!" Dex said, grabbing one. He rolled it into the light coming from the museum.

Bang!

A bullet hit the wall behind the twins, showering them with dirt and debris.

Daphna leapt on the deck behind her brother, who had it running. "That way!" she cried.

Dexter hit the gas, and they lurched forward.

Bang!

Another bullet whizzed by in the dark. They took a slow turn, then another, so the next bullet came nowhere near them.

"You cannot hope to hide from me!" the Secret Keeper wailed. "You cannot possibly hope—!" But his voice was already fading.

Dex took three more slow turns, drove for a while down a long straightaway, then turned again a few more times. Daphna strained her ears. It didn't sound like another motor had started up. It seemed the Secret Keeper wasn't going to try to drive a scooter. Just in case, they drove on a while longer until Daphna felt there was no chance he could have followed them even if he'd tried.

*"Pull over!"* she whispered loudly into Dex's ear. He did, and the two of them stepped off the scooter.

The twins looked up and down the tunnel they were in. It was deserted. They cut the engine but left the headlight on.

"Dex," Daphna said.

"I couldn't let him have it. I just couldn't."

"But—I don't understand."

"He can't open it now—not with five blades stuck through it at all different angles. Not unless he wants to risk scraping a name off when he pulls the knife out."

"Like his own name, for example."

"Exactly."

"You're a genius!"

"Or an idiot. I might have just destroyed our only hope. And if I didn't, they'll probably figure out a way to get that knife out."

"It won't matter," Daphna promised. "Because by then we'll have found the golden book."

"Heaven!" Dex remembered. "Did you go?"

"Mr. Brown—" Daphna told him, returning to the many crises still at hand, "he's with those—Mr. G's group. He's their leader, I guess. I thought they were regular people! He had a doctor *kill* Quinn, just for a few moments—We were just down the street!—to send him to Purgatory, the realm between this world and Heaven. That's where he said he thinks the golden book—The Book of Creation—is hidden. I was going to do it, but Quinn—he—he went to Heaven, but he's in a coma now. They came to the museum to find us so they could try again with one of us!"

"Wait," Dex said. "So, Quinn *didn't* go to Purgatory?"

"No. I don't think there is such a thing as Purgatory. I'm pretty sure I've read that many groups don't think it's a real place. I don't think Mr. Brown told us the truth about what they were doing."

*"So where is Nora?"*

"She must be in Heaven, since that's where Quinn went. He sort of woke up, but they said he was still there and gave him another shot. He said—he said—"

"What Daphna? What did he say?"

"When you were in Heaven—was there a particular book you were attracted to?"

"What? How—? Yes—"

"Dex, I think those books house our souls. In fact, I'm sure of it. Did you see the letters flowing through the book Dead Face opened? Those letters are DNA. Something came out of that book, some kind of— Quinn said there was a *dragon* there. I think it came out of that book. It's burning books up there. *Burning souls!"*

"I shouldn't have stabbed it!" Dex howled. "I should have just let him erase me so I could get her myself! Let's go!"

"Where?"

"To Mr. Brown. He can do the operation on me."

"But Dex," Daphna warned, "I told you—he's been lying. We have no idea what he really wants or where he's actually trying to send us. We don't even know if this Book of Creation is real. We need to figure this out ourselves. Like always!"

"But we have nothing to go on, and we only have ten days!"

Despairing, Daphna hung her head again, but then she looked up. "Wait!" she said. "There is one more thing I haven't told you, though it might not mean anything. Mr. Brown's group—we heard them talking about some kind of painting, something that must somehow jeopardize their search. They bribed or threatened the artist about it, so maybe we could find out who it was. I don't know if it has anything to do with the exhibition back there at the—"

"A painting is missing," Dex said. "From the Last Supper room, a really long and narrow one. It was weird to see the empty spot with just hooks hanging there. But if it's such a big deal, I'm sure they destroyed it, unless they didn't have time with all this—"

"I know where it is!"

# CHAPTER THIRTY-NINE
## *The Smuggler*

"It's in Mr. G's house!" Daphna was already back on the scooter. "In a wardrobe—in his basement!"

Dex didn't bother asking how she knew this. He moved to climb back onto the scooter, but Daphna stepped back off.

"Hold on a sec," she said, freeing a wad of paper from her back pocket. "We found a map of the tunnels. *All* of them."

Dex leaned over to see the rather large sheet Daphna was now holding up to the headlight. It looked like a jumble of scribbles and dots. He got on the scooter and started the engine. "Hurry, Daphna."

Daphna scanned the crisscrossing squiggles. It looked like chaos, but she could see the grid in the midst of it all. That was downtown. She closed her eyes and tried to recreate the turns she and Dex had just taken to get away from the museum. If she was close, she thought, looking back at the map, they'd be somewhere around—

"Okay," she said, folding the map again and tucking it away. She climbed on the scooter behind her brother and said, "You drive, I'll navigate. Go straight."

Dex went straight.

"When we turn," Daphna said into his ear, "we lean together. The better we do that, the faster we'll go. Can you see okay? LEFT!"

They took the turn perfectly. Not a wobble, not a weave. Dex increased the speed, already feeling more comfortable.

"So these tunnels do go all over town?" he asked over his shoulder.

"I think so," Daphna said. "Right!"

They took the turn easily again, and Dexter increased their speed some more.

Daphna gripped her brother as she had Quinn

just hours earlier. She was beyond happy to have him back and determined never to separate from him again, even if circumstances demanded it.

*Quinn.*

She couldn't think of him. But she couldn't not think of him, either. What if the riots had spilled into the little operating room? What if Dr. Lewis and Mr. Brown had succumbed to the rioting themselves? Was Quinn in Heaven?

Was he now suffering like everyone else there must be? Their mothers! Or was he in this mysterious realm? What was this dragon?

"Right!" Daphna shouted, having lost her concentration. Dex cut the turn hard, but they did not skid or slide.

"How do you know which way to go just from looking at that map for ten seconds?" Dex asked. But he wasn't surprised.

"Left!" Daphna hadn't memorized the map, but she was sure they were heading in the right direction. She never needed exact directions to get where she wanted to go.

Now that Dex wasn't worried about getting shot again, he was able to take in what he could see of the tunnels, though that wasn't much. It was actually somehow better that way. Streaming past the headlight were what looked like wooden supports. The walls were earthen and gave off a moist, thick smell. How could all this be under the city his whole life? Would there never be an end to secrets in this world?

"Dex," Daphna said. "If we get separated again, even for ten seconds, we call each other. Okay?"

"My phone! It's still in the museum."

"In that throne room or whatever it was?" They were moving along expertly.

"No," Dex said. "I never took it down there. I hid it upstairs before we ever went down."

*"So you knew what they were going to do to you?"*

"Are you crazy? I had no idea."

"Then when did you text me?"

Dex pulled over and stopped. He turned around on the scooter and said, "What are you talking about?"

"What do you mean what am I talking about?"

Daphna asked back. "Why do you think I came for you?"

"Why *did* you come for me?"

*"What?* You texted me the word, 'Help.'"

Dex turned back around and started the scooter again. Tears were filling his eyes.

"What?" Daphna asked.

Dex let a few tears fall, but then he could speak. "Nora must have smuggled it downstairs," he said over his shoulder. "Which means she only pretended to faint and texted you curled up on the floor."

"Wow," was all Daphna could say back.

Dex let a few more tears fall as he drove. Was Nora's life over? No, he wouldn't think of it. She'd finally stood up to her father. She, who seemed so weak and ineffectual, was the one who figured out it was him. And it was *she* who took him on, and all by herself. To save him?

To save everyone?

And what did she get for it?

No, these thoughts weren't helpful, either. He'd get her back if it was the last thing—

"Stop!"

Dex stopped the scooter. Daphna jumped off, so he did too.

The headlight revealed a large, dented metal plate of some kind lying on the tunnel floor. A hole the same size as the plate was exposed in the dirt wall above it. Something was inside—clothes?"

"That's the wardrobe?" Dex asked. "In Mr. G's house?"

"Yes," Daphna said. "His basement." She cupped her hands. "Here, I'll help you up, then you pull me in."

"Okay."

Dex got a grip on the ledge, then stepped into his sister's hands. She hoisted him as best she could, and he scrabbled his way in through the coats.

Then he turned, ready to reach for his sister, but before he got the chance, she cried out in pain.

Dex heard his sister's body hit the ground, but when he leaned out to see what had happened, someone grabbed his ankle and yanked him in through the wardrobe.

# CHAPTER FORTY
*Reunion*

Daphna lay on the ground, dazed. She'd been looking up at the bottom of her brother's sneakers as they disappeared into the wardrobe when something—some*one*—decked her.

"Dex!" she called, but was silenced by a brutal kick in the stomach. It was followed immediately by another. And then another.

After the next kick, she vomited blood on the tunnel floor.

"I knew you'd be back!"

Branwen.

She kicked Daphna again, this time in the head. She was wild, rabid, completely insane.

Daphna curled into a ball and wrapped her arms over her head, trying to gather some semblance of thought.

Branwen kicked her in the back of the neck, then in the lower back. She kicked some more, anywhere and everywhere.

"Dex!" Daphna screamed. *Where was he!*

Branwen had circled round and was now trying to kick her in the face. She wasn't talking now. She was beyond threats and taunts. She was just trying to kill Daphna, plain and simple.

"Dex!" Daphna had never felt pain like this, even when she'd been shot.

One, two, three, four kicks to her arms wrapped over her head. Daphna had no choice but to come out of her curl and try to fight. But the moment she did, Branwen leapt on her chest and grabbed her by the throat.

Daphna couldn't call out any more. She could only look into Branwen's eyes. In them she saw something much more awful than a Pop deranged by grief. They seemed almost to have fire inside them.

Daphna's arms were dead weight now. She offered no resistance at all.

She was finally going to die.

After all she'd done, Daphna still did not know where she would go when her soul left her body.

But it was okay.

Her rib was only inches from the earth.


Dex was dragged through the hanging clothes. He hit his head on the sharp corner of some large object in the wardrobe, then fell out onto a concrete floor. Then he was yanked up onto his feet and punched in the face.

He fell back to the floor, stunned and bleeding from his nose into his mouth.

Mr. G stood over him, livid.

"I've been cut off completely now!" he screamed. "Do you understand what that means?" He bent over, picked Dex up again, then slammed him back down.

"All these years! My life's work! My part in history! MY REWARD! It's over! All *over!*"

Mr. G leapt on Dex's chest and grabbed him around the throat.

Dex couldn't muster any resistance at all.

He was finally going to die.

Dex was sure his soul would suffer for his failings, but it was okay because it would only be his soul that paid the price.

Someone would bury his body.

# CHAPTER FORTY-ONE
### *The Lake of Fire*

The darkness was profound. But something was happening to it. It was fading. A light was slowly washing it away. The light, diffuse at first, grew brighter and brighter.

Daphna knew this light, this *living* Light.

She stood inside it now. Her pain was gone. It never existed.

She was in Heaven.

Daphna fell to her knees as grateful tears streamed from her eyes.

She would stay that way until her mothers came for her. They'd show her to her Book. Or Quinn would come and together they would read every book in Heaven's library and none would be forbidden and no one would ever tell them to stop.

But no one came.

There was a faint sound in the distance.

Daphna rose to her feet and began moving through the Light. As she moved, the sound grew more distinct.

Then it was there, all around her.

Screaming.

In the distance, flames leapt up in the Light.

Daphna tensed to run, but someone grabbed her by the arm.

*Dexter!*

She could see that he had been weeping, too.

The twins looked into each other's identical eyes and understood that their lives, if they still possessed them, were balanced on a razor's edge.

*If we go looking for the Book of Creation,* Dex thought to his sister. *If we search for Quinn or Nora and it takes too long—*

*We'll die.*

Yet the twins remained there, watching fire devour the Light.

*The Lake of Fire,* Dex thought.

*We brought it here.*

They knew what to do, but they weren't ready to do it.

*Look!* they both thought.

Something was rising up among the flames.

Something massive and looming.

There then came a roar so loud, it shook the very vault of Heaven.

Dexter and Daphna took hands, turned round, and dragged each other back into their lives.

# CHAPTER FORTY-TWO
*One Punch*

Daphna opened her eyes. Branwen was no longer on her.

"Dead!" Branwen cooed. "Teal! Wren! She's dead! The Wicked Witch is dead! Dead! Dead! Dead!"

Daphna slowly rolled her head to the side.

Branwen's back was to her. She was looking at something in the scooter's headlight.

Slowly, silently—somehow—Daphna got to her feet.

She walked up behind Branwen and tapped her on the shoulder.

When Branwen turned around, Daphna reared back, then knocked her out with one punch.

A piece of paper fluttered to the tunnel floor. Daphna touched her pocket. Branwen had taken Quinn's note, which she'd somehow forgotten about.

Daphna picked it up.

It was not a note. It was a photograph Quinn must have taken from the mess in Mr. G's secret room. It was of Daphna as a young girl standing in the entrance of the Central Library. It took a moment for what she was wearing to register, but now it did: white shorts with white stripes down the sides and a white top. And the little white visor. And the white tennis shoes, too.

An angel in white.

Daphna tucked the picture back into her pocket.

# CHAPTER FORTY-THREE
## *The Painting*

Dexter opened his eyes. Mr. G was no longer on him. He was there, though, at the wardrobe, wrestling something out of it.

The painting.

Dexter closed his eyes while Mr. G dragged it past him to an open spot on the concrete floor. With his back to Dex now, Mr. G laid the painting down, squatted next to it, and lit a match.

Somehow, Dex got to his feet. There was a trophy lying on the floor—that gold-plated cup Branwen was going to brain him with earlier that morning at school. Dex scooped it up, and before Mr. G could touch his match to the canvas, Dex knocked him unconscious with it.

Dexter staggered back to the wardrobe and collapsed into it, planning to hurl himself into the tunnel, but two hands appeared on the ledge when he reached it. He knew those hands.

Dex peeked over and saw his sister's face.

The twins exchanged smiles they barely had the strength to produce, though Daphna's fell away at the sight of blood all over her brother's nose and chin. Dex got to a sitting position and dragged her up into the wardrobe. They lay there together under the coats, trying to recover.

*"Branwen,"* Daphna finally thought.

*"Mr. G,"* Dex thought back.

Neither tried to communicate for another minute. They just lay there, breathing, trying not to hurt.

After a while, Daphna said, "There are reasons some people won't riot—they're all out there rioting, by the way—but not absolutely everyone."

"Yeah?"

"It has to do with selflessness. If you have compassion for someone, like you have for Nora. If—if you are in love with someone—"

217

"Like you are with Quinn."

"Dex—he's in love with me, that's true, but—"

"It's fine. It's good. What's the third reason?"

"Meditation or—"

"Prayer."

"Right."

"Did you say, 'dragon'?"

"Yes."

"I thought so. That painting is on the floor, by the way. Mr. G was going to burn it."

Daphna didn't reply to this. She hurt too much.

"I guess that golden book isn't going to find itself," Dex said.

"No, I guess it won't," Daphna agreed.

The twins sat up, both wincing.

They sighed, then stumbled out of the wardrobe and over to the painting.

"Let's take it upstairs," Daphna suggested after seeing Mr. G.

Dex agreed. He picked up the trophy again—just in case—then one end of the painting. Daphna took the other end, though she almost couldn't manage to lift it because her sides hurt so much. Then, limping and unsteady, the twins maneuvered the unwieldy frame up the steps, through the kitchen, and into the living room, where they set it on the floor.

Noise outside attracted their attention to the window. The rioting had restarted on the school grounds. Kids and adults were trashing the building, which was on fire.

A deafening clap of thunder forced the twins to look up.

There was fire in the sky now, too.

Dex and Daphna went back to look at the painting.

The Last Supper.

They stared at it awhile.

"I don't get it," Dex said after looking over the rendering of Jesus sitting with his disciples at their table. They all looked decidedly biblical. "This doesn't seem like it belonged in that freaky exhibit. It's totally normal."

"I've seen tons just like this in history books," Daphna said, equally baffled.

"So what's the big deal? Why would they care

if some guy paints what a million other people have already painted?"

"There must be a difference," Daphna assumed. "A small one maybe."

"And what does it have to do with the book they want?"

"Maybe it has a clue about where the Book is, and they don't want anyone else looking for it."

"Is that the clue?"

"What?"

"That. It looks kind of like a book—" Dex was squinting at the painting, not entirely sure if he was seeing what he thought he was seeing. He pointed to Jesus' upraised hand, which seemed to be holding a softly glowing golden square.

Daphna jerked upright. "That's not supposed to be there," she said. "That's not in any of the paintings I've seen. How could I miss that?"

"It's not a cup then?"

"Dexter!" Daphna cried, looking at the golden trophy cup still in her brother's hand. "Mr. Brown—he lied about this, too! They're not looking for any *Book of Creation*. That cup—the golden cup Jesus supposedly had at The Last Supper! Remember the painting of this at the Vatican? The caption said something like—"

"'This is the new testament in my blood.' The pastor mentioned that same thing this morning."

"Right! How could a cup be a testament written in anything? It's not a golden cup! It's a golden *book!*"

"You mean—"

"Yes!" Daphna confirmed. "We're looking for the Holy Grail!"

# ABOUT THE AUTHOR

David Michael Slater is an acclaimed author of books for children, teens, and adults. He teaches English to 8th graders, but you will not be required to write an essay after reading this book. David lives in Reno, Nevada with his wife and son. You can learn more about David and his work at www.davidmichaelslater.com.

www.ingramcontent.com/pod-product-compliance
Lightning Source LLC
Chambersburg PA
CBHW051647260626
47170CB00004B/1382